My Shadows Keeper

The Dawn of a Massacre

My Shadows Keeper

The Dawn of a Massacre

A Novel by

Ben Woke

My Shadows Keeper The Dawn of a Massacre

Black Diamond Publishing

Acknowledgment

I want to thank my sister, Donna, for helping me finally put this series together; I want to thank all of my sisters – Donna, Janelle, Alanna & Leslie for your support and walking with me through this fire; to my brother, Joseph, for being a big brother; to my brother, Oronde, for being a mentor – keep writing; to my brother, Kimani, for understanding; to my brother, Tee-Tee – keep yo' head up; & to my cousin, Yung-Greedy for knowing what this fire feel like – 'preciate the love. Last but not least, I wanna give thanks to karma for showing me the way – I couldn't have become who I am without you!!!

Sometimes I sit and wish that I was a kid again; how I would do so many things different. I must admit, I would only want to be a kid again if I could remain with the same knowledge that I now have. Imagine a ten-year-old child talking to you the way an elder would; a ten-year-old child that has more wisdom than either you or I. It would probably scare the hell out of you.

I know we can't turn back the hands of time, but what we can do is teach our kids the things that we now know, so when they are ten years old, they can scare the hell out of someone. This is the purpose of experience, generation after generation, to take what we've learned from our experienced elders and make it a part of our daily lives. And most importantly passing it on to the ones after us. Only then can we grow and better ourselves as a people. If one doesn't learn from his or her experienced elders, then what that experienced elder has learned in their long period of life will die in vain. Without the teachings of our elders our very own existence will die in vain.

We have to dedicate our lives to the knowledge that our kids will one day inherit. This being only half of the solution. The other half is how our kids decide to use this knowledge. Only then can we all move forward and break this brainwashing cycle we are in; kids roaming the streets day-in and day-out in search of nothing. The ones that are in search of something only have drug-dealers, gang bangers, and killers to look up to. I'll admit, this was me. I had no guiding light to guide me. The only God that I knew was money and survival...

...this is my story...

Table of Content

PROLOGUE
AWAKENING

JUNE 16th...1:12am
JO JOHNSTON HOUSING PROJECTS
NORTH NASHVILLE...

It was late. Kimani couldn't sleep due to the extremely loud noises his father and his father's friends were making downstairs. Even at this late hour, the atmosphere was live with music and laughter in the small project apartment and he could smell the potent marijuana smoke in the air. Though he was only eight, he knew a lot about guns and drugs; something no eight-year-old should know about.

Nights like these were common for him, and for nearly every other kid in similar environments. Sadly, nothing was out of place here. If gunshots weren't heard throughout the night, it was simply because he'd slept through them and they hadn't awaken him.

Kimani could hear his father arguing loudly with someone in the downstairs living room and knew from experience that with the tone his father used, along with his choice of words, that he was either high off drugs, leaned on liquor, or both.

More than likely both.

Kimani had no idea whom his father was arguing with, but at the tender age of eight, he was curious and wanted to find out. So, he pulled the covers off, got out of bed, and walked over to his bedroom door.

He hesitated to open the door, contemplating the consequences if he got caught. He knew that if he was found out of bed, he would get his ass beat. *What the heck,* he thought to himself. His father, being intoxicated off lean and drugs would find a way to beat his ass anyway.

Kimani opened the door a crack and peeped around to see if anyone heard him. With the sound of the loud music, he knew no one would, but with a father like his, it was better to be safe than sorry. With no one in sight, he snatched open the door and walked over to the top of the stairs. From this vantage point he could see almost everything in the small living room down below.

Noticing his father, and three of his father's friends sitting around the living room, Kimani eagerly watched. He observed his father breaking down powdered cocaine on a porcelain plate while talking on the phone. Kimani watched him as he sat in his favorite chair with that plate of cocaine in his lap, and the telephone up to his ear. Listening to the argument his father was having over the phone; he took it all in with curious eyes.

It was impossible to hear both sides of the conversation, but he could hear enough of one side to be able to discern what was being said. That was more than…

"Bitch ass nigga. I told you, you'll get yo' fuckin' money when I give it to you," his father spat.

Kimani watched as he slammed the phone down hard on the receiver and threw the plate of cocaine down on the table before standing up. This was his cue. He knew not to get caught out of bed. Running back to his bedroom, he quietly, and very quietly, closed the door behind him. He thought about his father's conversation and demeanor as he got back under the covers. With low hopes of making it through the night without incident, he closed his eyes and willed himself to sleep.

He was awakened suddenly by the sound of a loud blast, then several more. Gunshots, he knew. Heart racing, Kimani hurriedly threw back the covers and went to the door. Wondering why his father would be shooting a weapon in the house, he worked up the nerve to open the door before looking around. With no one in sight, Kimani eased over to the top of the stairs for the second time that night. What he saw would stain his memory for the rest of his life.

His father's body was sprawled out on the floor at the bottom of the stairs. It was a gruesome sight, like none that he'd ever seen before. The only way that he could even recognize his own father was by the clothes that he wore. His head had been splattered into small chunks all over the wall and lower steps.

Kimani was frozen in place, helpless. His mind was there, but his body had become numb. He could only stare at the spot where he knew his father's head should be. The neck – what was left of it – was still gushing spurts of blood, regurgitating its life's fluids. The body still jerked in convulsion long after Kimani knew that his father was dead.

It was moments like these when it seemed that time all together ceased to exist; a reality where nothing moved. The only thing that was real to him was the small narrow tunnel that extended from his distorted mind to that of the gruesome scene before him. He had become deaf to the loud music. The only sounds still lingering was from echoes of gunshots heard a lifetime ago. This moment was strange. His body felt numb as if reality itself had a delayed effect. Even the jerking of his father's lifeless body seemed to be in slow motion.

Kimani stood there paralyzed.

As if suddenly jolted awake, he noticed for the first time his father's killer. The man had probably been standing there the entire time. Posed over his father, the stranger wore a torn tank-top and dirty blue-jeans. He was skinny but muscular, and he had extremely nappy hair. Kimani had no idea why he was paying so much attention to the details of this killer, but even with the sawed-off shotgun the man carried, it was the dusty hole-infested shoes the man wore that stood out to him the most.

Kimani watched as the killer spat on his dead father's body while issuing a few disrespectful words. The man was about to turn and leave – to go back to whatever hell-pit he'd crawled out of – but a killer's instinct, or maybe just bad luck, caused him to look up. Kimani stared eye to eye with the killer for what seemed like forever before the killer smirked and made his next move. The man slowly – there was no threat coming from this scared little kid – made his way towards the top of the stairs.

Kimani, heart pounding even more rapidly now, ran into his father's room. Without missing a step, he did the only thing he could think to do. He went to the small closet to grab his father's shotgun. He knew it was there and how to use it because he'd watched his father toy with it on several occasions. Cocking the piece of wood on the bottom of the weapon, Kimani went to the other side of the bed by the far wall and waited with the barrel pointed in the soon-to-be direction of his father's killer.

His heart was racing as the over-sized weapon shook in his small hands.

He waited.

With the lights upstairs off, only the light from the living room below spread minimum light into the hallway just outside the bedroom door. It was enough light to give Kimani the advantage of seeing the killer undetected. Even at the tender age of eight, he knew that this was an advantage.

Advantage or not, it didn't stop him from losing his bladder.

Kimani remained quiet, waited, and left the shaking shotgun pointed in the direction of the bedroom door. Everything seemed silent, except for the thunderous sound of his palpitating heart. He helplessly listened as the killer tauntingly tapped the metal barrel of his own shotgun on the hard-concrete steps and ascended the last of the stairs.

Clank... Clank... Clank...

The music from below, as if hoping to observe Kimani's fate, became silent in wait. Everything and everyone seemed to be against him.

Clank... Clank... Clank...

An eternity had passed and the killer finally came into view. He stood there, just outside the bedroom door. He obviously felt no danger coming from this seemingly helpless little boy. Enjoying the moment, the killer took his sick little time flushing out his prey.

Kimani stayed as still as his nerves would allow. His body shaking uncontrollably, the huge shotgun that he held was threatening to fall from his small grip.

As if by instinct – or maybe the sound of deep breathing – the killer turned towards the bedroom where his victim waited and walked through the threshold. Being blinded by shear darkness, he calmly reached over to turn on the light switch. He spotted his prey, and with an expression of shock on his face, the wrong end of a shotgun barrel.

Kimani, not wanting to give the killer the opportunity to react, pulled the trigger...

CLICK...

Nothing.

Kimani felt his heart sink to his ass.

Did he do something wrong?

Did he break the weapon?

How could this be happening to him?

With wide eyes, he watched as the killer shrilled the worse laugh he'd ever heard in his life. Not being able to take this nightmare any longer – being the little child that he was – he did the only thing he could do. He broke down and began sobbing uncontrollably.

The killer raised his shotgun pump in Kimani's direction with that maleficent smirk never leaving his face. Though shocked at this kid's resilience to survive, he lived by only one understanding in his line of work. In his world, it was *always* the bad guys that survived.

Kimani closed his eyes and waited for the inevitable to happen. He knew what would come next. Even in desperate times such as this, he wondered if he would feel the burning sensation his father once told him resulted from being shot.

His father?

That unforgettable image burned into his memory of a murdered man that he would never speak to again; a man that he always thought of as strong. More tears ran down Kimani's face as his mind struggled to understand. His heart raced faster and faster, the tightening muscles in his stomach becoming unbearable to withstand. Thinking of his father, he remembered him once say that *your life flashed before your eyes just before you die*. But there was no life here, only agony and hurt.

The killer finally stopped laughing that torturous laugh of his, one that Kimani knew he would never forget. Knowing that this would be the end and not wanting to witness that end, he closed his eyes as tight as he could and waited for death to come.

There was no time for thought, no time for hope, just the sound of the loud gun blast as the killer finally pulled the trigger.

Silence...

Eyes still closed but listening intently, Kimani heard something heavy hitting the floor followed by the clanking of metal on hard tile. There was no burning sensation his father once mentioned; there was no pain. If this was what it was really like to die, then dying wasn't so bad.

Working up the nerve to open his eyes, Kimani was shocked to see his father's killer lying motionless on the floor before him, dead. Baffled and confused, he didn't understand what was happening. Why would the killer kill himself? How was it that the killer was dead, and *he* was alive?

His mind was still racing, his body was still shaking uncontrollably, and still he couldn't seem to take his eyes off of the dead man's eyes as they stared off into hell's abyss. He had never seen eyes like those before; wide open yet dim. All he could think about was that he'd hoped his eyes would never look like those eyes.

With everything that was happening before him, it was the warm caress that he felt envelope him that brought him out of his reverie. It wasn't until he felt the warmth of the body holding him that things began to make sense. He was cold, and his draws were soiled, but the warm hug that he felt, and the consoling sound of his mother's voice was the one thing in this madness that gave him comfort. Still, he'd never cried this hard before.

With the sound of sirens off in the distance – someone must've called the police – Kimani continued to shake as his mother held him tight. Even then, he was still unable to look away from those dead lifeless eyes; a dead stare that would stain him forever.

Madness...

When the law finally arrived, they pronounced five people, including the killer, dead. With drugs found on the premises, the state took Kimani while an investigation was underway. It was ruled that the initial suspect entered the home and killed four people over a drug dispute. While in the midst of trying to kill a fifth, the suspect was shot in the back by Ms. Johnson who acted to save her only child. Fortunately, it was noted, she'd left work early from her graveyard shift, making it home just in time.

It took a while before Ms. Johnson regained custody of Kimani again, and sometime, still, before he regained a semblance of a normal mind. He had been introduced into a life of cruelty and violence, and little did he know, this life was just beginning.

From this point on, his world would never be the same again.

CHAPTER 1
GENERALS AND SOLDIERS

MARCH 3rd. 5:40am
JAMES CACEY HOUSING PROJECTS
EAST NASHVILLE...

NINE YEARS LATER...

♪ "I won't deny it/ I'm a straight rida'/ you don't wanna fuck wit me/ got the police bustin' at me/ but they can't do nothin' to a..." ♪

The sounds of Tupac stormed through the walls of James Cacey housing projects, triggered by the alarm on his state-of-the-art stereo system. Nearly half the song played before he even thought about opening his eyes. Even as he reached for the remote to turn down the volume on the four, fifteen-inch woofers, he continued to lay there looking up at the ceiling.

Blame it on the liquor and pineapple cush he consumed at the house party the night before. His head was beating like two gorillas in the bushes. Nonetheless, he knew he had to be at school in an hour and fifteen

9

minutes. Sometimes, just being out of the house before his mother got home from work would suffice.

He was fairly intelligent for his age, book wise and street wise. At only seventeen, he was a senior in high school and a veteran in the streets. He didn't care too much for school, but that was only because there wasn't much money to be made there. Besides, his credits were already complete.

Five minutes had passed before he finally sat up in bed and glanced up at the clock; 5:45am it read. He hated mornings. Reaching over at the ashtray, he grabbed the half smoked blunt he never finished the night before. Searching around for his lighter unsuccessfully, he gave up, got out of bed, and made his way towards the kitchen to light the blunt on the stove.

Half asleep, Kimani stumbled, tripped, and nearly fell on a pair of jeans lying on the floor before catching his balance. Kicking the clothing out of frustration, he watched as a wad of money and the lighter he sought came out of the pockets of the jeans and went sliding across the room. Relieved, he grabbed the lighter, sat on the edge of his bed, and put one end of the blunt in his mouth. With a smile on his face, he happily sparked the other end.

This was the usual for him, like breakfast to some. He allowed the smoke to linger in his mouth for a few seconds before releasing it, only to inhale it deeply through his nostrils. He smiled, looked at the blunt, and took another hit before releasing the smoke into the atmosphere.

Finishing the blunt, Kimani put the roach into the ashtray. Ready to get the day started, he grabbed his hygiene kit off the dresser and headed for the bathroom down the hall.

Living in the projects, there wasn't much in the small bathroom, but it got the job done. Feeling the effects of the cush already, he laid his hygiene kit on the sink and reached over into the tub to turn on the water faucets. He could hear the rust on the old knobs rubbing together as he twisted them.

He turned around to retrieve his hygiene kit but was confused when he noticed that the kit wasn't there. "What the fuck," he mumbled. It should've been right where he left it. He followed the same routine every morning, placing the same kit in the same spot as he prepared for his shower. Kimani stopped searching in the few places it could've been when he spotted the kit on the floor next to the toilet. Not even speculating how it could've gotten there – it was too early for that – he merely picked up the kit and sat it back down on the sink. Unzipping the bag, he laid his items out on the small sink, giving the water in the shower time to heat up.

While Kimani brushed his teeth, the mirror over the sink began to condensate from the heat build-up. After rinsing out his mouth, he reached down to turn on the cold water to splash over his face. He needed to wake up. With water dripping from his nose, Kimani used his hand to wipe the accumulated condensation off of the mirror.

Staring into the mirror, he didn't expect to see what he saw behind him. There was an intruder standing there watching him; a young child from the looks of him. Kimani's heart skipped a beat. Quickly spinning around to face off the young kid, he was stunned to find himself in the bathroom alone.

"The fuck?" he said.

Looking around, even glancing back into the mirror, he knew he had to be tripping. There was no way the intruder could've disappeared that fast. The intruder – a small boy, maybe ten years of age – was right there. And now he was gone. He was definitely losing his fucking mind. It was clear he needed to lay off the pineapple cush this early in the morning. Shaking his head, and pushing the thought from his mind, he continued getting ready for the day.

Freshly showered, dreadlocks hanging to dry, he grabbed the remainder of his things and headed back to his bedroom. Once in the hallway, he stopped in his tracks. Either he was really on edge this morning, or something wasn't right after all.

Glancing down the short hallway, he noticed that his bedroom light was on. He didn't remember turning it on either. He never did in the early hours. The same routine! Realizing that there may be an intruder in his mother's home after all, Kimani dropped everything in his hands and went directly for his forty-caliber automatic he kept under his mattress.

Quickly lifting the mattress, he grabbed the pistol and inserted the clip that was lying beside it. As he chambered a round, he knew in the back of his mind he could easily overpower the intruder. After all, he was only a young kid. But in this neighborhood, the smallest of kids did the most grown-up of things.

Living on the second floor of the building, a child was known to get off inside an apartment by climbing a nearby tree and going in through a window. Once inside of a home, that child could merely unlock a door and allow a gang of killers or robbers inside.

Kimani couldn't allow for any of these things to happen.

All in one motion of loading the pistol, he raised the weapon towards the bedroom door.

In situations like this, he knew that his ears could be his most vital asset. He listened carefully for any possible noise inside of the home. He heard nothing. He moved towards the bedroom door, Glock first, and peered into the hallway. The path was clear. He checked every room and every closet on his way down the hallway. He knew it would be a mistake to allow an enemy to get behind him. He checked behind every appliance and under every bed but came up empty handed. In the process, he checked every window and every door to ensure that they were locked.

When it was all said and done, he found himself paranoid and alone.

Maybe I did leave the light on, he thought to himself, though he didn't remember doing so. It could've been the hangover from the night before or the weed he'd smoked only moments ago. Either way, his palms and forehead were sweating, and his heart was trying to pound its way out of his chest.

He reluctantly exited the clip from the pistol and cocked the slid to extract the bullet from the chamber. Using the tank-top he was wearing Kimani wiped the bullet clean of any possible fingerprints before inserting it back into the clip. Grabbing his things off the hallway floor, he went to his room, placed the .40 caliber and clip back under his mattress and allowed himself to laugh at his foolishness. Again, he knew he was tripping.

He looked up at the clock on his stereo, it was 6:16am. He only had twenty-nine minutes to get ready for school and be on the bus-stop. As he got dressed, he thought about the morning so far. Paranoia could be useful sometimes,

13

but it could also be dangerous if you didn't know how to utilize it. One minute your heart was racing, and the next someone was either hurt or dead. On the other hand, if balanced, it could be used to sharpen your senses, but there had to be equilibrium. Like everything else in his life, he learned that lesson the hard way. Without such lessons there would've been a lack of self-preservation, the will to protect himself and survive.

Putting his thoughts aside, Kimani continued to dress. Sliding into a pair of freshly pressed jeans, he made sure to button and zip them up. With an icy-white tee-shirt on, he placed a custom-made North Carolina jersey over it. With the word *baNgside* and the number 90 stitched on the back, he knew he would be reppin' the set. An Eddie Bauer watch graced his wrist as he selected a pair of grey Tim's to go with his fit. With a spray of cologne, he was ready to hit the yard.

He grabbed his backpack and headed for the front door.

At 6:31am, James Cacey Housing Projects was as live as ever. Workers stood on the corners catching sell after sell. Homies ducked off in the cut rolling dice. Things never changed here. If there was a way to make money, it would be made.

Just like that.

With everything at the norm, Kimani moved on. There was simply no time to stop.

His hood was like no other hood in the city and larger than most. Everything from 4th to 12th, Shelby to Glenview, was controlled by the baNgside 90 Crips. At seventeen, he was only a lil homie on the set, but it didn't mean that he wasn't a force to be reckoned with. His hood was one of many established gangs in the city and had been for some time now. Notorious for making shit happen, gettin' money, and making shit happen, it was one of the many attributes that drew most youngsta's to it. A lot of hoodsta shit took place on these blocks, and a lot of the city's money circulated through these very streets. Over the years, it had become its very own economical system.

Kimani, who was just seconds from the bus-stop, noticed that something wasn't as it should be. There were no other students there waiting to be carted off to school. He looked down at his Eddie Bauer watch, 6:43am it read. He wasn't late, and he wasn't too early either. He could only hope that the bus hadn't run early today. If so, it would be another fifteen minutes or so before the next...

"What the fuck," he blurted aloud, looking at his watch again.

He was embarrassed now. Staring in disbelief, he casually noticed what the problem was. It was a fucking Saturday, and everyone in their right mind knew that there was no school on Saturdays.

As foolish and embarrassed as he felt, he continued to walk without missing a step hoping that no one noticed how dumb he looked.

He planned on walking around the corner and simply going back to his building, but that was before he spotted the platinum-colored '69 Lincoln Continental on a set of twenty-six-inch rims coming his way. It wasn't the cleanliness of the ride that made him stop – too often he saw clean rides in this hood – it was the fact that the vehicle began to slow down just as the passenger-side window gave way to the passengers inside. Only fifteen feet from where he stood, an arm leaned out of the window to reveal a .357 automatic pistol. This was one fucked up morning he was having.

Kimani froze. His life flashed before his eyes. Life. Death. If only his damn memory had been right, he would've been at home still in bed. Funny, he thought, how fate had a way of taking course. Just as he was concluding that thought, the passenger and his pistol emerged farther and everything around him seemed to slow down. He remembered this same sensation the night his father died almost ten years ago – the feeling of clutching fear – as bits and pieces of death crossed his mind. A million questions came to him as the car stopped and the passenger pulled the trigger.

Instantly Kimani's shirt became soaking wet as fluid rushed down his chest. He felt the fabric of his white tee sticking to his body. In this moment he worried about his mother and how she would feel when she discovered that her only child had been shot.

Kimani reached down and grabbed his abdomen expecting to feel pain but there was none. Instead of blood, his shirt was wet with water. These clown-ass nigga's were playing with water guns. He could hear the occupants of the vehicle laughing at his dumbfounded expression.

The passenger, the fool laughing the hardest, was Kimani's life-long homeboy, C-loco. The driver, Tee-Tee, was one of the older homies in the hood. He alone has put in more work than Kimani and C-loco together, and these two have put in their fair share.

Still, Kimani was livid.

"The fuck y'all playin' fo', Cuz? That bullshit ain't funny," he yelled. "Y'all nigga's goin' fuck around and get dealt wit'." He warned as his irritation sat in. He was angry, and they both knew it, but that only made them laugh even harder.

His heart was racing, and his breathing had become sporadic. Truth be told, he knew how lucky he was that these two *were* his homies and that they *were* playing. Though they probably wouldn't have made it out of the hood alive had they been the op', neither would he, more than likely.

C-loco looked at Kimani and attempted to talk through his laughter, although it wasn't as easy as he made it seem. "Damn, Cuz... you aight? You look like you knew yo' ass was through." C-loco pointed at Kimani and laughed harder to show how hysterical he thought the shit truly was. "It's all good, Cuz." He smacked the side of the door with his hand as he saw the look on Kimani's face. "Ain't no love lost, homie."

Kimani was breathing hard, trying to calm his nerves. It was hard being mad and happy at the same time. He watched as C-Loco eased his laughter and attempted to be more serious. Looking at him, he saw the drastic change in his expression. It was much more serious than before.

"Hop in, li'l nigga," stated C-loco. "Some wax got's to get handled and Bones want us to take care of it." C-loco mentioned the big-homie. "You down, or what?"

Kimani was tripping at his friends ability to go from play mode straight to beast mode. That had to be a sign of his own insanity. But insane or not, when the big homies name came up, shit got real.

Kimani could tell by the seriousness of their demeanor that something bad must have happened. He was a rida, and right or wrong, he was always ready to ride. "Yeah, nigga. I'm down. What it is?"

He reached for the door handle to the back seat only to find that it wasn't there, it was a kiss-door Lincoln. The entire back door was put on backwards. Correcting himself, Kimani opened the door and got in. "The fuck, nigga, yo' dumb ass didn't know how to put the door on right?" he jokingly asked Tee-Tee. After letting them get the best of him, he tried to put himself in a better mood.

The inside of the vehicle was just as clean as the outside; what's a fresh ride without the heart? A foot-long flat screen tv embedded the front dash and five smaller flats were embedded into the sun visors, stirring wheel, and behind the two-head rest for the viewers in the back seat. Kimani sat down on the plush leather, milk-white seats, shut the forward-facing door, and tossed his backpack down on the floorboard.

"So West craccin'? What it is?" he asked.

"What it was?" responded C-loco. He remained silent for another fifteen seconds or so before saying what no one wanted to say out loud.

Kimani was getting the impression that something really bad had happened. After what seemed like forever, he urged his homie to continue.

"T-Baby got caught up in that drive-by at the block party last night," C-loco revealed.

"What drive-by? And what you mean he got caught up? He aight, ain't he?" Kimani's heart began racing.

"You wasn't there. You left early," C-loco explained. "We was goin' handle this shit last night, but we wasn't able to find the bitch ass nigga responsible. Nigga's been up all night trying to find the Mark. Now that Bones got a fix on the nigga's location, he want us to go and handle the shit."

Kimani heard everything that C-loco said, but his mind was mostly focused on T-Baby, and his unanswered question. "T-Baby... he aight, right?"

"Naw, Cuz. T-Baby dead."

Silence.

Kimani couldn't believe the words that he was hearing. "He can't be dead, Cuz. I was just wit' him last night. We was just at the block party..." He felt numb, hurt, sorrow. Words could not explain the pain that he was feeling at that moment. When the truth of it all began to sink in, he simply closed his eyes and laid his head back on the head rest; another one of his close friend's dead.

T-Baby, 16, whose real name was Terry, got his tag when he was only ten years old. Even at that age he would try to run up and hop into a car when some homies were going to take care of some wax. The big homies would have to smack him in the back of the head to make him stay. Even then, he was reluctant to do so. They allowed him to do the simple things like running errands here and there, a message there and here. The big homie Bones wouldn't allow anyone that age to do anything more. For as long as Kimani knew him, all he ever wanted to do was be down with the 90's.

It was an appetite that cost him his life.

After a few moments of silence, Kimani spoke. "What up? What we goin' do now?"

It was Tee-Tee who responded, "strap up, nigga. We goin' on a ride to the south side."

"The south side?" Kimani asked. "Who the fuck nigga's responsible fo' this shit, Cuz?" Coming from the south side, it was a question he already knew the answer to.

"It was some bitch ass nigga from U.C.," said C-loco. "The word is, somebody from the block blasted on them fools and they wanted to get back." C-loco paused for a second before continuing, "if it's a battle they want, we goin' bring them the whole fuckin' war." He reached under his seat and pulled out a fully automatic Uzi with its four, one-hundred round clips. He always prepared for the worst.

"How we know they was the ones that did this shit, Cuz?" asked Kimani. Yet another question he already knew the answer to.

"It all came from up top," responded Tee-Tee.

It always came from up top. Kimani was merely trying to keep his mind off T-Baby.

Tee-Tee reached into his pocket and pulled out a pack of Newport's. He hit the bottom of the pack with the palm of his hand until a cigarette slid out. He placed the single into his mouth. Before he could reach for his own lighter, C-loco had his sparked and placed in front of him to allow him to focus on driving.

U.C., everyone knew, was short for University Court, a three-story south side housing project that was just as ruthless as James Cacey. They were also one of the baNgside 90's primary rivals. The two sets had road on each other countless times.

As usual, everyone was a victim, and often, more than not, an innocent victim. Like T-Baby. If anybody did anything to the others hood, the consequences would often be deadly for both sides. That's why damn near every time Rollin-90's struck, it was coordinated from the top. Everyone had to pay the price. No matter who it was, or how severe. Just like that.

The trio road down south 7th avenue before Tee-Tee turned right on Dew St. It's what everybody in the hood called 'The Cut,' one of several cuts in the neighborhood. It was where Tee-Tee had his latest spot. They drove to the nearest parking lot, parked, and got out of the vehicle. All three walked to Tee-Tee's building.

Though it was early, it was crowded out in this part of the neighborhood. From hustlers, to junkies, to the children that played in between, this was life in the hood. C-loco and Tee-Tee spoke to one another as they walked just ahead of Kimani. He couldn't hear what they were speaking of, but it didn't matter, with thoughts of T-baby bombarding his mind, his attention had been grabbed elsewhere.

He watched as a little girl – five, maybe six – sat on a porch of one of the project buildings up ahead. She was crying. Tears were running down her face like a leaking faucet.

It wasn't odd to see a child crying in these conditions. Due to poverty and hunger, it happened more often than not. But it struck him to his core to see that the little girl was staring at him. When he moved, her eyes moved with him. As the trio walked past her porch, her gaze followed his every move. Kimani, almost in a trance now, turned his neck as he walked past her unable to look away. For some reason he couldn't explain, he felt all of the sympathy in the world for her, almost as if his heart had been wounded along with hers. Oddly, her eyes reminded him of the dead man's eyes he stared at all those years ago, as if they were staring right through him. She had been helplessly neglected, like this cold world had chewed her up and spit her out.

Tat... tat... tat... tat... tat... tat... tat... tat... tat...

The sounds of gunshot blasts dominated the air. It brought Kimani out of his reverie as he ducked low and sought out the culprits. C-loco had his Uzi up and ready, but relaxed when he realized that some fools were just shooting their guns in the air. The three shook their heads, looked at one another, and moved on as someone else stated the obvious; something about them nigga's bull shittin'.

Just before they turned the corner to Tee-Tee's building, Kimani looked back one last time to check on the little girl. She was no longer there. She too must have been shaken by the gun blast.

He put her out of his mind and sped up to join his *Conrad's*. There were things that had to be done, and he was beyond ready to get them over with. Tee-Tee was unlocking the door to his spot when Kimani caught up with them. He, being the last one in, shut the door behind him and locked it.

Once in the apartment, Kimani and C-loco sat down at the kitchen table while Tee-Tee went into another room of the small project apartment.

Kimani, wondering how long this ordeal was going to take, reached into his pocket and pulled out a fat sack of the pineapple cush he carried. He grabbed one of the cigars Tee-Tee had lying around and proceeded to break it down. With T-Baby still on his mind, he quickly rolled up a fat blunt of the cush and blazed it.

C-loco, on the other hand, had what appeared to be an eight-ball sack of cocaine. Opening the small packet, he cuffed the open end of the bag between his fingers as the sack rested in his palms. Squeezing the opened end ever so slightly, he allowed a tiny portion of the substance to pour out onto the back of his hand. Bringing the powder up to his nostril, C-loco inhaled deeply.

Tee-Tee came back into the kitchen with a Tech-9 in one hand and a photograph in the other. He walked up to the table to take a seat with his *Conrad's* and placed the photograph on the table for the three of them to see. The focal point of the photo was of a dark-skinned individual with corn-rolls zigzagging through his head. He stood on a street corner surrounded by a crowd of people in what appeared to be University Court.

Kimani and C-loco stared at the picture in silence as Tee-Tee spoke, "this is Dirty." Tee-Tee tapped the photograph with his finger. "Word is, the bitch nigga pulled the trigger on my nephew. Shit, y'all niggas know what we gotta do. This bitch ass nigga gotta go." No one spoke. No one had to. They just stared at the photo. They all knew what had to be done. "Any questions?"

C-loco remembered a time when he used to get jitters preparing for something like this. Now, it was more like breathing really hard. He didn't have a problem with it, some people said he even craved it. Instead of pouring the cocaine on the back of his hand like before, he just simply put the bag up to his nose and inhaled deeply. It left residue on the tip of his nose and upper lip. The boy was mad.

Kimani never understood why C-loco snorted that shit, but he never asked why either. He watched C-loco as he got up, went to the sink, and poured himself a cup of warm water. Dipping his fingers into the water, he sniffed the drops off of the tips of his fingers and into his nose to help aid his drain.

At the table, Kimani looked at the picture of Dirty in silence. Knowing that the nigga was about to die by the hands of him and his *Conrad's*, he stared, unable to look away. He didn't even know the nigga, never seen him a day in this life, but it was a face that he would never forget. Thumping the ashes from his blunt into the ashtray, he hit it once again before sitting the blunt down all together. He gave Tee-Tee a look of readiness, and on cue, Tee-Tee gave him the Tech-9 he had been holding.

"Let's do this shit, Cuz," Kimani said with a little heart.

Tee-Tee smiled, stood up, then walked over to the back door.

"Yeah, fool!" shouted C-loco. "Let's go! Let's ride on these unicorn ass nigga's." He began walking over to the back door before stopping to look back at Kimani. "Nigga, let's ride, fool. The fuck you waitin' fo'? Just look at 'em like duck's, nigga. Quack, quack, mufucka'. Let's roll."

Kimani didn't say a thing. He simply stood up with the rest and walked out the back door. There wasn't any turning back now. Just get it over with and don't talk about it no more. Just like that.

Outside, they all walked back towards the parking lot. These nigga's didn't give a damn about being out in broad daylight with heavy artillery in their hands. When they looked someone in the eyes, the other person quickly looked away. People tended to mind their own business in this neighborhood, and for good reasons too. Just before reaching the parking lot, Tee-Tee stopped. Kimani and C-loco did the same. For no other reason that the latter two could see, they waited.

"What's up?" asked C-loco.

Tee-Tee never responded, he only continued to search the parking lot as if looking for someone.

Kimani, not wanting to ask about their halt, looked around to see if he could spot the little girl again. He didn't know why he was thinking about it, he just was. Why was she crying? Why was she staring at him of all people? It almost felt like she was trying to tell him something but disappeared when he failed to listen. Giving up his search after failing to spot her, he turned back to Tee-Tee and followed his gaze. Whomever he had been searching for, he'd found them.

Kimani easily spotted the person. Unlike everyone else they glanced at, this person didn't bother to look away. It wasn't until the individual got closer that Kimani realized who he was.

Ray-Ray was a twenty-year old homie on the set. Growing up in the hood, putting on for the baNgside came natural to him. He too was in his feelings about T-Baby.

His attribute to the block – O.G. Bones saw early on – was the gift of deception. It was easy for him to catch people off guard. Bones, being the mastermind that he was, molded Ray-Ray into the perfect soldier. One that followed orders and never asked questions.

Tee-Tee waited for Ray-Ray to approach. He never knew who he was to meet up with in situations like these, as Bones had stated before, people talked less that way. In times of war, by the time any information leaked – if it ever was – the mission would be done and over. There were spies everywhere, ears and eyes belonging to the enemy. If one wasn't too careful, you could lead your hitters right into an ambush.

When Ray-Ray finally approached, he first hit up with Tee-Tee – interlocking and manipulating their finger to chuck up the hood – before doing likewise with Kimani and C-loco. It was the way the baNgside often greeted one another, showing love for the set.

It was Tee-Tee who spoke first, "how you feelin', homie?" He didn't really want to know the answer to the question, he just wanted to ensure that Ray-Ray was the right handler before continuing.

"Cool as a fuckin' fan," Ray-Ray correctly replied. Again, if information got into the wrong hands – U.C. nigga's in particular – this whole mission could take a turn for the worse. Such security protocols had been established decades ago. Everything was always 'need to know' basis. Compartmentalized information kept the hood alive.

"Speak on it, Cuz," Tee-Tee urged. He was anxious to put this play into motion.

"It's been confirmed, homie, by eight different reliable sources. Dirty's our vic'." Vic' was short for victim; the person on the off list. Ray-Ray continued, "y'all got the blue light to go 'head and handle y'all wax. The nigga been posted on the block all mornin'. Cuz been sendin' sells his way to make sure it stays that way. The big homie watchin', if anything changes between here and there, you'll be paged."

Ray-Ray didn't have to ask if Tee-Tee knew the page ciphers, everyone with significant job descriptions had them – each a different set of codes – and it was mandatory that they knew how to decipher them. He turned slightly to his left, an indication that they were almost done, and continued, "get in, get out, and leave it as fucked up as possible. Big Cuz said he wanna meet up when y'all done. You know he goin' wanna know the details. Keep yo' head on a swivel. Watch yo' six."

Ray-Ray hit Tee-Tee up one last time, only this time they both swapped keys in the process; so subtle with the exchange that neither Kimani nor C-loco saw the move and these two don't miss much.

26

The trio walked into the direction that Ray-Ray had come from while Ray-Ray walked the opposite way. His job was done for now.

Forty paces and Tee-Tee raised the alarm transmitter attached to the keys Ray-Ray had given him. He pressed the unlock button on the transmitter and watched as a '96 Ford Taurus' lights flashed. It was immediately followed by a few blares from the horn. They walked over to the vehicle and got inside. With C-loco in the front passenger seat and Kimani in the back seat, Tee-Tee started the engine and they drove off headed in the direction of University Court.

It took them twenty minutes to reach the south side. Coming off the expressway, Tee-Tee turned left on Lafayette Avenue until they came up on Charles E. Davis Boulevard and University Court.

They had reached their destination.

An endless row of project buildings dominated the landscape off to the left; row after row of three-story project buildings nearly as far as the eye could see. Tee-Tee immediately pulled off to the side of the boulevard to survey the scenery. He left the car in drive for obvious reasons, they were in enemy territory and their intentions weren't welcomed.

Kimani looked at his watch. 8:04am it read. Too early to put in work if you asked him, but who asked him.

Tee-Tee looked from his driver-side, rearview, to the passenger-side mirrors and back. He repeated his observation of his surroundings as they waited, knowing that they were vulnerable just sitting there. On any other mission, they would've just drove and sprayed anyone in sight, but this wasn't just any other mission; they wanted one person in particular, then the rest.

C-loco looked around and noticed forty, to sixty people standing out on the block of Charles E. Davis. He scanned the area in an attempt to zero in on Dirty. It was a long strip, and it took him a second to find him, but once he did, he tapped Tee-Tee on the shoulder – a little hard, Tee-Tee thought – and said, "there that nigga go right there, Cuz. Standin' in front of the corner sto', right next to the pay phone."

Tee-Tee and Kimani nonchalantly looked in the direction C-loco was indicating. Trying not to draw attention to themselves, they watched Dirty as he had his right leg cocked back up against the wall of the corner store. From the looks of it, he was in the process of catching a sell. The three immediately recognized who the sell was; a junkie from around the way. O.G. Bones never ceased to amaze as a tactician.

Dirty was a slim nigga known for his shit talk and ruthless destruction on the battlefield. Every army had their gunners – a master grade-A warrior – and Dirty was that for U.C. They were individuals that seemed to get the impossible done; the ones that always seemed to be standing on their two feet when the smoke cleared.

Dirty stood there laughing and joking with his peers; they too would become casualties on this day. To the trio in the car, he appeared to have no remorse for his actions. For that, he would pay with his life.

Tee-Tee, being a big homie on the set, wasn't here because he had to be. For him, this shit was personal; he was happy to retaliate on the bitch ass nigga that senselessly killed his nephew. The more he saw Dirty laughing and joking, the more disgusted he became. He smirked, sucked his teeth, and then put his foot on the accelerator.

Kimani and C-loco placed red bandannas on their heads to mask their true identities and prepared themselves for what was to come.

"Yeah, nigga..." said C-loco. "... let's blast on these off-brand ass nigga's."

Tee-Tee used his control panel to let all of the windows down; shattered glass could be hazardous. It seemed like an eternity from where they were to where their target stood. Always the strategist, he would drive normal until they got within thirty yards from their targets before smashing the gas pedal.

They drove down Charles E. Davis Boulevard just one-hundred yards from their mark.

C-loco hit the slide to the Uzi he held and kept Dirty in his line of sight. This was the moment he had been waiting for. His heart raced, but never skipped a beat. He already placed Dirty on his list of kills in the archives of his mind; another notch on his pistol grip.

Sixty yards.

Kimani grabbed the tech-9 Tee-Tee had given him and held it up at the ready. Though he'd killed before, it still wasn't something that he enjoyed; he wasn't sure that he ever would. He thought back to that morning when he thought he was about to die and found – as always before – that he liked it better when he was behind the trigger.

When dealing with death as he was now, he often thought back to his father; an image of a murdered man that he would never forget. Of all the things that he had forgotten about his father over the years – the sound of his voice, the details in his face – it was his headless body that always stayed vivid. He put the memory aside for now.

Forty yards.

Tee-Tee turned the volume up on the stereo; his trademark in battle. *Brotha Lynch Hungs', 'rest in piss'* blasted through the speakers for any on-looker to hear. War was inevitable, and he felt they had already waited too long for this. Things like this had to be dealt with sooner than later; the longer one took to respond to an enemy was an advantage gained by that enemy.

He wanted to wait another ten yards before smashing the gas pedal to the floor and giving the order to shoot, but he had no time to give that order. The trio heard someone scream,

"DRIVE-BY..."

The element of surprise gone, it was now or never. Just short of his attack point, Tee-Tee smashed the gas as Kimani and C-loco leaned their upper bodies out the windows. There always came that time when shit just had to be done; this was that time.

Kimani could see their enemies pulling out their straps to bust back. He sprayed the tech in their direction. Striking three marks with one sway of motion, he watched them as they all three went down. Not having the time nor interest to stare, he moved on. There were other ducks to pluck. He took aim.

C-loco, wasting no time, pointed the Uzi directly at Dirty and pulled the trigger. The Israeli-made weapon's first burst of bullets struck Dirty square in the chest; they caused his body to jerk backwards and his life's fluids to spray on the corner store wall just behind him.

Drive-by's were the most effective guerrilla tactic known to urban warfare. It was strictly a hit and run affair. The targets afar appear to stand still making for an easy score, while the vehicle remained in motion making it difficult for the enemy to take aim. Unlike back in the day, with easy access to fully automatics, it made the tactic that much more deadly.

Tee-Tee swerved as bullets from the enemy struck the vehicle but kept his composure despite the loud sound of bullets hitting metal. He ducked down as low as possible, making himself a smaller target. He knew that their survival depended on his ability to drive. He wasn't trying to make this a one-way trip.

Just a few more yards, he kept thinking to himself.

Their enemies tried to blast back, but their weapons were no match for the heat coming out of the black Taurus. They continued to blast rounds at the enemy, trying to incapacitate as many as possible.

In all of the chaos, Kimani noticed that people were running for safety. Some just laid on the ground in hopes that they didn't get hit. Some were trying to blast back; that's where he aimed his sights.

But before he could pull the trigger, he stopped and stared in Dirty's direction. His heart stopped beating at what he saw. Directly in front of where Dirty's body lay dead – calmly sitting down on the street curb – was the little girl that he lost sight of earlier; the same little girl that was sitting on the porch crying; the same little girl that wouldn't stop staring at him. She was still crying, and she was still staring at him – with all intent – directly in the eyes. What bothered Kimani the most wasn't the fact that she had gotten clear across town before him, or that she still had sorrow pouring out of her eyes; what disturbed Kimani the most was that she didn't appear to be afraid like everyone else who hopelessly ran for their lives.

Instead of fright, there was hurt. All of the shooting, the screaming, the pandemonium, and she showed no attempt to run, hide, or to take cover. Unlike everyone else in the vicinity, she seemed to be in a world of her own. His heart raced, his mind raced, but everything else was in slow motion. He couldn't believe what he was seeing.

Then Kimani heard a familiar sound; the sound of space being pierced at high speeds. And just like that, more enemy bullets rippled the car. He felt the bullet as it struck him, slamming his body hard against the back seat. The suddenness of it along with the agony of the burning sensation caused him to scream out in pain as he dropped his weapon to the floorboard. He could hardly breathe at that moment; it felt like a thousand pounds of bricks were on his chest.

C-loco sprayed the rest of his magazine from the Uzi and immediately jumped in the back seat to check on his *Conrad*. After all of the killing, it was the possibility of losing another homie that made his heart skip a beat.

The left side of Kimani's shirt was quickly becoming saturated with his own blood. He looked down to see the blood for himself and the sight of it all scared the shit out of him. He was getting light-headed but willed himself to stay conscious for fear of never waking up again.

Again, moments like these made him think of the night his father was killed. He thought about that night often, and him standing at the top of those long flight of stairs. While his wound was burning like hell, he was sure his father didn't feel a thing.

C-loco reached down, and using a pocketknife, cut the jersey and white-tee loose from Kimani's body. Frantic, he yelled for Tee-Tee to get to a hospital. Tee-Tee, being the veteran of the three, knew better; getting the authorities involved was the last thing he needed. When C-loco finally got the clothing off, he used the torn white-tee to wipe the blood away from Kimani's body. Relieved at the small wound, he took a deep breath before looking at his *Conrad*. He then started laughing; his homie had only been grazed in the shoulder.

"Nigga, get yo' soft ass up. You goin' be aight. That ain't nothin' but a scratch, fool." C-loco pointed at Kimani's shoulder. "you huffin' and puffin' like yo' ass got hit in the lung or somethin'. Cry-baby ass nigga." C-loco always found the oddest times to laugh and joke about the oddest shit. Maybe it was what kept him sane; or insane depending on one's perspective.

Kimani, a little agitated and sore, sat up and leaned back against the seat. The vehicle smelled like strong gun-smoke; strong enough to leave a metallic taste in his mouth. Looking down at his wound, he saw that the blood had already begun to slow to a trickle as it began to coagulate. He felt his entire body, to be on the safe side, ensuring that he had no other wounds.

"Nigga, you cryin' over that lil shit?" C-loco continued, "imagine how that weak ass nigga Dirty felt when I wet his bitch ass up?" He made shooting gestures with his hands. "Did you see that shit, Cuz? My heat had that nigga's body jumpin'. I did that shit, fool." C-loco, claiming his score, started laughing about his work.

Kimani realized how easy it was to breathe now that he knew that he would be alright; mind over matter. He glanced over at C-loco as he continued to brag. Knowing from experience how ill this nigga truly was he looked away, shaking his head in disbelief. Some people just refused to understand; either that or they found that it was easier not to understand. Ignorance was bliss.

Looking out the window, he saw that they were leaving University Court and was glad that it was all over. Still holding his wounded shoulder with his white tee, he found himself thinking once again about the little girl. He pictured her still crying. Why she wasn't trying to run like all the other helpless people was the question that bothered him most. It was sort of eerie for him to see her sitting there like that; oblivious to all but him. Wondering how she got from James Cacey to U.C. before them – she didn't appear to be with anyone in either place – was something that nagged at the back of his mind. He couldn't answer any of the many questions tumbling through his head, and he wasn't even fully sure if he wanted to. But one thing was certain, sometimes he felt like he was losing his fucking mind.

Tee-Tee concentrated on driving as he spoke, "come on, nigga. Get yo' ass back up front and act normal. We can't afford to get pulled over. This shit over wit'." He chucked up the N's, then continued, "O.G. Bones goin' be satisfied. Let's report, get back to the hood, and watch these niggas on the news. We just made these bitches famous."

With that, the trio left the south side and headed back to the wicked-east. Kimani's watch read 8:16am. Still early. He was ready to get back to the house but knew that they had to report to Bones first, it could be hours before he finally got home. Resigned, he closed his eyes, laid his head back on the headrest, and thought about the morning's events. With C-loco back in the front seat, it became much easier for him to concentrate, and the one thing that stuck out to him the most was a simple question…

Why did the world have to be so damn cruel?

CHAPTER 2
REALITY

MARCH 3RD. 8:21am.
NEIGHBORHOOD LASER PRINTING SHOP

NORTH NASHVILLE...

He was tired. Only three and a half hours left until his shift was over, but he knew he would be leaving before that. His job was easy. All he had to do was print out a particular amount of copies for a particular customer depending on that customer's needs. Anywhere from 8x12's to poster-sized copying. Once the items were paid for, he would then either hand the items over on site or have them mailed via postal services.

Today was the day that he would be visited by a certain individual with a secure locked money bag. He was to receive the bag with no questions asked. After the bag was received, he was to give the deliverer of the bag simple directions to a certain location down the avenue. Compartmentalized information was all that he was ever given.

He was usually told to secure the bag in the safe at the back of the shop, where it would then disappear sometime in the middle of the night, but today was different. Instead of the bag disappearing in the middle of the night, he would simply take it with him.

A customer was just leaving when the shop phone rang. He answered it.

"Neighborhood Printing," he said in a professional voice. "This is Donte speaking. How may I help you?"

He listened, but no one said a thing. The phone line went dead.

Of course, he knew what this meant. He was about to be paid a visit. As if on cue, a large Hispanic male with swollen biceps walked into the shop. With the shop empty of customers, and the door now closed, Donte pressed a button under the counter that automatically locked the door and switched the electrical 'OPEN' sign to 'CLOSED'.

He hated this particular customer. He'd dealt with him before and felt like the man asked too many questions. Donte hated questions. Just as he expected, the man with the swollen biceps started to speak.

Donte quickly held up his hand to cut the man off. The man looked surprised but didn't say a word. Donte turned and walked to the nearest copying machine and pressed one, three times before pressing the green 'copy' button. The machine came to life with a low humming sound.

It was something that Bones taught him to do many years ago. He remembered the O.G. placing a hand on his shoulder and speaking, "the hummin' vibration of the machine catches any noise comin' out of this shop and scrambles it. Makes it impossible to be picked up by electronics." Bones cocked his head and continued, "you know, in case them boys got an infrared microphone pointed at my building; all they'll get back is static." Donte would never forget the way the O.G. looked out the window of the shop as if expecting something. "'You never know when the place is being watched, Cuz." Bones clicked his tongue for effect. Donte hated it when he made that clicking sound.

The thought of secure money bags, copying machines, and transactions all made him a little nervous. He didn't care though, Bones paid him too well to complain.

When he finally came back to the counter, the Hispanic man with the swollen biceps, asked, "what's yo' name, kid?" The man asked that same question every time.

"Donte," he answered. He didn't care, it wasn't his real name.

The Hispanic man put the bag on the table and watched as Donte grabbed it and put it on the floor beside him. Donte stared at the man expecting to get more questions. When none came, he said, "go to Sound Music Recordin' Studios. It's just two blocks that way." He pointed. "It'll be on yo' left. Ask for a Donnell Brooks. He'll tell you what's up from there." Donte continued to stare at the man. He just knew that he was bound to ask another question. And just like that, he did.

"Is the whole ten kilos of cocaine there? That pure white shit?"

Donte could barely manage to keep a straight face. He despised square mu'fucka's who tried to act hard; if they had to try then it just wasn't for them. He smirked, sucked his teeth and said, "I don't know what the fuck you talkin' 'bout, homeboy, but you might wanna hurry befo' yo' train leave."

Donte could tell that the Hispanic man felt the tension in the air; the man didn't say another word. Instead, he retreated towards the front door. Thinking that it would be open, he attempted to go through but found that it was locked. He ran into the glass face first before he could stop his momentum. Donte, laughing, waited a few seconds before hitting the button underneath the counter to let the man out. When he did, the 'CLOSED' sign changed to 'OPEN', and the copying machine stopped humming.

Donte reached for his cell phone…

…He answered the ringing cell phone. When no one said a word, he hung up, grabbed the package off the passenger seat and got out of the van. He walked with his head down and his U.P.S. hat pulled low over his eyes. With his full brown U.P.S. uniform on, he was about to drop off a specially delivered package.

Walking into the entrance of Sound Music Recording Studios, he went up to the man standing behind the counter on the far side of the lobby.

He delicately laid the package down on the counter-top. U.P.S. workers had to be careful with customer belongings. While he waited for the man behind the counter to finish up his conversation on the phone, he casually looked at the merchandise through the glass countertop before him.

When the receptionist finally hung up the phone, the two men stared at one another without saying a word. It was the U.P.S. man that finally broke the silence.

"I have a package here for a…" He looked at his clip board. "…Donnell Brooks. It says here… musical equipment from 'Music Friends'." The U.P.S. man looked back up at the man behind the counter. With the silence that ensued, he thought that maybe Mr. Brooks wasn't on the premises, but then the man behind the counter picked up the phone and dialed a three-digit number indicating an in-house call. He said a few words, hung up the phone, then looked back at the U.P.S. man.

"He'll be up in a minute," was all that the man behind the counter said.

It wasn't even that long before the U.P.S. man saw Donnell Brooks coming through a door at the back of the lobby. The man of the hour was coming to claim his package. Signing his name to the touch screen on the clip board, Donnell Brooks simply grabbed his package off the counter and went back the way he'd come.

The U.P.S. man saw a piece of merchandise through the glass counter that he liked but knew that he was pressed for time and turned to leave instead. When he walked through the exit door, the man behind the counter watched as he reached into his pocket and pulled out a cell phone. Making a call, he put the phone up to his ear. The man behind the counter never saw the U.P.S. man again…

…He was parked in a Krystal's parking lot just across the avenue from Sound Music Studios. He waited patiently, scanning all police frequencies as he did. Know thy enemy and friends of thy enemy, was a practice he took to heart. In his lap lay a black transmitter; a remote. He knew that once the switch was thrown it would be hell on Charlotte Avenue.

He'd been waiting patiently for his phone to ring. Once it did, he opened the line but didn't say a word. As he expected, there was silence on the other end. He hung up the phone and threw it onto the seat next to him. Turning the volume down on the scanner, the man picked up the transmitter, and kept his eye on the studio just across the avenue.

He focused as a Hispanic man stepped out of a tinted blue ford sedan and walked into the lobby of the studio, just as the U.P.S. man was getting into his brown U.P.S. stenciled van. As the Hispanic man disappeared into the building, he waited twenty seconds before lifting the safeguard on the transmitter. He was highly efficient in the art; this wasn't his first time manipulating such devices.

Placing his thumb on the silver switch, he pressed it and watched as Sound Music Recording Studios lit up the day with an explosion that was heard for miles.

The man with the transmitter got out of the car and walked into the Krystal's restaurant to get a bite to eat as if nothing happened. While people chaotically ran in every direction, and cars on the avenue crashed into one another, he calmly walked into the restaurant. Knowing that his next chess piece had been moved, the man with the transmitter reached for his cell phone…

They drove to a McDonalds on the twenty-six hundred block of Gallatin pike and pulled into the parking lot. C-loco had given Kimani one of the two white-tee's that he had on so as not to draw attention. The wound on Kimani's left shoulder had stopped bleeding, but it still left a small streak of blood on the new white tee that he wore. At this point he really didn't care; he had things on his mind and just wanted this to be over with.

The trio got out of the car and walked into the restaurant.

Walking up to the counter, Tee-Tee and C-loco ordered but Kimani discovered that he wasn't hungry. *How could they eat*, he wondered? When their orders came back, Tee-Tee led them around the corner to the back of the dining area. Kimani, the last to approach, came up to take his seat at the table. He noticed that someone was already sitting there.

Though from his angle, he could only see the back of the persons head, he had a gut feeling on who that person would be.

Sitting in front of O.G. Bones was a half-eaten meal and a ten-inch mini-pad with a high-definition LCD screen. Bones, Kimani noticed, watched the screen as he ate.

Bones was an older cat; at forty-seven years old, he kept his appearance up to par. You simply couldn't tell his age. His eyes, on the other hand, looked like they'd been around a while. They were focused and remained that way even when he smiled; they never changed. Eyes like that made it impossible to figure out what a person was thinking. He was clean-cut, with a well-groomed circle of waves in his head. Just as his teeth would always be perfectly straight and pearly white, the suits he wore would always be tailored and fitted. A business look for a business mind.

O.G. Bones was the very definition of a self-made man. Tee-Tee sat on the same side of the table as Bones while Kimani and C-loco sat on the opposite side of the table. For no reason at all other than to be nosy, Kimani wanted to get a look at the footage on the mini-pad and leaned forward to get a peep. When he realized he still couldn't see, he started to lean back but looked up and noticed that Bones had been watching him. He froze; in their world, meddling was worse than stealing.

Unbothered by the intrusion, Bones simply grabbed the mini-pad and turned it around for both Kimani and C-loco to see. What they saw on the screen surprised the hell out of both of them.

It was footage of the very drive-by that they committed only moments ago.

As the two watched the video in stunned silence, the person doing the recording was in the process of zooming in on the trio while they sat in their car off to the side of the road. The high-definition screen showed perfect detail as Kimani and C-loco both placed the red bandannas on their heads and prepared for war.

Kimani didn't like it; he didn't care for someone having footage of him committing such acts. But when it came to Bones, he dared not say a thing. The fact that Bones had the resources to not only devise such an attack but to gather the footage of that attack and have it here before they got here, showed what the O.G. was capable of. While Kimani didn't like it, weighing the alternative forced him to keep silent.

He watched bones with distrust in his eyes.

In turn, the O.G. studied the li'l homie's reaction. Pausing just long enough to wipe his mouth with a napkin, the big homie spoke, "three people in all dead by the hands of the Rollin-90 Crips." Bones continued to scrutinize the li'l homie. "That was good shootin', Cuz. You revealed some keen skills today. I'm impressed." He watched Kimani. "You keep this type of shit up and you'll have yo' own grounds in no time." Putting his elbows on the table, Bones steepled his fingers together.

Kimani knew that havin' his own grounds, meant that part of Cacey Homes would be his to control. He also knew that 'in no time', could be five, even ten years from now. Being a part of the baNgside 90's was a career; a lifetime career.

He couldn't get the idea of the big homie having this footage out of his mind, but what was he to do? It was just one of many ways that Bones kept dominion over the hood and control over his subjects. To be a man in Bones' position, Kimani knew, you had to be a monster with a devil's reputation.

Bones continued, "you shoot like a real killa, Cuz." He said to Kimani. "Remind me of me when I was yo' age. But answer this fo' me," the O.G. smiled. "Why did you stop shootin' all of a sudden, the way that you did? What was you lookin' at? You acted like you never saw a dead body befo'. I mean, if this gangsta shit ain't fo' you, Cuz, we can find a place fo' you down at the bottom of the hill."

Kimani thought about why he had stopped shooting; the little girl and the way that she stared at him, crying. However, he knew that he couldn't tell Bones this.

"I just ran out of bullets, that's all." He lied.

It didn't answer the entire question, and Kimani had a gut feeling that Bones knew it. He was relieved that the big homie didn't bother to press the issue. He watched as Bones simply nodded in agreement and went on talking to Tee-Tee about other business.

Kimani heard nothing of the conversation; he was too busy studying the video footage. What Bones had said made him think about the little girl. For some reason that he couldn't explain, she made him uneasy.

As the drive-by they committed commenced, he watched the vehicle close in on Dirty. Goose bumps began rising on his arms and neck as he suddenly became enveloped with fear. Squinting unbelieving eyes, Kimani watched the video as though he no longer trusted what he was seeing. The little girl that he so vividly remembered – the one that emitted so much pain on her face – was nowhere to be seen. His mind wanted to scream.

He knew exactly where she should've been, he could still see Dirty's body as it lay there dead. Not seeing the little girl next to him now caused his stomach to turn and sweat to bead on his forehead.

He briefly glanced up at Bones and Tee-Tee with a look of shock on his face. He could only hear bits and pieces of the conversation the two were having – something about a music studio – and was grateful that neither of them was watching him. He could only imagine the expression they would see.

Thinking back, he remembered the little girl sitting on the porch in James Cacey, and then later crying on the curb in University Court with that same blank stare. Not seeing her now on this recording when he knew that she should be there frightened the shit out of him. He thought before that he was losing his mind; the shit was official.

He watched the video closely as the black Taurus sped down Charles E. Davis Boulevard and made a hard left on Carroll street. Just as the vehicle disappeared around the corner and out of sight, he saw her... She stood there on the corner watching the trio as they sped past her down the avenue.

This shit can't be real, his mind screamed.

Captivated by the video, Kimani could only see the backside of her as she watched them turn the corner, but he knew without a doubt that it was her standing there. He felt cold chills riding his spine.

Who are you? Kimani silently asked in disbelief. And as if she'd heard his very thought, the little girl turned around and stared directly into the camera. Struck with horror at what he was seeing, Kimani jumped back as far as his seat would allow, knocking C-loco's drink off of the table in the process. Even with the sudden commotion, he had a hard time taking his eyes off the video and the little girl that seemed to be watching him through the screen.

Stricken with fear, Kimani forced his eyes off of the video and saw that everyone in the restaurant was staring at him. There was no way in hell he would be able to explain this one. Eyes roaming over to the set of seats adjacent to theirs, he spotted two of Bones' henchmen as the large individuals got to their feet with their hands tucked out of sight. Kimani hadn't noticed them before, but he also wasn't himself today.

"The fuck wrong wit' you, fool?" demanded C-loco, upset about losing his drink.

I wish I knew the answer to that, Kimani thought to himself. He didn't need someone to tell him that he was losing his mind, or that this shit was crazy as fuck, so instead of attempting to explain himself he just got up and walked out of the restaurant all together.

By the time he'd gotten outside, his heart was racing so fast that he had to lean up against the wall by the entrance to catch his breath. Luckily, he hadn't eaten, he felt like throwing up.

Kimani thought back to what Bones had said – *what was you lookin' at? You acted like you never saw a dead body befo'* – and realized that they couldn't see the crazy shit that he saw.

Trying to gather his composure, he forced himself to take deep breaths. He was suddenly weak, exhausted, and could barely stand upright.

What's wrong with me? He wondered.

Looking out at the few people in the parking lot, Kimani tried against all reasoning to find her – if she had watched him before, maybe she was now – and was relieved that she wasn't there.

Before he could contemplate the madness further, he spotted a familiar face coming his way. Ray-Ray was walking towards the entrance to the restaurant. Kimani found it odd to see him in a brown U.P.S. uniform but was too caught up in his own shit to ask why. Neither of the men spoke as they crossed paths, they barely even looked in the other's direction.

When Ray-Ray went inside, Kimani continued to scan his surroundings, afraid that the little girl was watching him. But in the end, all that he could see were the people moving up and down the street, busy in one fashion or another.

The little girl wasn't there.

In his confusion for his search for her, he did notice one thing that he wasn't expecting, the black Taurus that the trio drove there in was gone. It made him wonder how many soldiers Bones had in the parking lot, out of sight, out of mind. Understanding that he was probably being watched, Kimani forced himself to hold his composure and think about the crazy shit later.

A few minutes passed before Tee-Tee and C-loco came out of the restaurant. They didn't bother to ask him what the fuck was wrong with him, and for that he was grateful. The trio simply walked across the parking lot towards Tee-Tee's platinum colored continental – how the vehicle got there Kimani didn't care, he just wanted to go home – and hopped into the ride.

It took them twenty-minutes to get back to the hood. It wasn't much longer before Kimani was out of the vehicle with his backpack slung over his shoulder and heading up the steps to his building. He used the apartment key to open the door. Locking it behind him, he went straight to his bedroom and without taking off his shoes laid flat-out across his bed.

Tired and exhausted, it wasn't long before he was sound asleep.

CHAPTER 3
THE CODE

MARCH 3rd 11:23am.
JAMES CACEY HOUSING PROJECTS
EAST NASHVILLE...

He woke up suddenly when the alarm to his stereo sounded off. ♪"I won't deny it, I'ma straight rida..." ♪ He allowed the music to play a while, the way he always did, before reaching for his remote. Turning off the alarm, he sat up in bed and looked over at the clock. Still early.

Peering down at his wound, Kimani grimaced. He must've irritated it in his sleep because the gash had started bleeding again. Rotating his shoulder cuff, he noticed how stiff it had become. With the wound as stiff as it was, he decided to just leave it alone.

Content, he stood up and went to his mirror. Feeling himself getting dizzy, he watched as the reflection of the room through the mirror began to spin. Not wanting to fall, he placed his arms outwards to catch his balance. The dizziness faded slightly.

Slowly turning around so as not to lose his balance again, he paused, something was different. He started walking over to his dresser and in doing so was surprised to realize that it was gone. "The fuck." He mumbled, stopping in his tracks. As his head began to spin and the hairs on the back of his neck began to stand up, Kimani felt an eerie sensation creeping up on him. It was the kind of sensation he got when someone was behind him.

With as much speed as he could muster, he turned around and prepared to defend himself. He immediately regretted it. The dizziness he now felt was overwhelming. Gathering all the strength he could to remain upright, his senses became dominated with the strong smell of gunpowder. It was a smell that was out of place here, but no less potent.

Strange.

It didn't take him long to realize that nothing here was what it was supposed to be. Feeling the world turn upside down before once again righting itself, Kimani forced himself to focus and tried to make sense of what he was seeing.

He looked down at the bed but was shocked at the sight of it. It wasn't his bed. Slowly turning, so as not to bring on the dizziness once again, he took in the room with stark surprise. The bed, the toys, and the lack of furniture told him all he needed to know. This wasn't his room. Where his stereo was supposed to be, a crate supporting a black and white television set occupied the space. He remembered that little television set – and everything else in this room – like it was yesterday.

Peering back over into the corner of the room, he stopped. With utter shock, he watched his younger self soundly sleeping in a bed that belonged to him almost ten years ago. Little eight-year-old Kimani lay there with not a worry in the world.

He heard noises coming from the background, almost silent, but still audible. With a hint of that unforgettable sound, Kimani knew where and when he was. More important, he knew exactly what was about to happen.

Walking up to the bedroom door, he paused as he once did, hesitating to open it. When he finally did, he was surprised at how much louder the noise from the music downstairs had become. He knew for sure that it would awaken little Kimani, and looking back over his shoulder, he saw that little Kimani had begun to stir.

Moving forward, Kimani walked out into that familiar hallway. Oddly, the closer he got to the top of the stairs, the louder and clearer the music became. Everything here seemed strange and distorted, like God had taken this portion of reality and stretched it between his fingers. The steps leading to the downstairs living room were three times longer than they should be. It would take him forever to get down those stairs. That being said, he knew that it was something that he had to do.

The music from below became louder with each step that he took as if to warn him from approach. Kimani treaded on, one step after another. As he neared the bottom of the stairs, the music began to level out as it gave way to the conversation his father and his father's friends were having. He entered the living room; saw his pops sitting in his favorite chair with a joint in one hand and a plate of cocaine in his lap.

The phone rang.

"Yeah, who this?" A.J., one of his father's friends answered. His voice was slurred, it was obvious how intoxicated the man was. "Yeah, hold on," he said, holding the phone out for Kimani's father to grab.

"Who the fuck is it?" Kimani's father asked. "Can't they see I'm busy?"

"Cutter." A.J. responded.

Kimani's father's expression quickly changed. He reluctantly reached out for the phone and spoke into the mouthpiece. "Cutter? What's up, baby? What can I do for you?" Kimani watched as his father listened with a stern expression, the faces he made speaking volumes. "'Goddamn, Cutter, baby. Ain't no need to be snappin', I told you already, I'm goin' get you yo' money." Pausing to listen, Kimani's father moved the phone away from his ear, looked at the device with a smirk, and then put it back up to his ear. He continued, "fuck you mean you goin' send somebody over here to check me? Bitch-made ass nigga." He vented. "Fuck you talkin' bout? I done told you, I'm goin' get you yo' shit. That's that on that." Kimani's father slammed the phone down hard on the receiver, threw the plate of cocaine on the table, and then stood up.

Kimani felt the strong urge to turn around and run back to his room the way he did all those years ago, but his body refused to move.

Watching his father in awe – the details in his face, the raspiness of his voice – he wanted so desperately to say something to him. Only inches from him now, he knew that the urge was futile. If it were possible, they would've wondered what the fuck he was doing here a long time ago.

As real as this felt, as clear and vivid as it seemed, he knew that this was only a memory hid deep inside of his subconscious; a subconscious trying to reveal its secrets.

Kimani looked up towards the top of the stairs – they all seemed to be normal now – and saw a shape disappear around the corner. He knew all too well who that shape belonged to, but before he could contemplate it any further, the once strong smell of gun smoke dissipated, and he woke up.

He was awakened suddenly by noises within the house. This time he knew it was real; the excruciating pain in his shoulder told him so. He jumped out of bed and immediately went towards the bedroom door. From here, he could hear a rustling noise coming from down the hall.

Slowly making his way towards the living room, Kimani listened carefully as he went. It was clear that there was someone in the apartment.

Coming up on the threshold of the living room, he paused, it wasn't until now that he realized he didn't have his pistol with him. Today just wasn't a good day.

He listened. Silence. He could no longer hear the noise. Not wanting to hurry back for his gun, he made his decision and entered the living room. He didn't see what he expected to see; standing by the front door of the apartment was his mother. She stood still, staring in his direction, with her right hand lost deep within her oversized purse. Looking at him like he'd lost his mind, she said, "boy, what the fuck is wrong wit' you? Why the hell you creepin' up on me like that fo'?" She took her hand out of her purse but continued to stare at her son as if he was mentally ill..

Kimani knew why she was clutching; he also knew that she wouldn't hesitate to use it. Only in Brentwood did mothers walk around with pepper-spray in their purses. He finally let out the breath that he'd been holding and said to his mother, "Sorry, I didn't mean to scare you like that. I just woke up, heard some noises, and came to see what was up," he waited for an acceptance, but didn't get one.

It didn't take him long to realize why. She had been distracted by the blood that had accumulated on his shirt.

Looking down to see for himself, he paused before taking off the white-tee and felt the pain as the hardened scab was ripped from flesh. The nick had become a real nuisance. To make matters worse, the shoulder had begun to swell. What was once a small wound was turning out to be a real problem.

Realizing how nasty it looked, he swore to get it tatted once the wound became a scar.

Looking up, Kimani no longer saw his mother standing by the front door. Hearing noise behind him, he turned to see her coming down the hall with a first-aid kit in her hand. He hated it when she did that; her ability to move with silent feet.

His mother placed the first-aid kit down on the living room table and went into the kitchen to get a chair. She wasn't about to let her son sit on her white leather couch with all that blood. It didn't matter that the couch was still covered in plastic.

"Sit down boy," she said as she set the chair down next to the table. Opening up the first-aid kit, she pulled out a large alcohol pad and a pair of latex gloves. Putting the gloves on, she opened the alcohol packet and began cleaning the dried blood away from the wound. She then dipped a clean q-tip into a fresh bottle of iodine and began rubbing the substance into the wound itself. She was grateful that she'd caught it before it had gotten infected. After using plenty of the antiseptic, Ms. Johnson started wrapping the wound with a bandage and gauze. She had been a nurse for twenty-five years now and cleaning wounds was something that she'd become good at.

She was tired, had been on her feet all night, and knew that trying to pry information out of her stubborn son about his wound would be futile. So instead, she shook her head and leaving out of the living room, went to take a shower. She couldn't wait to get out of her hospital scrubs and wash the night away.

Kimani stayed seated in the chair thinking and wondering if his mother knew what kind of wound it was. He didn't want to have to explain it to her. The morning had been too crazy for him to explain, including the vivid dream of his father, the conversation on the phone, and the man named Cutter on the other line. He wondered if his subconscious mind was trying to tell him something. He'd never heard that name before and knew that he would never find a way to ask his mother about it. It was a long time ago and healed wounds were meant to stay healed.

Before he could give it any more thought, the phone in the kitchen rang. Kimani gathered himself, got up out of the chair, and went to go answer it.

"Hello." He spoke into the receiver.

"Hey, baby. Where you been at? I've been tryin' to call you all mornin." It was Sasha, Kimani's girlfriend for going on eight months now. It eased his mind to hear her voice. Without him realizing it, his shoulder was no longer hurting. "I've been out. I had to take care of somethin'. Why? What's up? Everything aight ain't it?" he asked.

"Yeah," Sasha said. "I just wanna see you. I'm horny and I hate wakin' up by myself. Do I have to spell it out fo' you?"

"I told you 'bout fuckin' wit' me, girl." Kimani smiled. "Got that ass whipped. Got that ass fiendin'. Now what you goin' do?"

"Stop plaayyin'." Sasha begged. Kimani loved it when she begged. "Are you goin' come over here and give me what I want?"

"You goin' back that ass up on it?" he asked.

"Umm. I'm goin' do a lot more than that, baby." Sasha admitted.

Kimani could hear the moaning in her voice. She continued, "I just want you to put my legs over my head and fuck the shit outta me," she said. Knowing just how to entice him, she emitted soft moan after soft moan. "Ummm. My pussy getting' wet baby. I need you. Are you on yo' way?"

"You damn right I'm on my way," he said. He hadn't learned how to say no to her yet. "Just give me a few minutes and I'll be out the doe'."

"Aight, baby. I'ma be waitin'," Sasha said, elated.

"Aight, girl. I'ma be there, shortly. Keep that thing wet."

"Aight, baby. I will."

"Bye."

"Bye."

Kimani, excited, had his hands in his pants trying to keep his manhood at bay. He looked up and saw his mother standing in the entrance to the kitchen, watching him. He didn't notice her there before. Embarrassed, he immediately removed his hands from his pants and stood up straight. He watched as his mother pressed her lips, shook her head, and turned around to head back to her bedroom. She knew her son didn't have it all.

Kimani allowed himself a guilty smile, before resigning to his bedroom as well.

He was thinking about Sasha, now. She was everything a man could want; 5'8, 140 pounds, and thick to death with flawless brown skin. She was by far the finest girl in the hood. After eight months, he was beginning to catch feelings for her, though he wasn't prepared to let her know that yet. A freshman at Tennessee State University, she was intelligent, and that was one of the many things that he'd come to really like about her.

They first met at Opry Mills mall. He spotted her in K-Jewelers, just as he was coming out of Men of Fashion. He remembered throwing his bags into C-loco's hands, then walking off in her direction.

"The fuck..." C-loco began to protest before realizing what Kimani was up to. "Yeah, nigga, you betta do that shit..." C-loco said. "And see if she gotta friend, too." He watched as Kimani reached into his pocket for a breath mint before walking up to make his introduction.

Kimani nonchalantly brushed his hand gently on the small of Sasha's back before speaking. "There are three things people are drawn to the most..." he said, looking her in the eyes. "charm, praise, and money." He watched her as she had a look of shock on her face. Snared by her beauty, he continued, "while that last one is the most impressionable to most, it's the other two that's mo' important to me." He made sure to smile as he continued, "ply her with money, and she'll be yours fo' good, or at least until the next man comes along who's willin' to put out mo.'. Now give her charm and praise, and you can quickly find yo' way into her heart. But the idea that love alone is enough, is too gushy fo' me. Balance... that's the key." He paused.

"And who the hell you supposed to be with that whack ass game?" Sasha said, "and what the hell you think you doin'?" She aggressively pushed his arm away from the small of her back.

"My names, Kimani..." he responded, shocked. He didn't expect her not to be impressed by his words. Still hoping against all odds and trying to remain focused, he gave her a somewhat hesitant smile.

"Nigga, please." Sasha continued to resist. Rolling her eyes, she walked off, leaving him behind.

"I must be confused." Kimani said, making a move to catch up to her, he wasn't about to let her get away. "I mean, you fine as hell and all, but I've seen fine girls befo'..." he could tell by her changing expression that had her listening. "That bein' said, never in my life has a person caused me to lose focus the way you have just now. I don't know what it is 'bout you baby girl that's got me actin' so irrational, but whatever it is, I'm anxious to find out if you will allow it."

He eased in front of her to see if she would try and walk off again. She didn't. So, he observed her as she stared at him with a new look of interest on her face. He could tell that she was calculating. Confident, he continued to probe. "It ain't just yo' beauty, love. As I've said, I've dated beautiful women befo'. Why don't we exchange numbers, let me find out what got me so damn hypnotized?"

Liking his persistence, Sasha finally cracked a smile. It was the smile that he'd been waiting for. He knew that from that moment on she was his. All he had to do was get her to fall. First impressions were everything, the rest took care of itself.

That was eight months ago, and they were still going strong.

After a quick shower, Kimani went into his bedroom to get dressed. The Kenneth Cole' fit he was putting on was new, he'd just got it last week, along with the pair of two-hundred-dollar Kenneth Cole boots. It was the heavy buckles that extended across the tongues of the boots that drew his attention to them.

Going to his bed, he grabbed the .40 caliber pistol and inserted the clip. Tucking it into the back of his waste-band, he headed for the front door. Sasha's warm body was all he needed to ease his mind. As always before, she was the perfect remedy.

Leaving his building, he walked through an open field that would bring him out on south 7th street. Sasha stayed down on 6th street and it would take him about ten minutes to get there. Walking down a sidewalk in between two buildings, he felt a vibration pulsing on his hip and looked down at the pager that hung there.

Pressing the little white button on the side of the pager, he watched as the numbers 2436-8-911 popped up on the screen. Frustrated, he began to decipher the numbers in his head; the numbers – when they came – were always coded and had to be deciphered. Realizing he was being called, he vented in frustration.

"Damn," he exclaimed loudly. He hated being interrupted when he was about to get his dick wet. Knowing that he would have to hear it from Sasha for not showing up, he cursed the day that he accepted the pager. Being on call was a part of his description, the responsibility he took on when he accepted his position. In the end, dicking Sasha down was all that it would take to get him back in her good graces. It was the arguments before then that he hated so much.

This is what happened when you were good at what you did, you were put on roll-call. After the drive-by he did a few years back in Edgehill, the O.G. had given him his current status. In the beginning he thought it would be all upside, but it turned out to be more responsibility than privilege. Tee-Tee and C-loco both carried pagers as well.

To an outsider, a nigga with a pager was either whack, stuck in the eighties, or broke. To a nigga in the know, it was simple genius. For one, any ciphered number coming through the pager could only be deciphered by the receiver. And two, it couldn't be tapped into from a remote location. The Feds would have to covertly swap it out with an identical one, without the user knowing it. Even then, they still had the code to contend with. With those codes only being known by the sender and receiver – and an ever-changing set of codes – it would be virtually impossible for the Feds to catch on.

1325 South 7th Street was a meeting place at the top of the hill. Like the money houses and the stash houses in the hood, the meeting places randomly changed. In times when things were really busy, they changed every other day.

Walking out onto South 7th, Kimani spotted Caccy-Laccy posted up on the corner. He was a young cat from Raleigh, North Carolina. When his parents died, he moved to the city with relatives and quickly found his way to the streets. He had it hard at first, being an outsider, he had to fight almost every day. But he held his own in the end. Caccy-Laccy hung up his cell phone when he saw Kimani approach.

"Cacky-Lacky." Kimani said. "What up wit' you, Cuz?"

"Not shit, Cuz, just tryin' to get my piece of the pie," said Caccy-Laccy. "West crackin' wit' you, boy? I heard yo' ass got shot. You aight?"

"Yeah, I'm good." Said Kimani. "Shit wasn't that bad, considering." He thought about Dirty's dead body as it lay on the curb and rotated his shoulder to show that he was good. "I got a meetin' wit' the big homie though. I need to use yo' phone real quick." Kimani didn't bother to ask Caccy-Laccy how he'd come to hear that he'd gotten shot. He knew that mu'fucka's in the hood always talk too damn much. Some people just didn't see the significance of keeping their mouths shut.

He grabbed the phone when Caccy-Laccy offered it and called Sasha to let her know that something had come up. After hearing her gripe and complain, they said their goodbyes, and he handed Caccy-Laccy his phone back.

She didn't even thank me fo' at least callin' and lettin' her ass know, Kimani thought to himself. He should've known it was coming as she often got in her feelings. "Aight then, Cuz," he said to Caccy-Laccy. "'Preciate that shit. You keep yo' eye open out here, fool. Crip or cry, nigga."

"Fo' sure, fo' sure. I'm a rida', Cuzzo. I always got my eyes open."

"That's what's up. I'm out then. Big N's, Cuz."

"N's," said Caccy-Laccy.

Kimani, resigned, made his way towards 1325 South 7th street. He was ready to get this shit over with.

The meeting spot was at the top of the hill. When he came around the corner of the building, he noticed that there were three cats standing outside the back door of the apartment when he arrived. There was no doubt in his mind that there would be more around front by the front door; evidence that Bones was more than likely on the premises. He hoped this meeting didn't have shit to do with the McDonald's incident. He still didn't have the courage to explain that shit.

As he walked up to the door, one of the individuals held it open for him. His presence had been expected. What the big homie wanted, he had no idea, but he began to get nervous. When Kimani went inside, he saw one of the henchmen that he noticed earlier at the restaurant, the one that was clutching for his weapon.

"Upstairs, and don't touch anything." Was all that the man said.

Kimani walked through the empty living room and went up the steps to the two-story apartment. He almost used the handrail for support but quickly remembered what the henchman said. He continued his ascent.

Once in the upstairs hallway, he noticed the door to the first bedroom slightly ajar. Stopping to peer inside, he saw that someone had been tied to a chair in a seated position. With a blind fold covering their eyes and blood staining their upper shirt, Kimani watched as a second person – a large white man – came into view and gave the captive a solid punch to the face. With the way that the captive was screaming and spitting out teeth, it was obvious that he was in a lot of pain. All Kimani could do to hold back the oohhh's was to put a fist up to his mouth.

It was dark in the hallway, but he could hear some movement up ahead. Squinting his eyes to better his vision, he spotted Bones' other henchman. The man had obviously been watching him the entire time. As Kimani walked up to him, the man stepped to the side and opened the door he'd been standing in front of to allow him entrance. Without saying a word, the henchman closed the door behind him.

Bones stood in the empty room alone. He had his back to the door, peering out the window, looking over James Cacey homes. From this vantage point, being on top of the hill, Bones could nearly see the entire neighborhood, his kingdom. He took his time as he stared out of the window. A simple power tactic designed to make Kimani wait.

After what seemed like forever, Bones turned around to face off one of his subjects.

Out of the blue, Kimani realized that Tee-Tee and C-loco wasn't there. He'd never met the big homie alone like this. Realizing that he was the only one that had been paged really put him on edge. He was hoping silently that he hadn't done anything wrong.

Bones, Kimani saw, had a smile on his face. It meant nothing. Bones could just as well be mugging him right now. By habit, Kimani looked down at the O.G.'s hands. They were out, exposed and relaxed. With anyone else, it would've told him a lot, but this was Bones he was studying. Bones, not one to miss anything, held up his hands – palms out – with that same smile on his face. After making his point, he dropped his hands and got straight down to business.

He spoke, "Kimani, I called you here for two reasons." Bones cuffed his right fist inside of his left hand. "One, I need to know if you aight? This mornin', the way you ran out of Mickey-Dee's?" he paused before continuing. "Now usually I wouldn't meddle in other people's affairs..." He lied. "...but I'm a li'l concerned about the way you been actin'. You'll understand, I have to keep the li'l homies in check, make sure y'all li'l niggas ain't losin' y'all minds and shit." Bones waited for a response.

"Yeah, I'm good, Cuz." Kimani answered. "Just got some crazy shit on my mind." He knew that was an understatement. "You know, ain't nothin' I can't handle. Just small shit."

"Just small shit, huh?" Bones was listening to Kimani's every word trying to catch something that could be easily missed. From a psychological perspective he was a master of the minds. But Kimani – like him – was good at hiding things; one of the many attributes he liked about the kid.

Kimani watched the smile that Bones displayed. He didn't like it. Once a person realized that coming from Bones a smile wasn't really a smile, it made it impossible for that person to truly trust him. The unknown has been feared since the beginning of time.

Bones continued, "you had me worried there for a minute, Cuz. The homie Tee-Tee told me that everything would be aight, that you just needed to... breath. You sure there's nothin' you wanna holla at the big homie about? Nothin' you wanna get off yo' chest?"

"Naw, I'm good," Kimani said. He thought about the little girl that he saw on the mini pad this morning, there was just no way in hell that he was going to talk about that to anyone.

"I'm fine wit' that if you are," Bones conceded. "Now that that's out the way, let's get down to business."

The words *let's get down to business* made Kimani's heart skip a beat. He still had no idea why he alone had been called.

"I need you to run an errand fo' me. You legit right? You got L's?" Bones asked.

"Yeah, I got a license."

"Good." Bones reached into his pocket and brought out a set of car keys. He tossed them to Kimani before continuing, "in front of this buildin' you'll find parked a navy-blue Chevy Caprice. I need you to take it to 9282 Gallatin Pike and have my stereo system hooked up. Four fifteens in the trunk, right, should shake shit up?"

Kimani clearly understood the significance of the question. He also knew that it was rhetorical, and that Bones wasn't looking for an answer.

"The whole process shouldn't take no mo' than forty minutes to finish," Bones continued. "Once you done wit' that, I want you to bring it back and park it exactly where you got it. After that you can do whatever."

"Do I ask fo' anybody in particular?" Kimani wanted to know.

"Did I say anything 'bout you askin' fo' anybody in particular?" Bones seemed irritated at the question. The silence he received from Kimani now was all that he wanted. "Let's get this shit done then, li'l homie, I got a deadline to meet."

Kimani recognized when he was being dismissed. He felt that he'd asked a legitimate question but didn't want to make a scene out of it and turned to leave instead.

"Oh, and Kimani..." Bones waited for Kimani to turn back around. "...Don't play wit' my music. Look in the glove-compartment, you'll find a li'l somethin' fo' yo' hard work."

Kimani refused to say anything else. He only nodded and simply turned to leave. Contemplating what it was he was about to do, he walked through the door with Bones following right behind him.

In the hallway, the bedroom door where the bloodied victim was being held, was opening up. An oversized white man with curly brown hair, tan slacks, and a white-collared dress shirt stepped out into the hallway. The man was so large, and the hallway was so small, that Kimani had to stop in his tracks, unable to pass either side of him. Rubbing his reddened knuckles, the man nodded in Bones' direction.

"Detective Anderson?" Bones said. "I hope that everything is goin' well?"

"We've got everything we need," Detective Anderson stated.

"Good, good," said Bones.

The burly white man stared at Kimani for a while before turning to the side to let him pass. Kimani glanced in the room and noticed that the bleeding captive was still tied to the chair, only the chair was lying flat on its back.

Who the victim was, Kimani had no idea, but he couldn't say that he gave a fuck either. Without missing a step, he went down the stairs and out the front door. Giving a quick prayer to the man tied to the chair, he pushed it out of his head and headed for the navy-blue Caprice.

In the car, he immediately opened up the glove-compartment to get out a map. On the back of the map was a directory, a quick way to find a street – big or small – anywhere in the city. But Kimani didn't need direction around the city; he grew up here and knew how to get around well. Bones had been speaking in code and he had been mentally equipped to decipher such a code a long time ago.

Finding Gallatin Pike in the directory, he counted four columns over to the right...

Four fifteens in the trunk, right?

... this put him in the N's of the directory. From there, he counted four spaces up...

should shake shit up.

...until his finger rested on Nolensville Pike. That was on the south side of town, potentially enemy territory. The first and last numbers of the address would reverse, making 2289 Nolensville Pike the properly deciphered address. Of course, the business of the stereo system would remain the same.

Kimani knew that he was about to pick up some work. He also knew that all of the coded conversation was to protect Bones' interest. In the event that their conversation had somehow been recorded, Bones would be able to clear his involvement.

Folding up the map, he placed it back in the glove-compartment. He couldn't help but notice the fat stack of hundred-dollar bills, every bit of ten-thousand he was sure. Kimani closed the compartment, started the car, and headed for his south side destination.

Pulling out of the parking lot, he noticed a tinted black Chevy Suburban pulling out behind him. What he didn't know was that a security detail of four individuals with fully automatic sub machine guns occupied the SUV. Nothing, not even a metro interceptor, would stop him from making this run.

Bones was smart. He wouldn't be in his position if he wasn't. Kimani was just ready to get this shit over with so that he could go meet up with Sasha. Thinking of her always seemed to make him think farther into the future. And because of that, he always dreaded a day when something would go horribly wrong. All he could do was try and prepare for it. Just a little longer and a little more cash, then everything would fall into place for them both.

The routes and procedures had been set in place a long time ago. In the beginning, they would simply meet face to face. The system was different then, much easier and far less dirty. After years of fighting the 'so called' war on drugs, the suits-that-be came to realize that it was all a lost cause and began to use the profits from those drugs to fund the war on terror. Because lives were at stake, the feds no longer played fair. Mothers, wives and even grandmothers would become a victimized product of this dirty game. Often times when participants refused to play their part, they would find themselves somewhere not found. It was war on a whole different front and not even the smart ones survived for long anymore.

However, when the enemy evolved you had to evolve further, constantly changing your strategy to keep them at bay.

This was one such strategy: an order form would be placed in a public mailbox on a public street at a precise time somewhere in the city. Like everything else in this business, those locations and times constantly changed. Within hours of that very drop-off, the mailman would come to pick up the days mail. Often times, regular mail would be mixed with the order forms, but that wasn't the mailman's concern.

The order forms would then go through a number of different channelers and safety precautions before making its way to its final destination. Fail-safe mechanisms would always be set in place on both ends in case something took a turn for the worse. For one, neither of the channelers knew the other. If something did go wrong and the hand off to the next channeler wasn't met on time, the buck would stop there. That route would never be used again, and that particular channeler would forever be marked.

Once the order made its way to its final destination and its contents were deciphered, the where-about's of the payment pickup would find its way along similar routes. No hand-to-hand transactions were ever made between buyer and seller. That was a job reserved for pawns.

A great general always adhered to one simple rule: soldiers were expendable, the hood was not. It had to survive at all cost.

Everyone else had left to go on their lunch break. He had the building all to himself. As he walked through the door that read 'EMPLOYEES ONLY', he knew he only had a short amount of time and went directly to his workstation. It was almost time for the pick-up to take place and he was ready to get this part of the day over with. He never imagined in his earlier years that he would be doing this type of work, but it was the sole reason he was given this job as an audio-technician in the first place; the sole reason he was making this kind of money.

Things were changing in the world and he was determined to be a part of that change.

The speaker box he constructed was large enough to accommodate four, fifteen-inch woofers. As of now, it was just a double walled box with four fourteen-inch holes in it. The magnets had been removed from the speakers. Between the thick layer of coffee beans covering the backside of the speakers and the narcotics being stuffed inside of the box, there simply wasn't any room for the magnets.

He went to his locker and used his key to open it. Inside of the locker were thirty kilos of cocaine and ten kilos of heroin, all stored away inside of a military duffle bag. He removed the bag with his left hand and relocked the locker with his right.

He was just a channeler, somewhere between seller and buyer. He noticed long ago that he was always under constant observation while in the midst of transporting. His employers didn't take chances. With only simple instructions to follow between the two channelers before and after him, the information he had would do the Feds no good because he simply didn't know enough about the chain.

The bag was heavy. He figured that out when he picked it up in Atlanta. The weight of narcotics he dealt with was enough to get a man an unimaginable amount of life-sentences, but the money that came along with it was more than enough to take that risk. He laid the bag down on the table next to the speaker box he constructed and opened it. Upending thirty kilos of cocaine and ten kilos of heroin onto the table, he immediately began to stuff them into the speaker box.

He had gotten good over the years at constructing them. It was a box within a box, with coffee beans stored in between the inner and outer walls to mask the narcotic scent. Why they wanted him to build the box at this juncture in the journey he had no idea, especially when he wasn't given that same courtesy in Atlanta. But it didn't matter, he wasn't getting paid to ask those kinds of questions. So he did his job and kept it moving. When the employee finished stuffing the box with the drugs, he placed the dummy speakers over the holes, and gracefully sealed them into place.

Kimani got off Nolensville Pike and pulled into the entrance of Car-tronics Custom Interior and Designs. When he got out of the car, there was a small white guy with a Car-tronics uniform on waiting for him. Just looking at him, Kimani thought a person would have never known what he was into; the world was strange like that.

"The keys, sir. Four fifteens should only take about an hour." Said the small Car-tronics employee. He knew that it wouldn't take that long, but he had to look professional about it.

Kimani handed the keys to the employee and closely watched as he drove the vehicle into the garage of the building and out of sight. *That mufucka' betta not fuck wit' my money,* he said to himself. He looked over his shoulder across the street and spotted the black suburban parked in a grocery store parking lot. The driver of the suburban flashed his headlights twice and Kimani looked away. He was secure.

Walking into the small lobby of the building, he decided to wait there for the employee to finish the installation. The lobby was clean, with about ten waiting chairs. He picked one and sat down. There was a flat-screen TV mounted on the wall. He watched as a commercial advertising a concert featuring some of his favorite artist aired. It would be taking place downtown at Bridgestone arena. Marking April 5th in his mental notes, Kimani decided it would be a nice place to take Sasha. She loved music just as much as he did.

Waiting patiently, nearly forty minutes had passed before the employee emerged with the navy-blue Caprice. Driving up to the entrance of the building, the employee got out of the car and walked into the lobby. He simply handed Kimani the keys, told him that services had been rendered, and thanked him for choosing Car-tronics.

The first thing Kimani did upon getting into the vehicle was check the glove-compartment; his money was still there. He smiled, placed the stack of hundreds into his pocket, and drove back to James Cacey with the black suburban in tow.

He parked the Caprice exactly where he was supposed to – Kimani made similar runs before – and lowered the air-suspension all the way to the ground before shutting off the car. With no back seats in the vehicle, and the large hole that had been cut into the floorboard where those seats once were, it would make it easy for someone to come up through the sewer's manhole just underneath where the car was parked. Sometime in the middle of the night, whether the laws were watching the vehicle or not, the narcotics would be extracted from the trunk without being seen.

With Kimani's job now done, he headed to Sasha's crib knowing that the team in the black Suburban was in for a long night.

CHAPTER 4
MY OTHER HALF

MARCH 3RD. 1:19PM.
JAMES CACEY HOUSING PROJECTS
EAST NASHVILLE...

Sasha was staring at herself in the bathroom mirror, wrapped only in a body towel. She had a strand of hair in one hand and the curling iron in the other. Just getting out of the shower, she prepared herself for a night out on the town. It was 'ladies free until twelve' night at club Neighborhood and as always, she knew it would be off the chain.

"If Ki' don't wanna' chill wit' a bitch like me, then fuck it. I'm goin' still do me. Can't no nigga stop my shine," she expressed aloud.

Sasha developed feelings for Kimani over the last past eight months. She knew that him letting her have her way all the time had a lot to do with it. She also knew that C-loco probably had a lot to do with him changing his mind about coming to see her. C-loco was always fucking shit up.

"Always puttin' them punk ass nigga's first." Sasha aggressively grabbed a new strand of hair and began curling it. "See if they give yo' ass some pussy and suck yo' dick, nigga."

She had just finished curling her last strand of hair when she heard a knock at the front door.

"Who is it?" she angrily yelled from upstairs.

"Girl, open the damn door. You know who it is," said the muffled response from the other side of the downstairs door.

"Took yo' ass long enough, nigga," Sasha said to herself.

She looked in the mirror one last time to make sure everything was in place; something wasn't. Reaching down to remove the towel from her naked body, she smiled at her sexiness. She knew how beautiful Kimani felt she was. She went downstairs to let him in.

"Damn, girl! You better knew it was me..." said Kimani. "... answerin' the door butt ass naked and shit." He stared at her perky nipples.

"Whatever," Sasha said, cheesing hard. "Come here and give me a hug. It took yo' ass long enough to get here."

Kimani walked in, locked the door behind him, and gave Sasha a hug as he seductively kissed her neck. Putting his arm around her soft body, he reached down to get a hand full of ass cheeks. Her booty was phat and soft at the touch. When she hugged him back, he grimaced at the pain in his shoulder but said nothing about it.

"Damn, baby, that ass softer than a mu'fucka'. What you been eatin', marshmallows?"

"Shut up. You stupid." Sasha laughed. "Where the hell you been at? I been waitin' on yo' ass all mornin'. I thought I was goin' have to use my toys."

"Damn, for real? I wanna see that." Kimani smiled.

"In yo' dreams, nigga." Sasha smiled back and shook her head. "If you would've come when I said..." she let the unfinished statement sink in.

"Well I'm here now, love," Kimani said. "Stop playin'. You know you wanna feel a nigga long strokin' that ass." He gripped her left ass cheek and began kissing her just under her lower ear; he knew how to make her squirm.

"Why you always do that?" Sasha asked. Though smiling, she really wanted to be mad at him at that moment, but he always knew how to make her give in. She was never able to resist his touches. Hating the fact that she was vulnerable around him, she loved the feeling that came with it. It was weird; sometimes she didn't know how to think straight. Horny, she grabbed him by the hand and led him up to her bedroom.

Following close behind her, Kimani smacked her on her ass cheeks as they went up the steps. She had a hell of a bangin' body – a phat ass and large breast – and knew how to use it to get what she wanted from him. Some would say that he was pussy whipped, but he didn't give a damn.

"You know we got's to hurry up," she warned. "I don't know what time my momma goin' get home." At the age of nineteen and a freshman in college, Sasha was still living under her mother's roof. Though she was grown, she still had to abide by her mother's rules and fucking nigga's in her house wasn't one of them.

"You know it don't take me nothin' but five minutes to bust a nutt anyway," Kimani joked.

"Nigga, please." Sasha started. "You'll never hit this pussy again."

"Damn, that's how you feel? You goin' do a nigga like that?" he asked as they entered her bedroom. "Just goin' cut a nigga all the way off? Besides, I don't know why we gotta hurry up, fo', if yo' moms show up, she can always join us," Kimani joked. "She be lookin' at a nigga sideways, anyway..."

"Don't be talkin' 'bout my momma ..." Sasha hated when he played with her like that. Turning around to hit him in the chest, she accidentally hit him in his wounded shoulder instead. Seeing the pain register on his face, she froze, not meaning to hurt him. "What's wrong? I didn't mean to hit you that hard."

"Nah, its aight." Showing her the bandage, Kimani tried to soothe her. "Some fools did a drive-by this mornin'. I got hit in the shoulder befo' I could get out the way. Moms patched me up real nice though." It wasn't exactly the truth, but it was the truth, nonetheless. Though the truth she heard wasn't the truth she thought she heard.

He really didn't need it, but Sasha helped ease him down on the bed. She began massaging both of his shoulders, being extra careful with the left one.

"Don't worry, baby. I'm goin' take care of you." She promised. "If you need anything, just let me know and I got you."

Kimani smiled. Even though he only told half of a truth, he knew the treatment that was coming to him far outweighed the guilt he would feel from lying. A few months ago, there would've been no guilt whatsoever, but things were changing; Sasha began to matter to him.

The events that took place earlier that morning were still fresh on his mind. That was a consequence of having a conscious; the effect he would feel.

Sasha, sensing his mood – she'd always been able to do that – decided to change the topic.

"Baby, you hungry?" she asked. "I wanna make some egg omelets and pancakes."

Kimani, realizing he hadn't eaten all morning, took the bait. "Hell yeah, I'm hungry." He rubbed his stomach. "You goin' put the butter on it like you always do?"

"Yo' spoiled ass," Sasha said. "Don't I always put butter on it?"

"Yeah," he admitted.

"Aight then," she said sarcastically; trying to get him in a playful mood once more.

Sasha got up and prepared to go downstairs to the kitchen. As she walked, she spoke over her shoulder, "and don't think I done fo'got what you said 'bout my momma. I'ma tell her what you said, too."

She left him sitting on the bed with a stunned look on his face. He watched as her ass cheeks moved up and down while she walked and noticed the subtle peep she gave over her shoulders to see if he was looking. One thing was for sure, she knew how to be seductive; it was his favorite thing about her.

When she was gone, Kimani got up and headed to the bedroom closet. Opening it, he squatted down and reached for the large safe. Pressing the electronic code into the bulky piece of metal, he listened as the steel bars gave way. He liked this particular safe; it was one of the best one's on the market. Bigger than most, it had been bolted to the hard-concrete floor from the inside. It wasn't going anywhere.

He came here at least once a week to drop off money, depending on how fast he was making it. Sometimes ten to twenty thousand went into the safe if it was a good week. Money often came quick for him; for no reason that he could understand, Bones paid him more than he paid other homies in his position; and the jobs he did for the big homie was only a portion of his income.

Kimani neatly placed the money into the safe. After months of grinding, the safe had begun to fill up; he would have to relocate the money soon. Closing the heavy fire-proof steel door, he listened as the bars locked into place. Standing up, he went to join Sasha downstairs.

He sat on the living room couch and listened as she did her thing in the kitchen. She was her mother's daughter; she knew how to cook. Reaching under the living room table, Kimani brought out his X-Box console then plugged it into the seven-foot high-definition plasma television hanging on the wall. Almost everything in this house with significant value, he'd paid for; he didn't mind keeping Ms. Reed on his good side. In return, he knew that she would do whatever she needed to do to ensure that it stayed that way. And so the game went.

Fumbling through his many games, he grabbed the latest 'Call of Duty' and put it into the console; he loved military coverts. He didn't know what it was about war that sparked an interest in him so much; maybe his mind was damaged. He never understood why him – like so many others – were captivated by something as evil as killing; why did a murder in the middle of the street bring such a large crowd? Was it simply human nature? Were human's naturally evil, living out their lives in an attempt to become good? Were we already in hell, trying to atone to earn our way into heaven?

A true testament to the conditioning of a sick society.

As the game booted up, he listened to Sasha working in the kitchen. If there was a heaven, it revolved around her; she was the angel that lifted his spirits and kept him grounded; she was the yin to his yang; the whole reason the sun came up each day.

He'd worked his way through the first mission when she finally came back into the living room. In her hands, two plates of pancakes, turkey sausages – she knew he didn't eat swine – and a pair of golden-brown egg omelets. Pausing the game, Kimani watched as she went, butt ass naked, back into the kitchen. Saving his position, he turned off the console and looked down at Sasha's creation.

Ole girl was the truth.

"Damn, baby. You did the damn thang." He said loud enough for her to hear. "No wonder I'm crazy 'bout you."

Bringing orange juice into the room, Sasha sat down on the couch next to Kimani and turned in his direction. "Whatever, nigga. You crazy 'bout me cause I got yo' ass pussy-whipped." She watched the smile creep up on his face.

"Pussy-whipped?" he asked. "You think you got me whipped? I'm only messin' wit' you so I can get close to yo' momma... aight... aight, I'm just playin' wit' you, girl."

Sasha had him in a chokehold so fast that he almost dropped his plate. Laughing, Kimani sat the plate down on the table and began tickling her; he knew how to get her to let him go. If there was one thing that she couldn't stand, it was being tickled. Succumbing, she just sat there pouting with her bottom lip sticking out. These were the type of games that they played; boy makes girl mad, boy apologizes, they reconcile, girl falls in love.

Kimani kissed her on the lips and apologized once more.

"I'm just playin', baby." He kissed her again. "Don't be mad at me. You know I ain't got it all." Leaning in close, he softly kissed her lips again and again, struggling to hold back his laughter. "You forgive me, love?"

"I'm goin' tell my momma what you said," was all that Sasha said.

Because she loved him, she struggled between pouting and smiling. She'd learned long ago that it was inevitable; she couldn't stay mad at him for long. After a moment of silence, she changed the subject to something a little more serious.

"Why don't you want a key to the apartment, baby?" she asked. She tried to get him to accept a key many times before. "My momma don't mind. She almost love yo' ass as much as I do, though I don't know why I would tell yo' ass that." She gave Kimani a side-ways look. "Anyway, it'll make me feel better. It ain't like I'm tryin' to make you come home every night or somethin'." She knew that was exactly what she wanted.

"I thought we went through this already," he said through a mouth full of pancakes. He swallowed before continuing, "I just prefer to call first befo' I come over. I ain't tryin' to just pop up."

"You just think I'm tryin' to lock you down or somethin'." Sasha protested.

"Nah, it ain't even like that." He took a bite of the omelet knowing that he would put them in their own spot before he asked her for a key to hers.

Sasha didn't want to press him the way she had many times before. Instead, she put her head on his shoulder and said, "Baby, I love you."

There was silence.

Raising her head up off of his shoulder, she looked at him out of the corner of her eye. She craved the day that he would say that to her. Until then, she would be patient as always; that's just how much she'd come to love him.

Feeling the heat on the side of his face, Kimani turned to see the crazy look that Sasha had been giving him.

"You know I care 'bout you, right?" he said. "You my other half. I wouldn't be here if I didn't care 'bout you. I know you got my back, and in return, you know I got yours. Believe that." Kimani reached over once more and gently kissed Sasha on her soft lips, smiling as he did. He knew without a doubt that he had feelings for her; he just wasn't ready to express those feelings. Maybe someday.

Sasha accepted his words; she always did. It was more of an 'I'm tryin', than anything, but it mattered to her. Besides, couldn't nobody tell her nothing... She knew her baby loved her. She gently laid her head back down on his shoulder and watched him stuff his stomach with her cooking.

Kimani finished eating, thanked Sasha, and watched as she took the dishes – butt ass naked – back into the kitchen. The way that her ass moved when she walked caused him to get excited. Ole-girl knew what she was doing.

When she came back into the living room, she was surprised to find Kimani standing there, naked. Aroused, he had her ready to fuck.

Kimani stared at the beauty, that was his girl, as she stood there enticing him. Between the whip-cream that she'd placed on her nipples and the split of her honey-comb-hide-out, and the way that she sucked the bottom half of her lip, Sasha had him throbbing.

"Damn, baby," Sasha said, smiling. "I spilled some whip-cream on me."

"We better get you upstairs and get you cleaned up, then." Kimani returned. "We wouldn't want all that cream to go to waste."

Nibbling on her lip, she made her way up the steps with Kimani following close behind. Bad shoulder or not, the homie was ready to put on.

He gently pushed Sasha down on the bed before hitting the remote to the CD player, "there's a right and wrong way to love somebody," the sounds of Keith Sweat emitted from the speakers. Kimani grew up on the oldies. Easing down on top of Sasha, he slowly licked all of the whip-cream off of her body. He felt her body begin to tense up. Kissing her on her soft lips, he gripped her hips – she had the softest hips – with the palms of his hand. From her neck to her collar bone, he kissed, loving the sounds of her moans.

Sasha wrapped her long soft legs around Kimani's naked body. She was getting weak, losing all control to the built-up pleasure she was feeling inside. Holding onto his muscular frame, she moaned louder, feeling her nectars begin to flow. She was feeling like this from the four-play alone, and she couldn't wait until he began to pound her pussy. All that mattered to Sasha in this moment was the love that she felt for her man.

Kimani kissed her from her shoulder to the bend of her arm before making his way to her breast. He gently sucked on her nipples, feeling her body rise up to his mouth. Snaking his tongue slowly across her breast, he stopped only to give soft kisses in between. He kissed, he licked, and began rolling his tongue across her other breast.

Sasha gripped the back of his head, not wanting him to stop; she loved the way he made love to her body.

Moaning softly, she craved more as he gave her what she wanted.

Using his hand, Kimani fingered her pussy, hooking his index finger just inside of her wet hole. When he felt her back begin to arch, he knew he was exactly where he was supposed to be.

Sasha used her pussy muscles to grind his finger. She was loving the sensation she was feeling. She felt the tingling as her pussy started to spit cum; he always made her cum. She relaxed her hand on the back of Kimani's head while he caressingly made his way down her torso. She was ever so anxious for the moment that his lips made contact with her clit; loving the way that he rolled his tongue on it.

She discovered long ago that he had mastered her body; he knew where to probe and how to kiss. His ability to pay attention to her feelings, adapt to her motion, and anticipate her climaxes, was what caused her to love the way he made her feel.

As he continued to kiss on her body, he massaged her breast with his hands. He began to slowly snake his tongue down the back side of her long legs as she – lying on her back – stretched them both to the heavens. Pausing just behind the bend of her knee, he kissed her there, feeling her body begin to shake. He slithered his tongue down the backside of her thighs, cuffing her ass cheeks with his palms. He could tell when she couldn't take it any longer.

Sasha, unable to control herself, grabbed Kimani tight by the dreads and forced his lips onto her wet pussy. "Oooh, baby... Yes... That's it, right there." She moaned, climaxing.

He hungrily sucked her clit'; curling his tongue in and out of her hole. Her cum began to drip down his mouth as he rolled her clit' between his lips and tongue, listening to her sweet moans.

Sasha started to convulse with every passing second. As the two moved in unison, she curled her toes and her eyes rolled back into her head. Submitting to this ecstasy, she screamed his name.

Expressing her love, she eased Kimani on top of her, kissing him on his lips. She, tasting her own nectars, became lost in the moment. She kissed him aggressively as their passions began to heat up. Reaching down, she grabbed him by his shaft and eased it into her wet pussy. She moaned – mouth wide open – when his manhood stretched her pussy wide; it was the perfect mixture of pleasure and pain.

Kimani stroked her slowly at first, dancing with her tempo. Together their flesh became one. He'd known Sasha long enough to know exactly where her G-spot was; he stroked her there. Her heels rested on his back, and her knees rode alongside his shoulder blades feeling the tightening of her vaginal walls. He had every intention of giving her pleasure, rhythmically stroking her wet pussy.

Without missing a beat, he lifted Sasha up on top of him and began bouncing her up and down on his dick. She went wild at his aggression. Holding him tight, she wrapped her long legs around his waist.

With her heavy breast pressed against his chest, and her arms wrapped tightly around his neck, she started cumin again, feeling his muscular arms gripping tight around her waist. She felt him deep inside of her; physically and emotionally. Tightening her walls around his shaft, Sasha's moans got louder and louder. Her body shaking, her inner thighs tingling, she begged for him to fuck her harder. Sensing the tingling from her climax, she pressed her pussy hard against his dick and held him tight.

Allowing her body to climax, Kimani tossed her over onto her stomach and lifted her ass high into the air. He watched as she spread her knees apart, giving her ass cheeks more freedom to move. Easing his dick into her soaking wet pussy, he aggressively began to pound her.

With her pink pussy walls gripping the width of his shaft, Sasha released sweet moans into the pillow before her. Her ass cheeks bounced back and forth as she slammed her pussy hard against his body. With the stinging sensation of him smacking her ass cheek, she gave in as Kimani banged her back out; pounding his dick in and out of her pussy.

Using the palm of his hand, Kimani pushed Sasha's head down into the pillow. She, moaning loudly, screamed his name through the pillow her face rested in. She gripped the bed sheets tight and tried to match Kimani's thrust, but with an arch in her back, all she could do now was scream and hold on for dear life. He was about to bust, and she could tell by the rapid thrust in his motion. She moaned louder and louder, urging him on, and waited for him to cum inside of her.

"Kimani... ooh Kimani," she moaned. "Harder... harder... yeah, baby... yeah..." Starting to cum with him, Sasha's moan became a scream. "FUUCK MEEEE!!!"

Kimani leaned over and stuck his tongue in her mouth as he released his sperm inside of her tight pussy. Feeling the sensation of his bust, he squeezed her ass cheeks unable to let go and felt the rush of his semen burst into her womb.

"Ooh, Kimani." Sasha continued to moan. "Oh shit, baby. That shit felt so gooood. Mmmmm... baby." She began seductively sucking on her finger.

"SASHAAA?"

They both froze.

Sasha looked at Kimani with wide eyes and disbelief. Her mother was home, and killing the mood, she screamed Sasha's name from the downstairs living room.

"Sashaaa?"

"Oh, shit. That's my momma." Sasha panicked, jumping up and going to her dresser to silence the music. She reached into a drawer and retrieved a night gown, quickly put it on.

"Damn, baby." Said Kimani. "I left my clothes downstairs; you don't think she'll see 'em? Do you?"

"I hope not." Sasha said with wide eyes.

"SASHA?" Her mother yelled again.

"Yeah, I'm comin'. Give me a minute." Sasha responded.

"I'm just checkin' to see if you here. You need to come get yo' clothes off my livin' room flo', though. I done told you 'bout leavin' yo' shit all over my house." Ms. Reed said matter-of-factly.

"Aight, momma. I'm comin'." Sasha looked down at Kimani, still lying in bed, and they both let out a quiet laugh. When Kimani heard Ms. Reed's footsteps climbing the stairs, he jumped up and jetted towards the bedroom closet. Hoping to remain incognito. He went inside and closed it just as Sasha was opening the bedroom door to confront her mother. He didn't know how Ms. Reed would react to him being in her home naked with her daughter, but he had a good idea, and didn't want to find out.

"Why you gotta leave messes around my house fo'? Have you seen my kitchen?" Kimani could hear Ms. Reed ranting. "What you think you got a house maid or somethin'?"

"Aight, momma. I'm goin'." Sasha pouted. Kimani listened as she stormed away.

He heard footsteps retreating down the hall as Ms. Reed made her way to her room. Listening carefully, he heard Ms. Reed's bedroom door close behind her. Allowing himself a sigh of relief – he knew how close they had come to getting caught – he laughed at the thought of Ms. Reed chasing him out of the house butt naked.

As the tiny space in the closet began to heat up and become stuffy, Kimani cracked open the door to allow fresh air into the cramped space. He instantly regretted it; staring eye to eye with a conniving Ms. Reed, he quickly closed the door shut hoping against all odds that she hadn't seen him.

"Um, huh." He heard her say through the door; it was too late for wishful thinking. "I knew yo' ass was up in here. Leavin' yo' clothes on my flo' and shit; got my house smellin' like ass. I don't know who you thought you was foolin'." Ms. Reed was letting him have it. "And what you laughin' fo'? I ain't said nothin' funny."

Kimani went silent. He simply didn't know what to say or do.

"Do you hear me, Kimani?"

"Yes, ma'am." He quickly said.

"Don't 'yes ma'am, me." Ms. Reed returned. "You ain't been 'yes ma'amin' me. So don't start now."

He jumped when she banged her fist on the closet door. When she finished ranting, he listened as her footsteps retreated away and was relieved at hearing the bedroom door, once again, close behind her. Fiending for some fresh air, Kimani burst out of the small closet and froze in his tracks; he was shocked to find Ms. Reed still standing inside the room by the bedroom door. She eyed him up and down before taking her time leaving out of the room and closing the door behind her.

Kimani was stunned.

He knew it all along; that lady was a freak just like her daughter. She didn't look bad by a long shot, but it only made him realize one thing: he had to stop fucking with Sasha about sexing her mother. Things could get out of hand real quick. He shook his head and simply laid back down on the bed to wait for Sasha to return.

Thinking about what just happened, many scenarios came to mind. He could only imagine how Sasha would react if she found out about this. Dismissing any ulterior motives from his mind whatsoever, Kimani fumbled at the thought as Sasha walked back into the room. He watched as she threw his clothing down on the bed.

"You don't think yo' momma knew they was mines do you?" he asked.

"Nah, we good," Sasha said. "But why you layin' in the bed naked, like that? She might come in here."

"Don't sweat it. It's goin' be all good." More confident now, he said, "bring yo' sexy ass over here."

Looking back at the door, Sasha walked over to the bed and cuddled up next to Kimani. Still weary of her mother, she pulled the covers up over his exposed body. "That shit was close," she said. "I just knew she was goin' come in here and see yo' ass. She would've killed me."

Kimani was smiling. "I told you don't sweat it, girl. I'm sure she know what's up wit' us anyway."

Being the keeper of information, he could either hold the peace, or facilitate chaos. Of course, he chose peace. He saw no reason to create such stress over something that he saw as irrelevant. He knew that he would never cheat on her with her mother anyway.

Sasha ran her hand through her hair and realized just how messy it had become. Knowing what she needed to do, she reached down with that same hand and grabbed Kimani's dick. She started stroking it and felt it swelling.

"Baby?" she began. "I wanna go out wit' my homegirls tonight. I need to get my hair redone after you just messed it up..." She continued stroking his dick. "... and I wanna have some fun."

"So, what you tryin' to say?" Kimani interrupted her. He knew what she wanted, but he didn't want her to feel like she had to beat around the bush with him.

"I need a couple of dollars..." she said. "Please?"

"I guess I can do that." Kimani admitted. He wanted her to have fun. "But why you strokin' my man's like that? What you tryin' to do to me, girl?"

Sasha, without hesitating, leaned over and smacked the tip of his hardened dick against her soft lips. Moaning and using her tongue, she began slurping up and down on his shaft, letting it slide down her throat as she did.

Kimani watched her work while she looked him in the eyes. Her performance was the truth; the way she moved.

He never minded giving her money. He wanted her to feel like she needed him anyway. It only made it easier for him to control her every move if need be. Loving the way that she sucked his dick, he tried hard not to think about her mother's recent intrusion. It was easier said than done.

When she finished, Kimani kissed her on the forehead before getting up to put on his clothes; he would have to shower later. He reached into his pockets and gave her five-hundred dollars; he would find a way to slip Ms. Reed another two hundred under her bedroom door for her troubles. Whoever said pussy came free didn't know what the hell they were talking about.

Knowing that he had things to do, he issued his goodbyes and made his way out the front door.

Sasha, alone, stood in front of her mirror and stared at herself; she looked a hot mess. With the money Kimani had given her, she would go to Kim's – her hair stylist and home girl down on Main – and get her hair and nails done. She thought about her and Kimani. She knew that she was his other half, and he was hers. She was satisfied, for now. To get what she wanted, she would love him even harder and do what she did best; Be patient and wait.

Things would change; things always did.

CHAPTER 5
THE HUSTLE

MARCH 3RD. 12:46PM.
SOUTH 7TH AVENUE
BOTTOM OF THE HILL
EAST NASHVILLE...

"Look, Cuz, go ask Boo what up wit' the re-up. We almost out."

"Man, fuck that. I'm waitin' on a hundred bite. You go ask him."

"That's fucked up, homeboy." Said J-Rocc. "You a lazy mufucka Tipsy. You got me twisted you think I'm a be makin' the re-up all day. You need to get up off yo' ass."

J-Rocc hopped up off the bucket he'd been sitting on, looked at Tipsy sideways, and started walking across the grounds towards the stash-house. If they ran out before they got a chance to re-up, they would lose out on a lot of cash; a clucker would simply move on to the next group to get the product they craved. J-Rocc couldn't afford to let that happen.

They were a man down today; usually they'd have someone whose sole job consisted of making sure that each sub-group of men like themselves stayed stocked with product. But today, J-Rocc would have to serve that purpose.

The system they operated allowed for a no hand-to-hand transaction hustle. It was fairly simple.

Each group consisted of eight individuals. Four of them were sellers grouped up in two's – they received the money from the cluckers for either crack, heroin, sherm, or pills. One man relayed the amount of that sell from that particular seller to a boarded-up window in an abandoned apartment around the corner. One man kept that boarded-up window stocked piled with product, and the final two men sat inside of the apartment to that boarded-up window doting out pre-purchased product through a small hole. That was only one group. It was an efficient system that kept the money separated from the product at all times.

Anywhere from thirty to fifty groups were operating in the hood at any given moment, depending on the day and hour. Boo, an older cat, commanded five of those groups – including his – at the bottom of the hill. The men in J-Rocc's group were spread out as far as possible, communicating using only hand signals.

Usually, the bottom of the hill dominated most of the sells. Whichever group created the most profits by the end of the week got a small bonus relative to their profit. Commission would never work in this line of business; the production method was the only way to generate a good hustle. J-Rocc knew that he had to keep them re'd-up in order to excel profit. He also knew that Boo wouldn't have it any other way.

J-Rocc walked into the breezeway of the building where his group's stash-house operated; there were four other groups that operated from this building as well.

Because his group was a man down, he would have to get the re-up from the stash-house himself.

He saw Boo sitting at the top of the steps when he approached. The two cats at the bottom of the steps allowed him access.

"Boo? West crackin', Cuz?" J-Rocc said as he walked up.

"Rich-Rollin', fool." Responded Boo. "What it is?"

"What it was? You know we 'bout out. We gotta re-up."

"Where the fuck is Don-Don?" asked Boo.

"Yo' guess is good as mines, big homie," J-Rocc answered. "We gotta keep it movin' tho'."

"Aight then," Boo conceded. "Go on in, li'l nigga."

J-Rocc walked past Boo and gave a signaled knock on the apartment door to his left. He turned his face towards the security camera. Hearing the steel bars unlatch from inside, he pushed the door open with a twist of the handle. He entered through the kitchen door ready to answer to Old-School.

This was the part of the journey that J-Rocc didn't mind re'ing up for. Standing in the kitchen with Old-School were two naked bitches, both skillfully whipping up product. With asses and titties like that, he figured Old-School had the best job in the world.

"What you need, li'l nigga?" said a scraggily voice to his left.

Old-School didn't take no shit. Some would say that he was too old – he was in his sixties – for this job, but J-Rocc didn't see a problem with it. He watched Old-School as he sat at the kitchen table with a head full of grey hair and only a few teeth in his mouth. Aside from that, the old fart could calculate numbers in his head faster than anyone J-Rocc knew.

That being said, J-Rocc knew that he had to have his own numbers right any time he re'd up. He discovered long ago that in this current system every group would always be in the rear; they would forever owe the house from their previous re-up. Still, they had to stay re'd up in order to stay in production. It was a system that would always have its foot on their necks; Old-School would never let them forget it.

"We out, Old-School," said J-Rocc. "We need another sack. The way shit bangin' tho', we goin' prolly need two."

Old-School reached for his cell phone and dialed a quick number. After a few seconds, he spoke, "how much you got on two?" He asked the person on the other line. "Good... Good. Go head and collect three and four. Get at me when you add it up." He listened. "Three? Aight then." He hung up the phone before dialing another number. When the person on the other line answered, he spoke, "we ready fo ' pick up on two... Yeah. Twenty-six-eighty... yeah. Hit me up when yo' count clear... Aight then... Wait, what? One should've been clear...forty-four hundred. Aight, then." Old-School hung up the phone and sat it down on the table before him.

"Shit lookin' good I see," he said to J-Rocc.

"Yeah, you know the bottom of the hill doin' they thang," answered J-Rocc. "We might be on the bottom, but we stay on top; you hear me?"

"Dig that, li'l nigga. Shit, go on back then, they'll know what you need. If Don-Don don't get his ass back, I'll see you on the next one." Old-School reached for his cell phone.

J-Rocc walked through a set of beaded curtains that separated the kitchen from the living room and stopped to allow his eyes to adjust to the dimness. He quickly spotted four nigga's, either sitting or standing, talking to one another. They all got quiet when he entered the room. Without moving his eyes, J-Rocc noticed five weapons, two A.K.'s leaning up against the wall; two Uzi's – one sticking out from under a couch pillow, the other on top of the coffee table; and one pump with the full barrel lying on the floor parallel to the couch. All of the weapons were in quick reach of its user. This particular stash-house supplied five groups in all; there was a lot of product there that needed protection.

"In the back, Cuz. You know the drill," the slinky one scoffed.

J-Rocc smirked at the one speaking before heading towards the steel door at the end of the hallway; he hated nigga's that tried too hard to be tough. He figured the ones that beat their chest the hardest were often the biggest cowards.

Coming to the end of the hallway, J-Rocc waited by the door. Just like in the other stash-houses in the hood, this door was an added precaution; the last stand. Modified with three-inch thick steel with reinforced bars and hatches, it would take a full demolition team to break it down.

A small slot on the door opened and a brown paper bag was pushed through it. With the re-up in his hand, J-Rocc turned to walk back the way he'd come. He paused as one of the naked female cookers brought a fresh batch of cooked product down the hall to the steel door. Watching as she passed, he was lusting as her ass cheeks switched from side to side. As thick as she was, however, he knew that he had to get back to work and made his way out the back door.

At the top of the steps, J-Rocc chucked up the N's with Boo one last time before heading down the stairs. Rushing to drop off the product at the pick-up window, he headed back to his post. All of this could've been avoided had Don-Don only showed up to work.

The system was efficient so long as everyone did their part. A clucker would pay any given amount to a seller like J-Rocc who would then relay that amount to the relay-man. The relay-man would then mimic that amount to the pick-up-window. The clucker, after buying, would have to go around the corner and out of sight to get their product from the pick-up-window, thus completing the transaction. The pick-up-window, like many other things in the hood, changed at random. In this case, it prevented a clucker from constantly walking off in the same direction. Very seldom a clucker would try and pick up some product without paying, but they were always dealt with accordingly.

A no hand-to-hand transaction hustle was a hustle that made it difficult for the narcs to contend with; it made it harder to prove that all of the pieces were linked. For J-Rocc, for instance, they would have to prove that he wasn't 'only' just receiving money from someone but was a part of a broader system.

Every two hours on the hour a group of three nigga's would come along on their route to collect money from the workers. That money would be taken to a money-house to be counted and cleared; at the end of the day, it would be shipped to a more secure location. As long as the money-house logs matched the logs of each commander – big homies like Boo – then the gears to the machine would continue to move.

J-Rocc and Tipsy only dealt with crack and heroin. But with other groups dealing in a variety of other drugs, there was a lot of money being made in this neighborhood. Tipsy was sitting on a crate catching a sell when J-Rocc rounded the corner of the building.

"West crackin', Cuz?" J-Rocc said. "What I miss?" Tipsy reached into his pocket and brought out two-hundred and twenty dollars just as a customer was handing him fifty more. He relayed the signal before turning to J-Rocc. "Two-twenty." Tipsy said, handing over the money.

"Damn, Cuz," J-Rocc said, shocked. "It's bangin' out here. I wasn't gone fifteen minutes. We piecin' this shit out like it's a cure fo' aids or somethin'."

"In a way it is." Tipsy laughed. "It'll make them fo'get they got the shit."

J-Rocc knew that there was a lot of money being made. He also knew that the only way to continue to make that money in such large quantities was to eliminate the competition. For that, O.G. Bones had his soldiers. While the money that they made funded those soldiers, it was those same soldiers that protected the money; a military and economic structure that went hand and hand. You couldn't have one without the other.

"What time you got, Cuz?" asked J-Rocc.

Tipsy looked at his watch "One-fifty-seven." He replied. "It's 'bout that time, too."

"Damn, Cuz. When you get that shit?" J-Rocc asked, grabbing Tipsy's wrist to get a better look at the watch he wore.

"One of my snow-bunnies bought this fo' me." Tipsy bragged. "You know I be havin' them hoe's spendin' that dough on a nigga."

"That sky-blue wrist-band killin'." J-Rocc paused. "But I ain't feeling no Michael Kors."

"That's cause you broke. You gotta have that dough to know 'bout this shit."

"Whatever, nigga." Said J-Rocc. "What that shit set you back fo'?"

"It was 'bout three on the market, but she paid like fifteen-hundred." Tipsy smiled. "Money ain't shit but paper to a white hoe when it comes to a nigga like me."

"Yeah, I hear you, nigga. But you and I know yo' ass eatin' that pussy, tho'. Yo' conversation ain't strong like that." J-Rocc was talking shit. "Who you think you is? Me?"

"That shit sound good. I don't see no diamonds on yo' wrist." Tipsy grabbed J-Rocc's bare arm. "Where yo' shit at, my nigga?"

"Watch out fool." J-Rocc pulled away. "I don't rock my shit to work."

"Yeah, aight. You got the juice." Tipsy started laughing as he looked down at his watch. "Anyway, it's almost two-o'clock; it's 'bout that time. How much you got?"

"Shit, 'bout seven-hundred." Said J-Rocc. "How much you got?"

"A li'l over a stack." Tipsy assured him. "Don't even trip tho', homeboy. The bottom of the hill in this shit together. We goin' be on top again this week, watch what I tell you."

Even though Tipsy was right about their group being one, J-Rocc didn't like being out-done by anyone. Looking up, he nodded in the direction of the three cats coming their way. "Look, there them nigga's go right there."

Tipsy looked up and spotted Tony, C.J. and Yucc walking with a determined gait. He and J-Rocc reached into their pockets and pulled out a bundle of money from their previous re-up; they were still in the midst of flipping their current order and it wouldn't be due for another two hours. Tony, the collector leading the trio, hung up his phone as they approached. He said, "the house say it's twenty-six-eighty." He began writing into a small book as C.J. and Yucc reached for the money.

"We almost done wit' the current run," Tipsy stated. "You may as well gone and take that too."

"Nah, it don't work like that, li'l nigga." Tony corrected. "You just sit out here and get that paper. Let me decide when it's time to collect. You do yo' job, and I'm goin' do mine. You dig?" Ever since Tony had moved up in his position, he found that he hated the average worker. They were at the bottom of the totem pole and didn't get paid shit. They had no clue that they were only the footstool of another man's throne. Every chance he got, he treated them like scum. "All that paper here, ain't it."

"Man, you say that same shit every time." It was J-Rocc who spoke up. "Ain't no nigga stupid enough to steal nothin' from Bones. Hell yeah all that shit there."

"Homeboy, let me make one thing clear," Tony began. "This my head on the line, fool. You damn right I'm goin' ask that shit every time. You gotta problem wit' that?" His right hand clutched the pistol on his waistband. "Let me know somethin', Cuz."

J-Rocc knew that Tony had a short trigger hand. Not wanting to instigate the nigga any further, he conceded.

"Nah man... ain't no problem. Everything there. You can count that shit yo 'self if you wanna."

"I don't count money, homeboy," Tony said, smiling. "I collect it." Knowing that neither J-Rocc nor Tipsy wanted any smoke, he walked off with his two muscle men in tow.

"Man, that nigga goin' get what's comin' to him, Cuz. He keep steppin' to me like I'm a sucka." J-Rocc vented when Tony and his crew walked away. "He goin' fuck around and make a nigga touch his ass up. Fuck that nigga, Cuz. He got me fucked up."

"I feel you, homie." Tipsy admitted, trying to calm J-Rocc. "That nigga do be trippin'. But don't sweat that shit right now, fool. We out here gettin' money, not sparkin' war wit' our own kind."

Tipsy's words didn't change much in J-Rocc's mind. He still had a look on his face that could, and would, kill. Even though Tipsy felt where his *Conrad* was coming from, he knew that shit would blow over soon. They were here to get money; he would leave the warring to the military faction.

CHAPTER 6
SNITCHES AND DITCHES

MARCH 3RD. 1:12PM.
SOUTH 7TH AVENUE
BOTTOM OF THE HILL
EAST NASHVILLE...

They had the three suspects bound, handcuffed, and in the back of the paddy-wagon; the criminals didn't even see it coming. Two of the undercover officers were dressed as homeless men; one pushing a shopping cart, the other apparently asleep by the dumpster. Three of the undercovers were cluckers walking up to buy product. And the rest awaited close by in unmarked vehicles ready to pounce.

The code word was, "I need some work," spoken by one of the undercover's. It wasn't long after that the first three suspects standing outside of the apartment were taken into custody. Of course they knew something was wrong. No clucker ever came to a stash-house asking for work. But unfortunately for them, it was too late to do anything about it. With a looping sequence that was quickly fed into the security camera outside the apartment door, the tact team had a short time to prepare a home invasion with the element of surprise still in their favor.

The S.W.A.T. team was ready and in place seconds later. Third year Sergeant Carlos Ramirez and his team took lead at the front door of the apartment, while Corporal Donald's and his team took position at the back.

Sergeant Ramirez took out his FOALSAC; fiber-optic-available-light-scope-and-camera. It would give him a fisheye look into the apartment without generating any light or sound. The FOALSAC device look like a very thin hypodermic syringe with a receptacle underneath that was roughly the size of three stacked dimes. Inserting the thin tip of the device just under the front door frame, he snaked it through until it reached the other side. Once there, he could then observe the room from the mini LCD screen mounted on the front panel.

The tiny receptacle underneath contained a small lithium-ion battery to film and record whatever the camera saw. He could sweep the device up, down, left, or right, each time he wanted to look around, or press the pic-button each time he wanted to take a picture.

Corporal Donald's worked the back door using the same device.

Lieutenant Connelly, team leader for the entire operation, knew that they were more than likely being watched by someone in the neighborhood, someone who could easily alert the suspects inside. Time was of the essence. The element of surprise was always the best offense. The leading tactical officer quickly devised a plan – with the current given detail – and put it into play.

"As Intel states, the chances are good that these doors are reinforced with steel bars. Burning it will probably do no good. We're going old school with this one." Lieutenant Connelly turned to one of his men. "Sergeant Osprey?"

"Sir."

"Get some plastique's set up and ready to blow; on the double."

"On it sir," stated the Sergeant.

Sergeant Osprey turned to two of his trainees and ordered them to set charges on the front and back doors. They immediately placed them where the handles and hinges would more than likely be.

With a small metal shield placed over each explosive to direct the blast inwards, the charge would be powerful enough to blow the doors right off of its frame. A magnetized quarter-inch sized clock was attached to the mechanism. When the pin guard was removed, it would start a ten second count down at which time an electrical charge would surge from the clock, through the metal, and trigger the explosives.

Sergeant Osprey's team removed the pin guards when commanded and stepped out of the way.

Lieutenant Connelly's tactical team moved forward to ready themselves as the first one's through the door. When the charges blew, and the doors fell inwards, the first man of each team would toss in flash-bang grenades to temporarily disorient the suspects; a tactic that would leave the team with yet another advantage.

Lieutenant Connelly gave a verbal countdown to prepare his men. When the countdown was over, the explosion came, and the first men of each tactical team tossed in their flash-bang grenades.

"Detective Anderson? This is Lieutenant Connelly." Sergeant Squires said to Anderson, gesturing towards the lieutenant with a wave of his hand. "He was in charge of the drug bust that took place over in Cacey Homes this afternoon; three suspects dead, and eight taken into custody. The chief wants you to spearhead the investigation." Sergeant Squires looked at Connelly and patted the Lieutenant on the shoulder. "If you need any direct information, he's your guy, Anderson. I'm headed down to interrogation. You girls have fun."

"Thanks Sergeant," stated Detective Anderson. He looked over the lieutenant with the stack of folders in his hands and tried to assign a character with him. He couldn't quite figure the man out. The lieutenant was fit – probably stayed in the gym – and appeared to be in his forties by the graying at his temples. He stood nimrod straight without faltering – more than likely military – but was a mystery beyond that. The Detective simply watched as the lieutenant stared back at him.

"Lieutenant..." Detective Anderson gestured. "...my office is this way."

The lieutenant followed the Detective to his office on the third floor of the building without question; he was definitely military.

The building was relatively new; barely five years old. The Detective watched his own reflection through the recently buffed floors while working out how exactly he was going to approach the debriefing. He knew nothing about the drug bust ahead of time, but now that he knew, he figured he was going to have to do some digging around to gather viable information for Bones. Luckily for him, he was going to be spearheading the investigation himself.

Off of the elevator, down the hall and seated behind his desk, Anderson asked Connelly to present what he had.

The lieutenant did so, handing over a large stack of folders; eight white ones for each of the suspects taken into custody, and three red ones for the ones that refused to go down. Once Connelly had given Anderson a quick summary of what took place, he simply waited for the Detective to respond.

"Any known ranking members that we know of?" asked Detective Anderson.

"Yes," responded Connelly. "One. He goes by the nickname, Boo. He's been in our gang files going on twenty-three years now." Connelly tapped one of the files now on Anderson's desk. "His real name is, Lewis Dotts. Age thirty-eight. He has a criminal record that we could feel the shelves with. Last arrest was a little over a month ago – a gun-possessions charge. Made bond before the ink dried. We did a background check on the mother that made the bond, and she's apparently on welfare." Connelly recited the memorized file with ease. "While making a fifteen-thousand-dollar bail while on government assistance isn't illegal, it does raise a few red flags."

Opening Dott's file, Detective Anderson looked up at Connelly. The lieutenant was sharp, and he would have to tread carefully with this one. Looking at the suspect's mug shot, Anderson confirmed for himself who he was looking at. He knew of Boo. He also knew that Bones would be highly upset about this particular arrest. Flipping through the file, he listened as the lieutenant continued to give a detailed rundown on the raid.

"When we finally managed to get inside of the apartment and the gunfire ceased, we encountered another problem that we did not expect; the room at the back of the apartment had a steel door bolted to the frame."

"A steel door?" asked Anderson, shocked.

"Affirmative," said Connelly. "And just as we were about to set up another round of plastique's, we noticed a foggy substance pouring through the cracks of the door. Concerned, we retreated outside until we could don the appropriate chemical apparatus." The lieutenant paused, reliving the moment. "We initially thought that the perpetrator set the room on fire with himself inside, but as we were clad and back in position, he announced his surrender and came out of the room wearing his own gas-mask." The lieutenant shook his head before continuing. "The foggy substance quickly spread throughout the apartment. Once it dissipated enough for us to secure the scene, we went into the room and found a large vat full of acid, still bubbling from some... reaction."

"Reaction?" Asked Anderson. "Reaction to what?"

"We assumed that the suspect behind the door disposed of the drugs into the acid."

"Are you serious?"

"It seems so. We also assumed that all the drugs were stored in that room until it was to be cooked."

"Until it was cooked?" Asked Anderson "Why do you say that?"

"Well, contradicting our Intel, the only drugs recovered on the scene were a few ounces of crack that were still being cooked on the stove-top in the kitchen."

The Detective had to laugh at that one. "Well, I'll be damned." He noted. "Without knowing what was in the vat, we can't even prove that they were attempting to destroy evidence. The little fucks are getting smarter and smarter." Before he could say anything further, Sergeant McLeod from interrogations burst into the room.

"Anderson," he called. "We got one talking."

The Detective and Lieutenant both looked at one another, before getting up to leave the room with Sergeant McLeod heading towards interrogations.

In less than a minute, they were all three in observation room one. Anderson turned and watched the interrogation through the one-way mirror as the trio were assessed of the situation by Detective Dently. Listening in on the interrogation, Detective Anderson made sure to pay close attention.

"...I need a damn name, Terrence." Sergeant Squires demanded.

"I told you already. I only know him by Bones. He runnin' the whole neighborhood. When he say somethin', it get done. I can point him out to you, but like I said, I don't think nobody know his real name." Terrence was shaking from head to toe.

"And does this Bones character let a no-shit mother-fucker like you get close to him?"

"I've been close to 'em once, but that was last year. And even then, he was surrounded by a lot of people that will kill fo' him; 'checkin' up on erbody' he said. Still, it was only fo' a second. And if I did get close to him fo' longer than that, he won't say nothin' stupid. He ain't dumb..."

WHAMMMMM!!!

Sergeant Squires reached over the table and smacked Terrence hard across the face. "You answer my questions and nothing more. Do you hear me, you piece of shit?" The Sergeant didn't mind the bullying approach. He turned towards the one-way mirror. "Get me some tissue in here. The little fucks bleeding everywhere."

Terrence couldn't move with his hands being cuffed to the top of the table, but even if he could, Sergeant Squires doubted he would've tried anything; his lip was shaking uncontrollably after only a few questions.

"Who's this kid?" Anderson asked Sergeant McLeod from the observation room.

"His names, Terrence Shelters. No prior criminal record; a few misdemeanors," McLeod explained. "He's only eighteen years of age. Stays with his mother at their last known address of, 1601 south 4th avenue. Also, no siblings, he's an only child."

"Terrence Shelters, you say?"

"You got it."

"We have to see if we can get him to perform for us," Anderson said. "Better yet, I'll do it myself." Anderson walked out of the observation room, leaving Connelly, McLeod, and Dently behind.

Terrence looked up when the newcomer walked in; the guy was massive.

"Terrence Shelters?" Detective Anderson offered his hand but retreated when he realized that Terrence was cuffed to the table. "I'm Detective Anderson. MNPD drug unit." He looked Terrence over. "Sergeant Squires, what the fuck did you do to him? He's bleeding all over the place."

"He tried to escape. I had to stop him." Squires laughed at his own joke.

"Uh-uhh," denied Terrence.

The Detectives both looked at their suspect with surprise. It was clear that he wasn't very cleaver.

"Are you alright son?" Anderson asked the shaken Terrence. The kid looked at Squires before looking back at Anderson and nodded his head. "If I would've known the Sergeant was doing this to you, I would've come in here a lot sooner."

Anderson could tell that the kid was comforted by his words; after the treatment he'd been receiving, he would feel comfort in anyone. The Detective reached into his pocket and pulled out a napkin to hand to him. Terrence leaned forward to wipe his mouth with his cuffed hands.

"Sergeant Squires?" The Detective motioned. "Could you give Terrence and me a few minutes alone? I'd like to discuss a couple of matters with him, if that's alright with you." Anderson wanted to make Terrence believe that Squires was the one in charge; since Terrence undoubtedly feared Squires he figured he would be more apt to confide in him.

"Sure thing, Anderson. I can do that," Sergeant Squires said.

Detective Anderson never took his eyes off Terrence as Squires got up to leave the room. When he heard the door close, he spoke, "now, Terrence, I'm not in charge of this investigation." The Detective lied. "That's Sergeant Squires' responsibility. That being said, I'm going to need your full cooperation so that I can keep Sergeant Squires out of this room. Do you understand what I'm saying to you, son?" Terrence vigorously nodded his agreement. The Detective continued, "now, like I said, I'm not in charge of this investigation, but when I heard what it was that Sergeant Squires was doing down here, I felt obligated to come and straighten things out. I'm just here to help you out. Do you understand me, son?"

"Ye... Yeah." The kid could barely speak.

"Good," said the Detective. "Now, since you don't have enough information to offer us, you're going to have to go and get that information for us." When Terrence said nothing, the Detective explained further. "Terrence, what we need from you is to become a confidential informant. Do you know what this means?"

Silence.

"It means," the Detective continued, "that we're going to have your beautiful mother come down here and pose like she's the one making your bail. Usually we'd just let you go, but you said it yourself, this Bones character is a smart cookie. We don't want for this to look too suspicious." Anderson loved scare tactics. "By now, Bones knows you've been arrested, so if you're held too long before getting booked, he's going to suspect something. So we're going to make this quick. Once out, we need you to act normal. That means doing everything that you would do on any other day. Don't deviate." Anderson paused to allow the slow-witted Terrence to catch up.

The Detective didn't bother to tell Terrence that he already had two under-covers inside of Bones' operation. While he gave Bones the information that he paid for, his two undercovers gathered the counter-information that could become useful; a little insurance in case he had to cover his own ass. It took them five years to get in the position that they were now in, and finally – Anderson felt – they were the power pieces he would need if necessary.

When Terrence nodded his confirmation, the Detective continued. "Our officers here at the precinct will be hooking you up with the appropriate devices needed. A wire under your shirt will suffice, for now. You will need to wear this device at all times. We never know when the words we'll need will be spoken. We'll train you on how to operate the device; how to keep it charged and so forth. Do you understand?"

"Yeah," Terrence said. He was becoming more and more confident.

Anderson noticed the calmness Terrence was beginning to show; his words were smoother; his breathing was regulated. The Detective continued to coax him on what he needed him to do.

"Your objective will be to get as much information as you can on this Bones character. We'll give you as much direction as we feel you'll need to better help manipulate your target." The Detective paused, smiled, and then continued, "there was two and half kilos of crack, and a half kilo of heroin in the apartment you were busted in, Terrence." Anderson felt no need to tell Terrence about the vat of acid. "You try and get cute on us, son, and we'll find your ass and make this all stick. You do as we say, and I can promise you that you'll never see a day in prison."

"Right now," the Detective continued, "this current investigation is the only thing stopping the FEDS from coming in here and taking over this entire operation. Once they do that, Terrence, there's nothing I can do to help you. So, I remind you, once again, don't try and get cute on us. You're not smarter than us and you never will be. Are we clear?"

"Yeah," Terrence agreed.

"Good. For your sake, I hope so." Anderson warned. "You cooperate and I'll do whatever I need to do to make this go away. Now you get comfortable. I'll send my techs in here to chat with you shortly."

"Aight," Terrence said. He looked like a sad child.

Smiling, Anderson got up and walked out of the room. He quickly confronted the other Detectives in observations and had them write up the necessary paperwork to be presented to the chief for execution. With instructions given, Anderson walked out of the precinct with one thing in mind. He got into his unmarked and drove down the Boulevard to the nearest gas station. Once there, he picked up a payphone to page Bones to inform him of his soon-to-be predicament. This was the very work that he was being paid for. The reason Bones constantly stayed ahead of the curb. A minute and a half after the page was sent, the phone rang.

"Detective Anderson, so nice of you to call me. Is yo' end secure?"

"I'm at a pay-phone."

"Good." Bones knew it didn't matter. He had the technological equipment required on his end to manipulate the phone line. This particular call, for instance, was coming from Lo Che Siang, somewhere in Indonesia, and a voice analysis would never penetrate the vocal alteration program designed to change the sound of his vocals. Bones was forever secure. "It seems as though I had a minor set-back today. Some of my best workers went down. You mind tellin' me what the hell I'm payin' you fo'?"

"It was a top priority independent investigation..." Anderson pleaded. "... privileged information that only a few knew about. I can't control what I don't know. That being said, I am good at what I do know, and what I do know is something I'm sure you'll be interested in."

"I'm listenin'."

"Terrence Shelters. He'll be making bail some time by the end of the night. State endorsed, I might add. He's a squealer Bones. Had he known too much about you, he would've spilled his entire guts. That being said, he's going to be looking forward to getting to know you a whole lot more, if you know what I mean. And so sad, he's only eighteen."

"He say anything important?" Bones asked. "Anything that could hurt?"

"So far, we only have your alias, and the fact that you're the head of your operation. Nothing concrete though. Until we can gather better Intel, it'll all be treated as nothing more than speculation. I'll make sure of that."

Bones paused in an attempt to control his anger. Having to clean up behind someone else was something he hated to do, but he knew that it was necessary. He calmed himself, already knowing what had to be done.

"So my grass is getting' too high, huh?" Bones started. "I'm gonna have to send some people in to cut it down, then. I don't want it gettin' so high that I can't see what's goin' on around me." Bones gave it some thought, and then said, "you have my number, Detective. Use it if anything else develops."

Bones disconnected the line without waiting for an answer and immediately reached over to power down the rerouting device. He had amassed a number of technologies over the years – thanks to his suppliers – that would aid in his ability to remain ahead of the competition. With Terrence on his mind, he flipped through his rolodex for the perfect professional to eliminate his problem.

Within minutes, his secure line began to ring. He quickly answered, "I need to see you in my office ASAP. Code word, T-C." Bones simply demanded before hanging up. He would relay that code word to his security down in the lobby and to his henchmen outside of his office door; anyone not using that particular code word would be turned away. As of now, only C-loco would be walking through the door to his downtown fourth floor Financial Consultant's Office; a business for businessmen.

He developed this company some nine years ago to counter-weigh the growing expansion of his empire. The money he was making from the streets was becoming too expensive to clean without the aid of businesses such as this. In the nine years since, he created many more such businesses with the same purpose as this one; to mimic the Financial Consultant business; it was a game that became heavier and heavier as the years went by.

Twenty minutes later, he and C-loco were sitting face to face across from one another.

"What up, big homie?" C-loco inquired.

Bones didn't respond immediately. Instead, he looked over at the one window in the office that gave a view to the outside world. He flipped a switch underneath his desk that manipulated the mechanism attached to the large windowpane. The glass not only fogged up with a misty tint, but it began to lightly vibrate; scrabbling any frequencies possibly directed at his office. Not ever willing to take chances, it was a technology that gave him the privacy he needed.

Every morning he had his office swept for electronic bugs. There was also a built-in sensor inside of the door frame to scan anyone entering the room; if they were wearing a wire, he would be notified immediately. He had to take every and all precautions working as a financial consultant.

Bones steepled his fingers, looked at C-loco, and then spoke, "I have a vic' fo' you." He carefully watched C-loco, happy to see that he wasn't surprised. "I can't stand a snitch around me, C-loco. I mean, I'm good to everyone. Wouldn't you agree that I'm good to everyone?"

"Hell yeah, no doubt," said C-loco. Seeing the anger in Bones' eyes, he wouldn't dare say anything to the contrary.

"I want fo' this one to hurt very much, Cuz." Bones insisted. "I want fo' him to know that we know; I want fo' him to beg; I want fo' him to plead; I want fo' him to ask fo' mercy; and I want fo' him to regret his actions befo' he dies." Bones recited each statement louder than the one before it. "I'm puttin' you, C-loco, in charge of makin' this shit last fo' as long as possible." The O.G. allowed for his orders to sit in. He was always the dramatists; he knew what captivated people's attention. He continued, "he'll be out of jail befo' sundown. I warn you, though, take grave care cause this one may be being watched very closely. One-time tryin' to penetrate my defenses. But I'm goin' fix that shit."

"Sho'-nuff. Consider that shit done. Who this nigga anyway?" C-loco asked.

"Terrence." Answered Bones. "Terrence from down on fourth?"

"He was guardian at the bottom of the hill; one of Boo's," explained Bones. "But them boys ran in my shit today. I took a major lost in production, not to mention one of my best crews. I want fo' this shit to hurt, C-loco. You make that bitch squeal. You hear me?"

"I got you, big homie," assured C-loco. "Consider that shit done."

"Good. I knew I could count on you. I give you by morning. And be careful, C-loco, it'd be so sad to lose you, too." Bones lied.

"I got you, Cuz."

"That's what's up. Here..." Bones tossed C-loco a fat stack of twenty-dollar bills. "Five-thousand now and another five-thousand when it's done. You can get the other half from Tee-Tee."

"Bet that." C-loco happily accepted. "That nigga good as dead."

"I can't stress this enough." Bones reminded him once again. "Be careful. Take yo' time and plan well. Morning." He paused. "You're dismissed."

With those last words spoken, C-loco got up and walked out of the office, imagining how he would handle the situation. First, he would go to Tee-Tee and get a weapon of his choosing. Then, he would go and talk to Ms. Shelters – to check up on his friend, Terrence, of course. He would wait for Ms. Shelter's to invite him in; that, she would do, because as everyone knew, she was a kind lady. He would talk to her and say the nicest things until the time came when she would have to ask him to leave; after all, she had to go and pick up her baby boy. Once she was gone, C-loco would creep back into the fourth avenue apartment – probably through a window that he would have left unlocked – and wait for Terrence and his mother to return home. The rest would be a topic for the ten o'clock news.

C-loco knew that he was an artist when it came to shit like this. To most, it would be a night of horror, but to him, it would simply be another notch on his pistol-grip.

He was a man cultured to reap the benefits of a twisted world.

Kimani left Sasha's crib at a quarter 'til four. He had money in his pocket, and clubbing – for a change – on his mind. There was no doubt whatsoever that he and C-loco would find something to get into tonight.

He walked across 6th avenue and headed towards his crib. He had thoughts of hoping that his mother would let him borrow the truck for the night. How he was going to ask her, was what he had to figure out. Though he had enough money to buy his own vehicle, Kimani always chose to remain low-key. Unlike most young cats his age, he didn't care much for shiny pennies.

Walking across the street, he was nearly hit by a car that came to a screeching halt just inches from where he stood. Out of instinct, he reached for his forty caliber at the small of his back.

"The fuck you doin', homie?" he demanded. He could care less that he was the one in the wrong. Glaring at the driver of the vehicle, his attitude quickly changed when he recognized the occupant. He removed his hand from the small of his back, and immediately started shooting jabs. "Didn't yo' momma teach yo' ass how to drive, nigga? You almost fucked up a nigga boots."

"Shit, didn't yo' momma teach yo' dumb ass how to look both ways befo' crossin' the streets?" C-loco countered. He tapped the gas petal, quickly hitting the breaks, forcing Kimani to jump back. He laughed at the expression on his homies face.

"Watch what the fuck you doin', nigga. That shit ain't funny," Kimani demanded, looking down at his boots. The cars on the avenue began to back up but no one bothered to say anything or blow their horns in protest. He walked over to the driver side window. "Fuck you headin', anyway?"

"I got some business to handle fo' the big homie," said C-loco. "Just a li'l bump that needs to be flattened. Why? What's up?"

"Shit. Just askin'." Fo' a moment Kimani saw the death in C-loco's eyes, but just as quickly, it was gone. He knew his homie and knew the madness that he harbored within. Glancing over on the passenger seat Kimani spotted a roll of duct tape and a silenced Sig-Sauer p-28 9mm pistol. It verified what he already sensed. "Look Cuz, hit me up when you get done wit' that."

"Bet that," said C-loco. "It won't take nothin' but a second, anyway. Where you goin' be at?"

"Prolly at the crib. You know the number."

"Yeah, yo' broke ass need to get a cell phone..."

"Whatever, nigga," stated Kimani. "You just make sure you hit the house phone up."

"Aight, fool. I'll do that. Give me a few hours. And make sure yo' ass there, too," C-loco reminded. "If I call and you ain't, yo' momma goin' be askin' a nigga a thousand questions and shit. She be interrogatin' a nigga."

"I'm goin' be there, fool," Kimani stated. "A nigga'll fuck around and go to Neighborhood's or somethin'."

"Neighborhood?" C-loco gave Kimani a sideways look. "Since when did yo' ass start clubbin' and shit?"

"Nigga, since yo' momma turned me out." Kimani began laughing at the blank expression C-loco wore.

"Yeah, aight." C-loco wasn't laughing.

"Look, Cuz, gone and handle that shit. Just make sure you hit a nigga up when you done."

"Bet. N's up, Cuzzo."

"N's." Kimani agreed. He watched as C-loco drove off, turning left on Sylvan Avenue. The traffic began to flow again as Kimani made a silent prayer for the soul that was on the off-list; only God could intervene now.

He paused and listened. He thought that he heard some noise.

Silence.

There it was again. Someone was definitely coming. Rushing across the small living room, he opened the closet door located just underneath the stairwell and quickly hid inside. He wanted this to be a surprise, and a surprise it would be.

The muffled sounds were coming from the other side of the front door; they were getting louder and louder, but he could hear them crystal clear from inside of the small closet. C-loco listened as someone entered the home. Moments later, the door closed, followed by the sound of the lock being turned into position. Probing with his ears, he could hear Terrence and his mother in the middle of a conversation.

"... this reminds me, baby, that friend of yours came by earlier to ask about you. He wanted to know when you were gettin' out of jail."

There was a hesitant pause. "Who you talkin' 'bout, momma?"

"That... Smoco, C-loco, or whatever his name is. I don't know why y'all use these crazy names."

"What all he say?"

C-loco could sense the nervousness in Terrence's voice.

"Not much. He just stayed over by the window the whole time. He wanted to know what you were bein' charged wit', and when they were lettin' you out. I told him it would be later on tonight. He sounded very concerned. He's such a good friend, baby."

This was it. It was now or never. C-loco reached for the doorknob and was about to open it when he heard Ms. Shelters getting closer. It was her that opened the door right out of his grip. When she spotted him, she just stood there.

With her purse in one hand, there was a confused and shocked look on her face. She never felt nor heard the suppressed bullet as it struck her square between the eyes.

C-loco quickly stepped around the falling body and spotted Terrence running towards the stairs. He thought it was only in the movies where the victims in danger of their lives ran up the stairs instead of through the front door and out of the home all together. He raised the silenced Sig-Sauer 9mm pistol and stopped Terrence's sprint with a piercing shot to the right knee.

Terrence went down hard at the bottom of the stairs. He emitted a scream so loud that C-loco was worried it would alert the neighbors. With three quick steps, he rushed up to his mark, and knocked him unconscious with the butt of the pistol.

Terrence's screams ceased; and the world around him went dark.

He was awakened suddenly by an excruciating splash of boiling salt-water to the face. The pain was too much.

He couldn't vent the agony by screaming, because his mouth had been gagged with duct-tape; not to mention something had been shoved into it. He tried to move, he wanted to remove the duct-tape from his mouth but realized that his hands and feet had been bound to a chair. He was in a seated position, tightly restrained.

The salt in the boiling water began to eat through his flesh; he could feel his skin as it melted from his face. He tried to close his eyes, to squeeze away the excruciating pain of this torture, but found that he couldn't. His left eye lid had already been eaten away, and the right one was in the process of melting. The pain and the realization of what was happening became too much for him to bear. Terrence lost consciousness again, and for the first time in his life he slept with both eyes open.

The world was painted red with all of the blood and puss that clouded his vision. Beginning to wake, he felt the collapse of his left eyeball as the pressure in it gave way. His face was blistered, his skin was still melting, and with his lone right eye he could barely make out the person in front of him sitting at his mother's kitchen table.

C-loco saw that Terrence was waking up. He put his sandwich down and walked over to where he had him tied to a chair in the middle of the kitchen floor. He spoke, "what up, homeboy? You aight, ain't you? Can I get you anything?" He teased. "No? Aight, aight. Well let's get straight to the business, then."

C-loco pulled up a chair and sat down directly in front of Terrence.

"Check this shit out..." he started. "I was out mindin' my own business when I get a call from the big homie. You know what the big homie said to me? He said, 'C-loco'... cause that's my name, right? ... 'I need fo' you to take care of somethin' fo' me'. And I was like, 'yeah, whatever Cuz'. So, he said, 'I got this snake mufucka that's tryin' to bite me. I've been good to the li'l bitch. I feed him all the rats he want, he ain't never need fo' nothin'. But the li'l bitch still tryin' to get at me. Why he wanna bite me, I don't know, but I can't let that happen." C-loco paused before continuing. "So here I am, homeboy. What you gotta say 'bout that?"

Silence.

Terrence's mouth had been stuffed full and he couldn't release the slightest of sounds.

"Oh, I almost fo'got, you can't talk," C-loco paused for effect. "You got a dick stuck in yo' mouth."

As if from the recognition alone, Terrence felt the pain coming from between his legs. He looked down and noticed that his pants had been pulled to his ankles and his inner thighs were soaked with blood. He knew that from the moment he saw C-loco come out of the living room closet that his life was over. He realized now that death would be a privilege compared to this.

"Yeah, that's right, mu'fucka'." C-loco taunted him. "It's yo' shit, nigga. But don't stress, I cauterized it fo' you. You ain't gotta worry 'bout bleedin' out. I see why yo' dick-eatin' ass never got no pussy though, you snitchin' bitch."

C-loco got up and grabbed the rainbow salt off of the table and splashed a handful of the grainy substance in Terrence's face. He watched as the little grains took its course and smiled at the agonizing screams coming from underneath the duct-taped mouth of his victim. The salt grains began to melt deeper into Terrence's flesh as he squirmed to get away.

"That's right, mu'fucka'. Scream!" C-loco laughed. "Cause yo' ass done fucked up. You turn yo' back on the hood, nigga, and the hood'll turn its back on you. What? You thought you was goin' get away wit' it? You thought you was goin' be free while everyone else had to suffer?" C-loco paused. "Here, mu'fucka'."

C-loco slung Terrence's wire-recorder at him. He was surprised to see the wire itself sticking to the melted flesh; in all of his years, he'd never seen that one before.

"Snitchin' bitch." C-loco continued to torment his vic'. "Why you do it fo', homeboy? Huh? What's that? I couldn't hear you." Said C-loco. He found sometimes that the words were worse than the torture. "Don't worry though, my nigga. I got you. We goin' fix you up real nice. I'm goin' tell you what I'm goin' do fo' you. Since the big homie don't like you no mo', I'm goin' make sure you never have to see him again. Is that cool wit' you?"

C-loco got up and walked around to the back of his victim. Terrence attempted to follow his movement – too frightened to let him out of his sights – but he was too well restrained. C-loco, squatting down, gripped the small paring knife he used to cut his sandwich in one hand, and grabbed Terrence's right index finger with the other. Very slowly, but deliberately, he thrust the small blade in between Terrence's fingernail and nailbed, pushing the blade in deep. Terrence fought to get away from the pain – the chair legs holding him, scuffing up the tiled floors – but C-loco was too good at his job; he was bound too damn tightly.

He was on his third finger with the paring knife when Terrence finally lost consciousness again. C-loco would wait; at well before morning, he had nothing but time. Terrence would wake and he would finish his other hand, talk to him some more, then find something else to do with him.

Washing his hands and arms, C-loco sat back down at the kitchen table to finish his sandwich. He was disgusted to discover that the bread had gotten hard. Getting up, he threw the stale sandwich in the trash. In the end, he would sterilize the entire apartment by setting it ablaze, so fingerprints and DNA wouldn't be an issue.

Rubbing his hands on his jeans, C-loco went to the refrigerator to find something to drink; working hard made him thirsty. He opened the fridge. Everything inside had been moved around to make room for Ms. Shelters' dead corpse; with a few broken Bones, she fit fairly easy. C-loco nudged her head to the side so that he could reach the jug of orange juice. Popping open the top, he drunk thirstily, closing the refrigerator door and sitting back down at the kitchen table.

When Terrence woke, C-loco would make sure to torture his ass some more before using the paring knife to slit his throat. He knew from experience that the human body's nervous system could only take so much pain before shutting down; his techniques would then become useless. Until then, C-loco had a purpose; to make an example out of any up and coming snitch.

When it was all said and done, the entire city would know that snitches wound up in ditches.

CHAPTER 7
DOWN ASS CHICK

MARCH 3RD. 7:23pm.
JAMES CACEY HOUSING PROJECTS
EAST NASHVILLE...

"Where you tryin' to go, Kimani?"

"I'm just tryin' to get out on the town, momma. It ain't goin' hurt nothin'. I'll be back befo' mornin' and I'll put it on a full tank of gas."

Ms. Johnson just stared at her son, considering whether or not she was going to let him use her truck for the night. She knew that he was responsible enough, plus he had his license and she had full auto-coverage, but it always made her nervous. Shit, she worked hard for her Escalade.

Kimani studied his mother, trying to determine what she was thinking. When he saw her roll her eyes and press her lips together, he knew he had her.

"I guess." She gave in like he knew she would. "But if yo' ass don't bring my truck back in one piece... so help you God, I'm goin' make you wish you did. Do you hear me, boy?" Not waiting for an answer, she continued, "go the speed limit. And don't have all them crazy ass friends of yours up in my truck. I'm not playin' wit' you, Kimani."

"Aight, momma. I got you." Kimani looked at his watch. 7:25pm. C-loco should be calling any minute now. "I'm goin' take care of it. Where the keys at?"

"In my room on my dresser." Ms. Johnson gently touched her son on the cheek. "And baby... be careful wit' whatever you about to get into."

"Everything goin' be cool, momma. Trust me. Ain't no need to worry. I got this." Kimani leaned forward and kissed his mother on the forehead. "I love you. Thank you. And I'll be back sometime by mornin'."

Seeing his mother smile, he turned to go to his room to find something fresh to wear. He would take a shower, throw on a clean 'fit, and prepare to see what the night had to offer.

By the time 8:15 came around, he'd began to worry if C-loco – not having yet called – was alright. Doing what Kimani knew that he was doing, he couldn't help but wonder if something went horribly wrong.

Kimani went to the kitchen, grabbed the phone from the receiver, and dialed C-loco's number. He put the phone up to his ear and anticipated a ringtone but got an actual voice instead.

"Hel... Hello."

"C-loco?" Questioned Kimani.

"What up, nigga? Fuck you pushin' buttons in my ear fo'," responded C-loco. "And where you been at; I been callin' yo' ass all night?"

"I was just 'bout to call you. Fuck you been at? I been sittin' here waitin' on you."

"Shit, I been callin'. Y'all the only mu'fucka's in the hood still gotta house phone; answerin' machine kept pickin' up and shit. Might be them alphabet boys. Knahmean?"

"Yeah, whatever, nigga." Kimani dismissed the idea. "So, what we goin' do? Shit still crackin' or what?"

"I got V.I.P. tickets to Neighborhood, nigga. 90% Neighbor discount. Ciroc on the house, titties in my mouth." C-loco declared. "You owe me fo' this one, Cuz. Word is, that Trey Songz boy goin' be performin' tonight, so you know it's goin' be plenty bitches up in there." C-loco paused. "Do Sasha know you goin' to the club, my nigga?"

"Whatever, fool. Look, I got the truck fo' the night..."

"Aw Shit."

"... so you at the crib right?"

"And you know this, mannn." C-loco was clowning.

"I'm a be blowin' the horn in a minute then, Cuz. Make sure you ready."

"I stay ready, to keep from gettin' ready," C-loco said. "You can believe that."

"Bet that, I'm on my way, then."

"Aight, Cuz. You know where I'm at."

"Aight then, fool."

"Aight."

Kimani broke the connection. He went to his mother's room to get the keys to the truck, and to let her know that he was about to leave.

"Momma?" he called, walking into the room. "Yeah," she answered, sitting on her bed.

"I'm 'bouts to ride out. Is there somethin' I can do befo' I go?"

"Yeah," she said, "hand me my purse."

Kimani did as he was asked, grabbed the keys off of the dresser in the process, and wondered if his mother was going to try and give him some money. She often did, and he always declined.

If she only knew. He thought to himself.

Ms. Johnson grabbed her purse and began digging inside of it. Just as Kimani was about to protest – to tell her that he was straight – she brought out an I-phone. She handed it to him with a smile on her face.

"I picked this up at the mall today. I almost fo'got to give it to you." She smiled. "I got me one, too." She showed him the purple case accessory she'd chose. "I have my number programmed in yours already. You shouldn't have no reason not to call." Seeing the smile on her son's face, it made her smile even harder.

"Damn, momma ..." Kimani paused. "I mean, dang, momma. How much did this cost you?"

"Boy, you worried 'bout the wrong thing." Ms. Johnson assured. "All you have to do is make sure you enjoy it and call me every day. Ain't no excuse for a son not keepin' in touch wit' his momma."

"I 'preciate this, momma. Now I'm goin' have to snatch you somethin' nice."

"Boy please. You just make sure you finish graduatin' this year. And give me a hug."

"Easy enough." Kimani admitted. He knew he would end up buying her something anyway; he always did. Leaning over the bed, he gently kissed his mother on the forehead before giving her a hug. "You know I saw this bracelet in the mall the other day..."

"Stop it. I done told you." Ms. Johnson was tickled; she didn't know what she was going to do with him.

Kimani kissed his mother one last time, and then walked out of the room. Manipulating the screen on his new phone, he made a mental note to download all the needed apps later.

In his room, he went to his dresser and picked up a bottle of Dolce cologne. Spraying the misty substance on his inner wrist, he rubbed them together before smearing the remaining residue on his neck. Sitting the bottle down, he sized himself up in his floor-to-ceiling mirror.

He had on a pair of bright-white Armani slacks and a matching Armani dress shirt with a sky-blue vest and matching gator belt. He observed the way the pieces highlighted the pair of old-school sky-blue big-bloc gators. He knew he would be turning heads tonight.

Thinking about all of the females that would be up in the spot, he allowed himself a guilty smile. With his dreads pulled back, and his white teeth gleaming, the boy was dressed to impress. He continued to get ready.

He corrected the platinum clasp that held the front of his shirt collar together and tightened the matching cusp-links at his wrist. With his big-face diamond encrusted Breitling watch and diamond encrusted pinky-ring decorating his hand, Kimani selected some platinum pull-out inserts and snapped them over his teeth. He didn't care for the shiny pennies, but that didn't mean that he didn't know how to be fly.

He walked over to his mattress and brought out the .40 caliber pistol. At his dresser, he opened the top left drawer and moved a stack of boxers off to the side. At the bottom of the drawer were several thirty-two-round extended clips and two standard ten-round clips. Though there would no doubt be a large crowd at Neighborhood's tonight, he opted for the two standard clips. There was just no telling when a person would need the extra ammo.

With the leather holster that was tucked at the small of his back, he secured the pistol, snapping it into place. He put the extra clips into their respective slots. With the sky-blue vest pulled down over the holster, he observed through the mirror the small bulge that it left. It was hardly noticeable, so he knew he would be alright. Mind content, Kimani picked up his new phone and walked out of the room.

He peeped in to say good-bye to his mother. With his phone in hand, he headed out the front door locking it behind him. It would only take him about five minutes to get to C-loco's crib up on thirteenth.

The night air was a good seventy degrees; perfect if you asked him. Getting into the truck, he immediately started the engine and blasted that new T.I. through the stereo system. He adjusted the mirrors and seats and secured his seatbelt before placing the truck in park. It wasn't long until he reached his destination.

He pulled into the driveway of C-loco's crib, blew the horn, and watched as C-loco peeped his head through the window blinds. It was mere seconds before the passenger door opened and C-loco hopped into the truck. Kimani could only stare at him; he never saw the front door to the home open nor his homie leaving out of the apartment.

"Goddamn, nigga. You look like a tall ass milk jug wit' the blue top." C-loco joked. C-loco was always joking. "All a nigga need now is a bowl of cereal."

"Ahh, this nigga got jokes. Don't hate on the Arm', nigga," Kimani shot back. "This 'fit alone'll pull mo' ho's than you can. I got a stack on it."

"Hell, you goin' have to have the 'fit, cause yo' conversation ain't 'bout shit."

"I ain't got the baddest chick in the hood fo' nothin', fuck you talkin' 'bout," Kimani stated. "Armani didn't pull that, Kimani pulled that."

C-loco had no counter. Everyone knew that Sasha was a bad bitch. As silence stole the air, Kimani allowed himself a triumphant smile. He pulled the vehicle out of the driveway and they made their way towards Neighborhood's.

It wasn't twenty minutes before they were pulling into the parking lot of the club. The first thing that Kimani noticed was the line of club-goers that extended around the corner and out of sight. Most of them were women hoping that they looked good enough to be chosen and ushered through the entrance.

"Cuz, it's a good thing you went and got those V.I.P. tickets." Kimani pointed out. "Look at that mu'fuckin' line, fool. We would've never got up in there. That bitch gots' to be packed tonight."

"What you expect? That Trey Songz nigga up in there," C-loco explained. "Every bitch in the hood tryin' to get fucked tonight."

Kimani began searching for a place to park. Finding a spot far away from the entrance, he left the truck running in park. He reached into his pocket to bring out a sack of cush; only then did he realize that he forgot to stop and get a box of Swishers. He turned to say something to the homie about it but was interrupted by the cigar that C-loco hovered in his face. Grabbing the Swisher from him without question, Kimani immediately began to break it down.

Weed rolled, and window cracked for ventilation, Kimani put fire to the end of the blunt and inhaled deeply.

"Hurry up, nigga." He heard a whispering voice urge from outside of the vehicle. Peering into the dark in the direction of the one talking, Kimani quickly spotted the source of the whispering. Two men jacking the rims off of a '73 Chevy Impala. Someone was going to be heated when they discovered that their twenty-six-inch rims were missing from their candy burnt-orange super-sport. The two men had the ride sitting on bricks and the rims in the trunk of their car in less than five minutes. Kimani and C-loco both watched the entire ordeal as they passed the blunt back and forth between them. Some shit was simply better than TV.

Entertained enough, Kimani put the truck in drive and eased his foot off the break. Pulling up to valet, they readied their V.I.P. tickets and walked the blue carpet. Just as he expected, they had everyone's attention. Ushered inside, bypassing the metal detectors, the two were taken to their booth without incident.

C-loco did his thing tonight, Kimani had to admit. Having already taken care of the bouncers, they were allowed to remain armed. Being prepared for the worse was a necessity in their world. The only downside to having bouncers in your pockets was that others would have also had their bids in. The bouncers would be well paid before the night was over.

A waitress came up to them to take their orders. C-loco ordered a plate of hot-wings and nachos, but all Kimani wanted was some peanuts, a whole cup of them.

"Peanuts?" inquired C-loco, looking at Kimani sideways.

"Salt, nigga," Kimani answered. He looked down at the set-up. The table was made of mahogany wood, with a plush blue semi-circled bench between it and the wall. He was always content with the idea that his back was up against the wall.

In the center of the large mahogany wood table was a chrome bucket filled with ice. Two bottles of Ciroc rested in the ice, while eight crystal glasses sat upside down on a sky-blue tablecloth surrounding the set-up. It was a nice center piece for the two Neighborhood high rollers.

"Damn, homie. You showed yo' ass off, boy," admitted Kimani. "Spendin' like yo' pockets real long. I wish I had it like that."

"Cuz, you know this ain't shit to a roller." C-loco pulled out a stack of hundred-dollar bills to show Kimani. "I'm here to roll, fool. You goin' roll wit' me or what?"

"Shit, if you say so, homie. Where that bitch at wit' them peanuts?"

"Nigga, what's up wit' you and these mu'fuckin' peanuts?"

"I told you, fool," answered Kimani. "It's the salt. I need that shit fo' my stomach when I drink."

"Aw, look at the baby..." C-loco joked.

"Yeah, fuck you, nigga." Kimani still hadn't sat down at the table yet; still trying to peep out the scenery. He didn't like crowds, even if they were still on their side of town.

C-loco noticed his homeboy's tension. He knew what he was thinking and why he was thinking it. Looking out over the crowded club, he said, "man, sit yo' ass down. It's goin' be all good up in here tonight. I don't even know why you trippin'." He shook his head. "That's why yo' ass need them peanuts, talkin' 'bout yo' stomach. Nigga, yo' ass just crazy."

Kimani reluctantly sat down but stayed at his end of the bench. Reaching towards the small of his back, he brought out the .40 caliber pistol and sat it down on the seat next to him. He never took his eyes off the crowd.

The waitress finally came back with their orders. C-loco was about to holla at her and get her number until she turned around and he saw that she didn't have an ass. A damn shame too. He didn't waste any time digging into his order as the club music banged through the over-head speakers.

"... can't hear a bitch." Said a near inaudible voice off in the distance. Curious, the two looked up and saw Keisha coming their way from the dance floor.

"What you say, girl?" C-loco asked as Keisha approached.

"I said, why y'all act like y'all can't hear a bitch?" She repeated.

"Shit, the music loud as fuck in here," said C-loco. "What yo' tired ass doin' up in Neighborhood's, anyway?"

"The same reason every other bitch up in here... I'm tryin' to come up." Keisha offered herself a seat at the table. Ole girl didn't sugar coat shit.

"Where yo' broke ass nigga at?" asked C-loco.

"Who J.J? Nigga, didn't you hear me say I was tryin' to come up? I don't need no nigga runnin' up behind me."

"I hear that shit." C-loco popped the top to a bottle of Ciroc and poured a shot for Keisha. He could tell that she was already slizzard, but that was the point. A person drunk did a lot of talking. Besides, he had to fuck with a girl from around the way. "Here, drink that up."

"Aw shit..." She happily accepted the glass. "I 'preciate that. You ain't like the rest of these stingy ass niggas up in here." She took a sip of the drink. "Did y'all hear 'bout that nigga Terrence?" Without waiting for a reply, she continued, "There was a fire. They said he been snitchin' and shit, but, he ain't gotta worry 'bout that no mo'. Somebody done knocked ole-boy noodle out his head."

"For real?" Asked C-loco. He was glad she was making it easy for him. "What happened?"

"You know my homegirl stay down on forth, right..."

"Nah, but go 'head," said C-loco.

"... I had to go down there and pick her up so we could come here..."

"I don't care 'bout that part."

"... and the police was everywhere. They had the whole block shut down. Stoppin' cars and searchin' people and shit." Keisha paused just long enough to take another sip of Ciroc. "Anyway, it was crowded. I asked somebody what happened, and they said that Terrence and his po' ole momma got killed. They said Terrence been snitchin'. It's fucked up, though, they didn't have to kill his momma like that."

"Damn, that is fucked up. Do they know who killed him?" Asked C-loco.

"Naw, but this Detective – I think his name was Amerson, Anderson, or somethin' like that – was askin' questions and shit." She paused. "But you know ain't nobody tryin' to say nothin'. And what, end up like Terrence and his momma?"

"That is fucked up." C-loco repeated. "That nigga was young as fuck, too. But you said wasn't nobody sayin' who did it."

"Naw, everybody was nervous and shit. Every time the police walked up to them, they just walked off." Keisha drank the rest of her Ciroc. "After they put the fire out and went inside, there was a whole bunch of cocaine in the house. I seen them seal it in some bags."

C-loco thought about the cocaine he'd left on the scene. It was something that Bones had instructed him to do. He didn't understand why, nor did he care, but he figured Bones had his motives.

Kimani wasn't entirely focused on the conversation, but when he heard the Detectives name spoken, he turned his attention their way. He remembered the brown curly-haired man he saw on top of the hill that morning and peeping C-loco's strange demeanor about the subject – along with the run-in that he had with him earlier crossing South 6th Avenue – he began to put two and two together. Bones had clearly used C-loco to get at Terrence and his mother. Realizing all of this, he quickly came to terms with the true reason C-loco was here tonight; and it wasn't to have fun. He watched his homie as he paid close attention to what the streets had to say.

It wasn't long before C-loco stopped asking questions and seemed to have lost all interest in Keisha. It was Kimani who shifted the topic.

"Who all up in here, Keisha?"

She looked over at him as if noticing him for the first time. There was no doubt in Kimani's mind that this girl was as dumb as a rock.

"Let's see..." she started, "*Conrad*, Li'l-Paso, Macc-90, Time-Bomb, Low-key, Caccy-Laccy, Dulen, Nine-times..."

"Caccy-Laccy up in here?"

"Yeah, he over at the bar." She pointed.

"Aw yeah, who else up in here?"

"George, Noocy, Edward..." Keisha's eyes lit up. "Oh, and yo' girl Sasha up in here, too."

"Fo' real?" Kimani sat up straight. "Where she at?"

"She was just on the dance flo' wit' my homegirl and 'em." Keisha pointed in the general direction of the dance floor on the far side of the club.

"If you run into her," Kimani warned. "don't tell her I'm here, aight." He wanted to watch Sasha and see how she carried herself in his absence. He wasn't on some stalker shit, he just happened to be in the position that he was currently in. He always felt she was a down ass chick, and his instincts were usually right, but there was nothing like seeing it for yourself. "Here you go." He popped the second bottle of Ciroc and poured Keisha another shot.

"Aw shit, 'preciate that, Kimani. Y'all ain't like the rest of these stingy ass nigga's up in here." She downed the glass.

Kimani could see C-loco mimicking Keisha word for word, out of the corner of his eye. He did his best to hold back his laughter.

"Look, I'm goin' get back on this dance flo' befo' I miss somethin'." Keisha got up to stagger back into the crowd. "Y'all nigga's be cool."

"That bitch talk too damn much." Kimani looked at C-loco when Keisha left. "I know she goin' say somethin' to Sasha."

"Shit, fuck it," offered C-loco.

"Fuck it," admitted Kimani. He turned up the bottle of Ciroc for the first time, and then popped a few of the salted peanuts into his mouth. He stared at the crowded club uneasily, trying to determine just how many people were up in this bitch; at least four thousand by his estimate.

Trey Songz was up on stage banging out hit after hit and the motion of the club was moving right along with him. Kimani's eyes kept venturing towards the large suspended cages. There were four of them in all – one each in the four corners of the club – all with two skimpy-clad females inside seductively dancing with one another. Let him tell it, they were all looking directly at him.

Neighborhood's was the shit; if there was one thing this club didn't lack, it was entertainment.

A scuffle off to the right caught his attention as two men began to tangle with one another. Bottles went flying and fist started swinging before the bouncers were able to break the two men up; using the rough-housing approach, the bouncers aggressively escorted the unruly men off of the floor and out of the club. Fight over. Kimani continued to scan the crowd.

"Look, Cuz, there go yo' girl sittin' at the bar..." C-loco said.

"Where?" Wondered Kimani, following his homies gaze.

"All the way to the left." C-loco nodded in the direction. "Damn, who that bitch she talkin' to? Ole-girl fine as hell. You think Sasha'll hook a nigga up?"

Kimani panned to the left of the bar until he spotted Sasha. She had on a tightly fitted royal-blue dress that came just short of her knees. Her hair was styled, and her make-up and lip-gloss was just right. By far, his baby girl was the finest thing in the city.

"Shit, she might if I tell her to." Kimani took a swig of the Ciroc.

They both watched as a light-skinned cat approached Sasha from behind, placing his hand at the small of her back. Kimani felt a twinge of jealousy pinch at his heart and he was tempted to go and say something to the nigga, but a reasonable mind prevailed. If he had to be at her side at all times to prevent her from choosing-up on someone else, then their relationship wasn't worth fighting for, anyway.

He could see C-loco looking at him out of the corner of his eye, though.

"Cuz, who the fuck that nigga think he is?" C-loco started to stand up. "Don't he know who the hell he fuckin' wit'?. "

Kimani put out his hand to stop C-loco. "Nah, chill out, fool. It's all good. Besides, look, she turned the nigga down. He walkin' away." Kimani knew that C-loco didn't give a damn if there was a large crowd of witnesses or not; the boy was ready to go. "Don't even trip, Cuz. You can't blame a man fo' bein' a man." He knew how fine Sasha was. It wouldn't be the last time that she was approached.

Kimani watched her. She was right back to her beautiful self, smiling and enjoying the night. He wouldn't lie to himself; it was a good feeling seeing her loyalty first-hand. Though he wasn't ready to admit it aloud, it made him grow that much weaker for her.

Just as he was beginning to enjoy that feeling, he spotted Keisha's loud-mouth ass walking towards his girl. "Damn, Cuz. Look who bumpin' down on her..." He nodded. Before he could even finish his statement, C-loco began laughing.

"You know that bitch goin' spill her guts." C-loco joked. "She don't know how to shut the fuck up. You would've been better off hitting her ass in the head wit' that Ciroc bottle."

Already knowing what Keisha was about to say, he watched as she turned in their direction and pointed. Kimani and C-loco both quickly shifted their eyes.

"Damn! I told you that bitch talk too damn much. She done blazed a nigga." Kimani looked over to see the uncontrollable laughter coming from C-loco. "Aw, that shit funny to you, nigga?"

Taking another swig of his Ciroc, he subtly glanced back in Sasha's direction; he noticed that she had her cellphone out and was manipulating the screen.

He immediately felt a vibration at his hip. Out of habit, he reached for his pager before realizing that it was his new cell-phone vibrating. The screen read 615-555-8130. Wondering how she got his number; he answered his new phone for the first time.

"Hello."

"Hey, baby." Sasha sounded a little intoxicated.

"Who is this?" he asked, trying to sound surprised.

"What you mean, 'who is this'? What other girl goin' be callin' you?" She was definitely tipsy. "It better not be no other girl callin' you."

"Girl you know I'm just fuckin' wit' you, yo crazy ass... "

"Nigga, I ain't crazy, you crazy." She returned.

"...you know how you get when yo' ass be drinkin'."

"How you know I been drinkin'?"

"Because I know you." Kimani admitted. "I can hear it in yo voice."

"*Anyway*..." Sasha exaggerated the word. "How long you been in Neighborhood's? And when did you start clubbin'?"

"Not long. How did you know I was in the club?" Kimani feigned.

"Ain't none of yo' business. Besides, I got people."

"You got people?"

"You betta know it."

"I bet they drunk as hell too." Kimani could hear Sasha start to laugh.

"I ain't that damn drunk." She defended herself. "I saw you tryin' to peep over here. You ain't foolin' nobody."

Kimani laughed. "So, what's up?"

"Not shit. Just have to keep pushin' these punk ass nigga's up off me. I keep tellin' them I got a man."

"You betta know it." Kimani demanded. "How long you been out here?"

"I don't know. Fo' a few hours, now." She said. "What's up wit' you though? Can a bitch come and chill wit' you?"

"Shit, you know where I'm at." Kimani offered. "Bring one of yo' homegirls fo' my homeboy. Who you got wit' you, anyways; I know yo' drunk ass chillin' wit' somebody."

"My girl Kim wit' me."

"Yo' girl Kim from down on Main?"

Silence.

"Why you wanna know if it's my girl Kim from down on Main fo'? You sounded real excited when you said that, boo." Sasha was slizzard. "You want me to put her on the phone so y'all can talk?"

"Nah, girl. Quit trippin'." Kimani said. "You need to stop drinkin'. I just wanna know who my homeboy 'bouts to hook up wit'. I can't be hookin' him up wit' no booger."

"So, you must think she look good then... "Sasha continued. "...if you goin' hook him up wit' her." She paused. "I can hook y'all two up if you want me to."

"Girl, you trippin'. I told you she fo' C-loco."

"She betta be fo' that nigga. Don't make me have to snatch a bitch hair up out her head." Sasha let that sink in before finishing. "Act like you know, nigga."

Kimani witnessed his girl get down before and knew that she had them hands. The thought of it made him laugh.

"Why I always gotta get the crazy ones?" he thought aloud.

"Shut up. I told you I ain't crazy."

"So y'all comin' over here or what?"

"I'm comin'."

"And can yo' friend be introduced to my homie?"

"We on our way."

"That's what's up." Kimani gave a sigh of relief. "You know where we at..."

"Um-hum."

"...I'll see you when you get here." Something occurred to him out of the blue. "Hey... "

"What?"

"How'd you know I had a cellphone, and how'd you get my number?"

"My momma-in-law gave it to me. Why?"

"Aw, so you done went and got married on me." He joked. He heard Sasha blow out an agitated breath before disconnecting the line on him. He smiled and placed the phone back on his hip. He didn't know why, but he loved getting her worked up. Getting a response from her and being able to have an effect on her was like glue to them. The day she no longer got mad, he would worry.

"Who's Kim?"

Kimani turned to see C-loco staring at him.

"Damn, my nigga. Where'd you hear that shit from?"

"From you, fool. All that lovey dovey shit you talkin' over there. Tell that shit to Oprah." C-loco stated. "Who's Kim?"

"Go 'head on, nigga." Kimani shot back. "Kim's one of her homegirls. She owns a salon down on Main and she goin' introduce herself to you. You a lucky mu'fucka', too. Baby girl the truth." Kimani visualized how phat her ass was. Turning towards C-loco, he didn't notice Sasha and Kim as they approached the table from the side.

C-loco, on the other hand, did see their approach. "So, on a scale of one to ten, how bad would you say Kim is?" He loudly asked Kimani.

"Shit, I'm tellin' you, Cuz. Baby girl like thirty-eight, twenty-four, forty-two, and fine as fuck..." he paused when he saw the conniving look on C-loco's face; that expression didn't look right. Turning around, he saw Sasha standing there watching him. He tried to give an innocent smile but could tell that it wasn't working. C-loco played too damn much.

"Hey baby..." Sasha said sarcastically. Though she'd heard the compliments that her man was giving, for the sake of her friends freshly done hair, she pretended not to hear a thing. Plus, she knew that C-loco was full of shit. "... and what's up, C-loco, wit' yo' no good ass."

"What's up, baby girl?" C-loco replied smiling. "What the hell you been drinkin' on? Yo' ass slizzard."

"Nothin' but some Alize. I let Kim get me drunk every time. By the way ..." She looked at Kimani. "This is my homegirl, Kim..." She looked back at C-loco. "I think it's time y'all meet. Kim, this is C-loco." Sasha gave Kim a nudge – a little too hard Kim thought – towards C-loco.

"What's good, baby girl?" C-loco got up to shake Kim's hand. "It's nice to meet you. As you just heard, I'm C-loco..."

"Kim." Kim replied.

"... and I swear to you, either I'm having de'ja'vu or I've been dreamin' 'bout you."

Kim smiled as she took her seat next to C-loco. He grabbed a glass off the table and politely poured her a shot of Ciroc. She happily accepted and took a sip of the liquor.

"So how long have you been down here, baby?" Sasha asked Kimani, taking her seat next to him.

"We been Rollin' fo' 'bout an hour now..." Kimani admitted. "... compliments of the homie, C-loco." Or Terrence and his mother, he thought silently.

"I've been out here for too damn long and to be honest, I'm ready to go. Ain't nobody up in here talkin' 'bout shit." Sasha gave Kimani her best puppy-doll face that he'd become so accustom to seeing. He knew, that she knew, that she could too often get her way with it. And she knew that he knew that she knew. Talking about her friend the way that he had, she would make him work hard for it before it was all said and done.

"Where we goin'?" He asked, watching the smile on her face.

"It don't matter..." she responded. "... anywhere but here. As long as I'm wit' you, I'm happy. Whatever you wanna do, baby." Her comment really meant, whatever *she* wanted to do.

"It sounds good to me. I ain't feelin' this place, no way." Kimani looked at his watch. 10:38pm; it was still early. They had time to get a bite to eat and hit One-Hundred Oaks for a quick movie. After tonight, he would probably go all out, booking a downtown hotel and spending the rest of the night pleasing her with a panoramic view of the city lights. "When you wanna leave?"

Sasha smiled.

"Let me check on Kim and make sure she goin' be aight."

They both looked in Kim and C-loco's direction; with Kim already sitting on C-loco's lap, it wouldn't be an issue.

"Well damn, never mind, then," said Sasha.

'I'm goin' let C-loco know that I'm 'bouts to ride out, make sure he goin' be able to get back to the hood and shit." Kimani looked back in their direction once more. "From the looks of it, he should be all good, though."

Kimani and Sasha both got up to leave.

Kimani was going to do whatever needed to be done to make things up to Sasha, tonight. She was loyal as hell – a down ass chick – and of that, there was no doubt. So whatever he had to do, he would do. That was just the cost of caring for her.

Just as they were about to leave through the entrance, they passed the light-skinned individual that tried to push up on Sasha. Kimani overheard him bragging to some chick about how he had a candy flip-flop orange Super-Sport sitting on a set of twenty-six-inch spinners.

With his babygirl at his side, Kimani could barely keep his laughter to a minimum as they both left the club scene behind.

CHAPTER 8
DISCOVERY

MARCH 4TH. 1:26am.
METRO NASHVILLE
POLICE DEPARTMENT
CENTRAL SECTOR/
DOWNTOWN NASHVILLE ...

"Hey Mark?" Detective Connie Wilkes asked. "Who are those two guys over there?"

"Over where?" Asked Detective Mark George.

"Over there." Connie nodded in the direction of the two men standing at the entrance of the Criminal Investigation Organized crime unit. With the explosion on Charlotte Avenue and the death of a fellow cop, it was much busier than usual at 1:30 in the morning. To see someone that you didn't know at this late of an hour, usually meant that something of importance was going on.

"If I'm not mistaken, they're from T.B.I," said Detective Mark. "They're probably here to take our case right out from under us." He looked at his watch. 1:31am. "It's getting too late to have to go through this bullshit."

"Poor Gomez." Mourned Connie. "He wasn't on vice a full three months. I remember when he first passed his exam and practical. He was so excited." She reminisced.

"Yeah, he was one of the good ones." Admitted Mark. He and Connie both regretted the lost; Detective Gomez was a good friend to everyone. Being new to Nashville – transferring from Atlanta – Mark and Gomez had quickly become good drinking buddies. But now that he'd been murdered, they were tasked with bringing his killer to justice. "Sons-of-bitches are going to pay," he retorted.

"How long do you think it'll be before we gain any leads?" Connie asked.

"Hopefully within the next twenty-four hours; it's vital," stated Mark. "Someone needs to be bounded over to the D.A.'s office." He looked over in the direction of the two agents. "Although, by the looks of it, it'll more than likely go federal."

"Doesn't look too good, T.B.I.'s involved, and the chiefs highly upset. Somebody's not going to be getting much sleep." Connie observed.

"Yeah, I know what the hell you mean," Mark replied, rubbing his eyes.

Connie tapped him on the shoulder and immediately sat up straight. "Look normal..." she urged. "...they're heading our way."

Detective Mark turned and watched as the two men walked over to them. They were both clad in blue suits, and from the bulkiness of their chest area, he could tell that they were both armored.

"Detective Connie Wilkes and Detective Mark George?" The leading agent asked. "I'm Special Agent Benedict. This here is Special Agent Swallows." The large agent pointed to his much smaller partner. "We're here from the Tennessee Bureau of Investigations. We were told by the chief that you two could be of assistance to us. We have a few questions regarding the explosion that took place this morning." Agent Benedict sifted through a folder he carried before handing it to his partner.

"So the case has gone Fed then?" Connie asked.

"Yes, it has," admitted the lead Agent.

"Well then, have way. I'm all ears." Cut in Detective Mark, upset about the change of jurisdiction. If anyone should be able to bring a murderous cop-killer to justice, it should be one of their own.

"First of all..." started Agent Benedict. "...it's late, so I would like to get straight to the point. I need to know everything that you two know regarding this case that may be useful to my partner and I, and I mean everything."

"Well, Agents, that's where things get a little complicated," Mark stated.

"Complicated?" Benedict asked. "How so?"

"Well, we simply don't have anything."

"Nothing?"

"Absolutely nothing," admitted Mark.

The Detective allowed himself a slight smile. He had authority issues. He simply didn't like superiors, especially those from other agencies that high-jacked his investigation.

"Alright then, what can you tell us?" The Agent settled.

"Uh... that we don't have anything that could be of any use to you ..." Being sarcastic, Mark pointed at Agent Benedict's partner. "... or him."

The lead Agent's face began turning red. Tugging downward on his blazer, he spoke, "exactly how long have you been working here, Detective?"

"Here at this building in particular?" Mark asked, "or here as in... the MNPD?"

The Federal Agent didn't answer. Instead, he bent down and placed both of his hands-on top of Detective Mark's desk. With the intent of letting his presence be felt, he intentionally placed his face a foot from the Detectives before continuing. "You think you're the first smart-ass I've come across, Detective? Let me remind you of something. As of zero-nine-thirty-four yesterday morning, my partner here and I, were called in off of a two-week vacation and back to official duty. You ever been to Cancun Mexico, Detective?" The Agent didn't wait for a reply. "I immediately caught the next flight back into the States and landed here in Nashville shortly after. Rendezvousing with Special Agent Swallows, here, we were met with the chief of the Nashville police department, your superior, and were given full and complete cooperation..." The Agent continued to glare at the Detective. "On top of that, we officially have complete jurisdiction over this entire investigation. So, unless you wanna be flagging down speeding vehicles on the boulevard, Detective, I suggest you show me a little respect. Now..." Special Agent Benedict stood up to his full 6'5" height and kept his haunting gaze squarely on Detective Mark. "...let's try this again. Do any of you, Detectives, have any information for the T.B.I. regarding my investigation?"

Detective Mark, realizing that he was defeated, conceded. "I'm sorry to have to advise you, Agents, but we..."

"Mark, Connie?" Corporal Swiss interrupted, running up to them with a smile on his face. "We may have just discovered something. You two need to see this."

"What are you talking about, Swiss?" Connie asked.

"The bombing footage. It's not much, but..."

"It's something," finished Special Agent Benedict. "And it's about time, someone with a little sense around here."

The Agents, ready to get their investigation under way, followed Mark and Connie as they made their way into the monitoring room with a smiling Corporal Swiss in the lead.

"What do you have? Speak to me, Swiss." Mark urged the still smiling Swiss.

"Just wait and see," Swiss said. "This may be what we've been waiting for."

In the monitoring room, Corporal Swiss walked over to his station with his new company in tow. He had been working all day, night, and morning trying to find anything that would reveal some type of lead. Now he felt they may have what they've been looking for.

"By the way..." Connie noted. "...we have guest. This is Special Agent Benedict and Special Agent Swallows from the T.B.I. This case has just gone federal."

Special Agent Benedict smiled before speaking. "Why don't we just get on with this? It's getting pretty late."

"Yes, yes," admitted Swiss. "Well, I was watching the crime scene of the explosion from a security camera surveillance system. It was mounted on a power-line pole just across the street in a Krystal's parking lot. Lucky for us, the camera is on a network system. Quick access makes my job easier." Swiss paused before continuing. "Nearly the whole time I've been watching the footage in slow motion, trying to catch something that would be otherwise easily missed. Terrible mistake," he admitted while manipulating his keyboard. "Had I been watching the damn thing in real time, I probably would've noticed this..."

"Just wait a second..." Special Agent Benedict interrupted. "We've yet to see this footage. Take us through this from the top and one step at a time. We need to be brought up to speed."

"Fair enough." The corporal agreed. Tapping a few keys on his computer he pressed the play button and adjusted the resolution to the ten-foot monitoring screen in front of them. They all watched as the crime scene at Sound Music Studio's was brought to life.

They observed the U.P.S. man walk into Sound Music carrying what appeared to be a square foot package of some kind. It was Corporal Swiss who spoke, "by the way, Agents, the box you see the U.P.S. man carrying is not believed to be musical equipment." The Corporal tapped some keys on his keyboard and the video began zooming in. "That's as close as we can get it and still have decent resolution." He continued to give the Agents the run-down. "To confirm our assumptions that the U.P.S. man is a possible suspect, we attempted to track him down through the U.P.S. company; needless to say, they didn't have a scheduled delivery to Sound Music. He's not one of theirs. Unfortunately, we can't get a good enough visual to determine who he is. We're left in the dark there as well."

Swiss turned towards the Agents before continuing, "license plate to the brown U.P.S. van he was driving was a fake. No luck there either." Turning back to his keyboard, he tapped more keys, fast forwarding the video up a few frames. He continued, "the guy goes in for one-hundred and sixty-two seconds before coming back out empty handed. He drives away. But, we still couldn't get a good look at him. As you can see now..." The corporal slowed the frames down to normal speeds. "... undercover Gomez goes in shortly after this guy leaves and, sorry to say, the rest is..." the Corporal sighed.

"What exactly was Gomez doing going into a music studio?" Benedict asked.

"Well," the Corporal answered. "We were conducting a drug operation. Detective Gomez was our undercover consumer. He was sent to this location by a suspect in a laser printing shop just up the avenue. We had officers stationed outside the printing shop, and immediately sent them in after the explosion. But when they converged on the building, it was already up in flames. Needless to say, the second suspect of the day eluded us." Swiss heard the Agent grunt. He tapped the pause key on the keyboard and watched as the footage on the screen froze. Turning around to face the Agents, he continued, "Now, the odd part..."

"Odd part?" Benedict asked.

"Yes," said Swiss. "The owner of the laser printing shop is a one-hundred and twenty-two-year old lady from Franklin, Tennessee, died of respiratory failure almost forty years ago."

"Let me get this straight, Mr. Swiss," said the Agent. "Are you telling me that there's no way for us to trace the owner of this shop?"

"Oh, yeah, there's a way." The two Agents both stood up an inch taller in anticipation. "Unfortunately, it'll lead you straight to the Greenwood cemetery."

The Agents both slumped. "Why is it you MNPD officers have a way of making Agents of the Federal government resent asking questions?"

Swiss looked baffled, wondering what he'd said wrong. "Swiss?" Mark interrupted. "This is all old news. You said that you had something new for us. Let's hear it."

"Yes." Swiss turned around and hit the play button on his keyboard. They all watched in horror as the Sound Studio complex exploded with enough force to shake the very security camera that was recording it. The Corporal zoomed out for wider coverage.

"My God!" exclaimed Agent Benedict. "That box had to be filled with Cee-Four."

"That was our conclusion as well." Remarked Connie. "And you can't just get it at your local hardware store either."

"Are you sure that there's a connection between the two?" Benedict asked.

"It's pure speculation thus far," admitted Connie.

"That being said, take a look at this..." Swiss interrupted, pointing at the bottom of the screen. "You see how everyone is running around as if in absolute traumatic shock?"

Connie realized what the Corporal was getting at and allowed her mouth to hang open.

"This guy here..." Swiss pointed. "... the one that just got out of that blue car? What's he doing?"

"He's... oh my God!" started Mark. "He's walking. What is... Wait! What's wrong with the picture? Why's there a glare over his face?" The Detective watched as the pin-point light in the footage obscured the suspects face even as he walked; when the suspect moved, the glare followed him. "Swiss, is there any way that you could clean that up so that we could get a look at this guy?"

"That's the problem," admitted Swiss. "I've tried that already, but there's nothing wrong with the pixels.

Whatever is causing this glare, it was recorded that way. Maybe it's a reflection of the sun ricocheting off of a piece of metal on a hat that he's wearing – I don't know – but if we can get a warrant to collect the surveillance from inside the restaurant, we might just be able to get a better look at the perp'."

They all watched as the man disappeared into the restaurant.

"Yeah," replied Connie, still watching the footage. "I'll get someone on that right away. Good job Swiss." She patted the Corporal on the shoulder. "We might just finally have us a real suspect."

CHAPTER 9
DECISIONS

MARCH 4TH. 1:32 am.
PRESTIGE FINANCIAL CONSULTANTS
DOWNTOWN NASHVILLE...

Bones looked at his watch. 1:32 am. He leaned back in his leather cushioned swivel chair and massaged his temples with the tips of his fingers. Though he was accustomed to being up for long periods of hours, he was tired and ready to call it a night. But discovering that the Hispanic consumer that they'd killed at the studios was a cop, created unexpected issues that had to be dealt with. It was clear that important decisions had to be calculated.

He thought about the previous events and the people that were involved. Mistakes, like the death of that cop could cost him much in the end with law enforcement officials, and Bones had to ensure that he didn't get stung. He'd learned long ago that hitting a hornet's nest with a short stick was always a fool's move.

He was sure that the laws had a facial on Terrell 'Donte' Baggins, because the laser printing shop had been watched for some time now. He was also sure that the law wouldn't be able to directly trace him to the shop; but Donte represented a whole new dilemma.

He wondered if Donte could be trusted in the event that he got apprehended. An old saying his father use to say came to mind, *when in doubt, take him out.*

Thoughts of his father brought back unexpected memories; some good, some bad. But all were learned from and learned from well. One incident with his father in particular stuck out with such clarity that it made him smile where it would've made others cringe.

Bones was only six at the time. He'd lived out west with his parents and half-brothers in Preston Taylor projects long before those white folks decided to tear them down. Those were the hard days – he remembered – when poverty was eating cold baloney without the bread. When eating cold baloney without the bread was considered a good day. It was the days when striped socks and thigh-high shorts was the shit, and the old lady who sat on her porch all day long put the fear of God in your heart if you did anything wrong.

Those days were long dead now.

Bones' father was about to walk to the store to get a case of cold beer for the night and Bones wanted to go along with him. His father agreed, and down 40th Avenue they went.

His father was longer and walked faster so Bones found that every now and then he had to run to catch up. It never bothered him though; he was young and had plenty of energy. When they got down on 38th, he spotted the neighborhood's wall; a stone cinder-block wall that stood seven-feet high and went on for nearly a third of the block. Just like a child that sought adventure, he reached for the wall and started to climb.

Ascending the bricks, he felt like a king on top of the world. From here, he was even taller than his father. Breathing hard, he suddenly realized that he'd fell behind as his father was some fifty feet up ahead. Responding fast, Bones scuttled along the top to catch up, keeping his balance as he went.

He quickly closed in on his father, and by the way that his father spun around with his hand at his waistband, he could tell that he'd startled him. He knew that he'd fucked up and figured his father would beat his ass for this. But unlike the many times before, his father remained eerily calm.

"There's two things I need to teach you right now, son." His father begun. "One, you should never sneak up on a man unless you're toting'..." His father revealed the .38 snub-nose revolver that he carried. "... and you got intentions of puttin' in work. You never know who'll get nervous and take you out befo' they realize who you are and what you're doin'. There's too many nigga's out here that react befo' they think, and I won't have my son fall victim to some bullshit like that."

Bones was in a trance listening to his father.

"And two," his father said, looking over his shoulder before continuing, "Well... jump down here. I'd rather tell you this face to face." His father put out his arms as if he was ready to catch his son. Bones hesitated for a second; it was a long way down and he wasn't very fond of falling. But trusting his father – the only man that he had ever looked up to – he jumped from seven-feet in the air into the open abyss.

His father, smiling, stepped out of the way.
WHAAMMMMM!!!

Bones slammed hard into the concrete sidewalk below. Laying there in agony, he reached for his father, seeking his paternal help. But as he laid there, his father only bent down to get face to face with him just as he promised he would. Hurt, but frozen by his father's dead stare, Bones could only watch as tears began running down his face.

"And two," his father continued, watching his son's painful expression. "And always remember this one, cause it's the most important of all the rules. Never..." he paused for effect. "...and I mean never, trust a man."

With that said, his father stood up straight and continued his walk down 40th Avenue leaving his son where he lay.

Bones often thought about that moment that took place some forty years ago. The scars on his knees, arms and forehead wouldn't let him forget. Needless to say, it was a tough lesson well learned. And needless to say, Donte couldn't – and wouldn't – be trusted.

Tee-Tee, who stood clear on the other side of the office, came over to have a seat in front of Bones' desk. He knew when Bones was thinking, and he knew when Bones was ready to discuss what he had been thinking.

Now was that time.

"Tee-Tee, tell me," Bones begun. "I wanna know yo' perspective on this... Donte business?"

Tee-Tee looked over to the only window in the office. When he saw the green light emitting from the infrared microphone filter, he turned back to Bones. "He's innocent, that's fo' sure," he said. "He never could've seen it comin'. But still, he's just a pawn, and that's all he'll ever be. At all times it's better to sacrifice yo' pawn than to sacrifice yo' king. If we think 'bout what all he knows, it's this… He knows that you're the one that gave directions to give directions. That's mo' than enough. If he's weak, which I think he is, then he'll mo' than likely spill his guts. I keep havin' thoughts of somethin' that you taught me a long time ago, Bones... 'when in doubt, take 'em out'."

Bones couldn't help but smile at the way his protege thought. If it came down to it, he wouldn't even have to give directions on what needed to be done; he knew that Tee-Tee would handle it with precision. Yet, he halfway liked Donte and that was more than he could say for a lot of people.

Studying Tee-Tee's train-of-thought, Bones smiled, he himself was thinking along similar lines. But when push came to shove, he had to be certain. It was his responsibility.

He continued,

"Learnin' that there was a cop involved, we can't take any chances, Tee-Tee; that's where we agree. But I wanna give him the benefit of the doubt; I need to sit him down and have a face to face talk. Who knows, he might just be a diamond in the rough." Bones paused, thinking about what exactly he had to do. "I'll tell you what we're goin' to do..." He began saying to Tee-Tee. "... we're goin' to..."

CHAPTER IO
CHOICES

MARCH 4TH. 8:46am.
JAMES CACEY HOUSING PROJECTS
EAST NASHVILLE...

Donte was walking down the sidewalk with his Sony MP3 player in his hands. Listening to his play-list, he thought about yesterday's events – pouring gasoline on everything and setting the shop on fire, and grabbing the secured money bag and his personal things before quickly exiting out the back door. Though he only knew of his individual role – and how to carry it out – he was aware that it was only a portion of a much larger master plan; even if he didn't understand fully what that master plan was.

To his astonishment, Bones let him keep half the money in the bag which totaled to some fifty-thousand dollars. Aside from having the money, there were more important things that he had to contend with.

Watching the news the night before, he was shocked to discover that the man that gave him the money bag was a cop. Learning that he was the one that gave the man directions to his own death scared the shit out of him.

Realizing that he was a cop-killer, it was a matter of time before they named him as a suspect. He was much too young to go to prison.

Donte stopped thinking about all of the money and prison-life when he spotted Loony, Solid and D-lo from the bottom of the hill coming his way. Why they were walking towards him and not at their post getting off the latest product was a mystery to him. But one thing was for sure, something wasn't right.

He took out his earplugs and placed them in his pocket as the trio approached. Not liking the looks on their faces, he spoke first. "What up?"

"What up?" Loony smirked. "The big homie, nigga, that's what's up. He wanna holla at you, fool."

"He wanna holla at me?" Donte asked. "And he sent y'all nigga's to come and get me?" He probed. He couldn't believe what he was hearing.

"Yeah, that's right. You gotta problem wit' it?"

"Naw, nigga. I'm just sayin'... what he want?"

"He want you, fool." Loony demanded. "Why you think we here? Now follow us and quit wastin' time; we missin' out on money."

"I'm sayin', though, Cuz." Donte persisted. "Why he send y'all three nigga's to get me?"

None of this was making sense to him. He knew that something wasn't right. With the explosion and the death of that cop that he saw on the news last night in the forefront of his mind, everything came crashing down on him at once. Bones didn't trust him. The fact that he sent these three as enforcers to retrieve him was evident enough. Bones wanted his ass silenced.

Without hesitating, Donte reached out and pushed Loony to the ground and immediately took off running in the opposite direction. Solid and D-lo, Loony's other two accomplices, immediately gave chase.

Loony didn't feel like running. He got up off the ground, picking up a nearby brick as he did. With the accuracy of an ex-high school quarterback, he struck Donte in the back of the head from some twenty yards away. He watched as Donte fell hard to the ground from the power of the blow.

Donte, being struck on the head, felt woozy. To make matters worse, when the trio caught up with him, they began to stomp and beat him repeatedly. He was already discombobulated from the blow to the head and panicked when he felt warm blood trickling down his neck. The trio continued to beat him nearly unconscious.

Solid, enjoying this shit, leaned to the side and gave Donte a wrestling elbow-drop to the face. He stood up and laughed, pointing at his victim.

Loony wasn't laughing.

"How the fuck... you goin' run... from the big homie, li'l nigga?" Loony retorted, repeatedly stomping Donte with his Timberland boot. "You know... that shit a violation. Now look at you... you fuckin' up... my mu'fuckin' Tim's, nigga." He continued to pummel Donte with the heel of his boot.

With blood gushing from Donte's mouth, he felt himself begin to lose consciousness. He felt darkness closing in all around him quickly losing the battle to stay awake. Just before his reality winked out, he heard somebody off in the distance yell

"Hey! Hey! Stop that. Freeeeze..."

The pummeling of boots stopped, and the sound of retreating footsteps were heard as Loony, Solid and D-Lo evaded the law. Donte attempted to tilt his head – tried to see who was yelling to save his life – and just before he passed out he saw two uniformed officers running to his aid; one was holstering his weapon, while the other was talking into his radio. The sky spun, light turned into darkness, and Donte's consciousness finally gave in to a world that was too painful for comfort.

"Baby... Baby? You just hold on. Everything's going to be alright."

Donte opened his eyes, but his vision was too blurry for him to make out anything. His surroundings seemed to ripple, like heat coming off of a boiler. As he lay down on top of a soft comfortable bed, he tried to focus. He thought that he heard someone speaking. He blinked one eyelid – the other was swollen shut – to try and clear his vision. It only helped a little, but it was better than nothing.

This time he was certain that he heard a voice.

"Ohh, you done finally opened your eyes. You took a fairly good beating. But don't you worry; we're going to take really good care of you. You're at Meharry Medical, baby. The EMT's brought you in just over two hours ago. My name is nurse Freeman... "The nurse pointed at her name tag. "... but you can call me Betty. I'm going to be your personal aid while you're here. If you need anything, baby, anything at all, you just push that red button right there." Giving Donte a welcoming smile, nurse Betty pointed at the emergency button just above his head.

Donte was amazed at how beautiful Nurse Betty was. He watched as she injected a clear substance into his I.V. drip.

Seeing the wonder on his face, she calmly spoke to assure him, "I'm just administering a dose of morphine to your I.V; it'll help ease some of the pain you're feeling. To be honest, I'm giving you a li'l extra cause you look like you're in a lot of pain. But don't tell the doctors I gave it to you, alright baby?"

Donte found it hard to talk but managed to nod his head.

Nurse Betty patted him on the shoulder and reassured him once again that everything would be alright. She turned, walked out of the room, and left Donte alone to his pains.

For the first time since gaining conscious, his vision began to clear, and he observed his surroundings. There were rough textured ceiling squares above him, cubicle textured walls, and healthcare posters with the average hospital propaganda displayed everywhere. There was a collection of cabinets, drawers and a soap dispenser on the other side of the room. Just in front of his bed was a thirty-inch flat screen mounted high on the wall. Donte reached for the remote next to his bed and hit the power button, but nothing happened. Figuring that there must be a main power switch somewhere, he put the remote down and reminded himself to ask Nurse Betty about it when she came back.

Body aching badly, he was barely able to move as he tilted his head towards the nightstand to search for a phone. Needing to call his mother to make sure that everyone was alright, he was disappointed to find that there wasn't a phone. He continued to look around the small hospital room.

To his left was a floor to ceiling curtain that partially divided the room in half to allow privacy for each patient.

Wondering for a second if there was another patient on the other side of that curtain, he quickly dismissed the thought and continued to look around. The one thing that stood out to Donte the most – the one thing that bothered him above all – was that the temperature was too hot inside the room; he was beginning to sweat.

It wasn't long before he realized that he had to urinate and decided to get up to relieve himself. Struggling just to sit up, he paused, suddenly realizing that his worst nightmare had become a reality. Looking down at his ankles and wrist, Donate cringed at the steel handcuffs and shackles restraining him to the rail of the bed. The first thing that came to his mind was that they knew who he was and what he had done.

His suspicions grew further when a tall white man with a gold police badge at his waist walked into the room.

Donte noticed the holstered weapon just under the arm beneath the man's blazer. On the man's left wrist was a cheap watch. When the man spoke Donte's real name – of which not many knew – Donte's suspicions grew to worry.

"Terrell Baggins?" The Detective paused. "I'm Detective Owens of the Metro Nashville Police Department." He opened his wallet and flashed his credentials for Donte to see. "Do you mind if I call you Donte?"

Donte's heart skipped a beat. He knew that the Detective was fucking with his psyche and he tried not to show that it was affective.

When he didn't answer the question, Detective Owens continued, "I think we both know why I'm here. So, let's cut through the introductions and get straight to the point, shall we? By the way, you are in police custody, as you can see..." Detective Owens gestured towards the handcuffs and shackles binding Donte to the bed. "...and you'll remain that way for a long, long, long time; unless, of course, you decide to cooperate and tell us what you know. Then maybe it'll just be a *long* time – with just one, long." Detective Owens held up his index finger. "But who knows, if your cooperation is very useful, as I hope it will be, then you may get off all together; which is a far cry from what you're facing."

Donte didn't say a word. He knew that even if he did cooperate and they did decide to let him go that he would just be signing his own death certificate; Bones was not a man to cross.

Detective Owens could tell that Donte wasn't budging. He continued to prod, hoping to find an opening, "Let me tell you what we know, Donte. We know that you were the one in the laser printing shop; we have pictures and surveillance. We also know that you were the one that directed Detective Gomez to the studio just down the street. There were three people dead in that explosion; not to mention that one of them was a decorated police officer with a wife and three kids. The murder of an officer alone in the state of Tennessee carries the death penalty. On top of that you're facing federal charges for the use of deadly explosives; the patriot act will doom you. Not that it would matter with you facing the death penalty and all."

The Detective smiled to show that he didn't give a damn either way. He wanted to show Donte that there was no hope aside from cooperating with him. Then, with skillful tact, he slowly gave him hope.

"You wanna know what I think, Donte?" He paused for a moment to see if Donte would respond. When he failed to say a word, he continued, "I think you had no idea that undercover officer Gomez was on his way to his death. I think you were only given limited information and had no idea what you were doing. I think you were as innocent as the people who involuntarily had their eardrums shifted by the blast; as innocent as the owners of nearby stores who had their windows shattered. I think you know who gave you the orders to direct Detective Gomez but didn't know the severity of the outcome. I think you know who gave you the order to set the shop on fire but didn't know that you were covering up a deadly crime scene. And I think that we, with your full cooperation, can make the courts understand that you are innocent – short of arson – and get you as limited time as possible. You're looking at three to ten years max Donte, oppose to the death penalty. It's your choice, son."

Donte thought about everything that Detective Owens was saying. He was right about him not knowing what was going to happen to that cop. Hell, he was right about him not knowing anything about anything; period. Still, he knew the repercussions of being a snitch; he wasn't trying to become a snitch. He would much rather take his chances in court.

He remained silent.

Detective Owens felt that maybe he was getting through to Donte and he didn't want to let up now. Once you begin to get someone's attention, you had to keep the pressure on to keep it. He sighed, gave Donte a sympathetic glance, and continued to coax him.

"Look, son." He began. "I'm trying to help you here. Can't you see that the people who set you up don't give a damn if you spend the rest of your life in prison or die by lethal injection for something that they've committed? To them, you're just a small part of the plan; a pawn! The question you need to be asking yourself is, do you want to spend the rest of your life in prison or possibly even be executed for something that someone else orchestrated? Or do you want to – at the most – serve ten years for a petty arson charge? We can make that happen, Donte, but we need your cooperation."

Donte was looking at his feet; a sure sign to Detective Owens that he had, and was, contemplating everything that had been said thus far. Whether he was rejecting it or accepting it was still to be determined; but he felt like it was the latter.

Observing, he could tell that Donte was afraid and he understood why; whoever was behind an explosion assassination like this had to be a very powerful and resourceful individual. He decided to take this interrogation down another path. Maybe one that Donte could appreciate.

"We have hundreds of safe havens, and the feds have thousands. With the severity of this case, if you choose to cooperate, you'll immediately go into protective custody. You and your closest of kin will be moved to say, Des Moines, Iowa. No one will know that you're there except the agents tasked with protecting you and the director himself; no one else will have access to your location. You'll be given a new social security number, a new name and a new identity dossier. Your current background history will cease to exist. Everything from education to medical will be given anew. No one will know who you are."

For the first time since the conversation began, Donte looked the Detective directly in the eyes; something the Detective had been waiting for. From this moment on, he knew that he had him. He turned up the heat.

"Listen to me, Donte. I wasn't going to tell you this, but, your family has already been moved to a secure location..." Detective Owens saw Donte's expression change. "...Detectives arrived at your house to find two individuals in the home with your mother and siblings. When the Detectives identified themselves, the two individuals ran out the back door. One of the Detectives gave chase, but the suspects eluded him."

Detective Owens gave Donte a concerned look. He knew he had his full attention. He continued, "I want you to think seriously about the predicament you're in, son. We can help you, but we need your cooperation. We need to know who's calling the shots. We need to know who's responsible for the explosion that took place on Charlotte Avenue, and we need to know who gave you the orders to do the things you did."

The Detective watched Donte for more signs that he was about to give in. He knew from his years of interrogation that this was the breaking point for him. He had done all of the pushing that he could do. Now, he had to stop shoving, and just let Donte fall his way.

He waited patiently for a few seconds, and just as the Detective hoped he would, Donte broke his silence,

"I don't know..." Donte paused to allow a storm of pain to subside. He grimaced, feeling the lightning bolts shoot all the way up his spine and into his cranium. Morphine or no morphine, he was feeling every ounce of pain in his body. He never thought it could hurt so much to talk – to even think of talking – but the pain was excruciating. Nonetheless, he looked the Detective in the eyes and spoke his peace, "I don't know... I don't know his real name, but, e'erbody in the hood call him Bones."

Silence.

"They call him Bones?" Detective Owens asked. He watched as Donte shook his head, yes. "And this Bones character – I'm assuming you already know what he looks like – do you know where, or even how, we can apprehend him?"

"Yeah." Donte admitted. "I see him in the hood all the time. I heard he got a few businesses 'round town, but I don't know where. If you can do what you say you can do, I'll take you to him. But I wanna see my family first."

Donte thought hard about what he was going to do. He knew that it was dangerous, but he didn't care. His family was in danger. He looked at this opportunity as a means to escape; the only way he could survive. He couldn't keep it in the streets. He was bound to lose any war with someone like Bones. He would do the only thing he felt would save the life of him and his family. It didn't matter to him that it would cost the lives of so many others.

"I wanna see my family." Donte repeated.

"You want to see your family?" The Detective asked.

"Yeah."

"Well, that won't be a problem, Donte. As a matter of fact," the Detective stood up. "We have them right here." He gave Donte a smile, showing crooked teeth.

Detective Owens was all smiles, Donte realized for the first time, except for his conniving eyes. The Detective looked at him, and then walked over to the floor to ceiling curtain dividing the room. Snatching the long curtain aside, he revealed what Donte had been asking for; his mother and two sisters lay on the floor unconscious and hog-tied. Turning around to see Donte's expression, he marveled at the horror-stricken fear painted on his face.

Donte stared at the Detective for a second, dumbfounded as to why a law-enforcement officer would treat a family the way that his was being treated. Trying to process the moment, it all dawned on him at once...

He heard the hospital room door open. Turning his head to the right, Donte's heart skipped several beats when he found himself staring face to face with Bones. As grown as he was, he wanted to cry right now; he wanted to cry for his mother and for his sisters; for the death that he would cause them. Looking over at his baby sisters and understanding that he was responsible, was too much for him to bear; he broke.

"No. Noo. Nooo." He started to cry, tears beginning to soak his gloomy face. He no longer felt the pain from his injuries; the agony of his body no longer a factor. Time itself came to a screeching halt as he...

Bones interrupted his thoughts.

"Donte... Donte... Donte?" Bones shook his head from side to side while making that annoying clicking sound with his tongue. He was appreciative of the horror he read on Dante's face. He loved how he had an effect on people. "I tried... I tried to be considerate to the fact that maybe, just maybe, you would stick to some kind of code of honor. But you know what they say... 'A man who stands fo' nothin' will fall fo' anything'. You should have known the consequences, fool. Either way, you will reap those consequences; four times over, I might add." Bones gestured towards Donte's unconscious family.

Donte wanted to plead – to ask for forgiveness – but he knew it would do no good. He just crossed a line that could never be backtracked. So instead of asking for forgiveness – instead of asking for the mercy of his beloved family – he did the only thing that he thought would do any good.

He screamed ...

"HELP... HELP... HELPPPPP!!!" Donte cried for help. He hoped that someone in the hallways of the hospital would hear his screams and storm into the room to help. But he only heard laughter. The Detective – enjoying every moment of this – was bent over holding his stomach from laughing so hard.

Bones, on the other hand, maintained a neutral posture with his hands in the pockets of his custom-tailored suit. His face carried the expression of a man who was being highly entertained; so entertained that he too began to scream.

HELP... SOMEBODY HELPPP!" Bones cuffed his hands mockingly around his mouth to intensify the scream. "HELPPPP..."

But no help came.

Donte couldn't take the torture any longer and began sobbing uncontrollably; his own tears blurring his vision.

Bones enjoyed moments like these. He ran over to Dante's bed and jumped up on it like a lion pouncing on its prey. He watched the terrified look on Donte's face as he stared into his one good eye. Clapping his hands onto Dante's shoulders so hard that it caused Donte to jump, Bones leaned down and got face to face with him. Memories of his father getting face to face with him when he was younger came to mind.

"I liked you, Donte." Bones began. "And I always felt like you would make the ranks. But you've really, really, disappointed me here today." Clicking his tongue, Bones continued, "luckily fo' me, I never fully trusted yo' ass. I never fully trust anybody, fo' that matter. Anyway, I was in my office and was havin' a conversation wit' Tee-Tee... You remember Tee-Tee, don't you? Well, never mind. You see, he brought up the topic of you not bein' trusted;

that you knew too much. He also suggested that you should be eliminated, and that he was willin' to put in the work."

"HELPPP... "Donte interrupted with more screams, hoping to draw someone's attention. He was startled and quickly silenced by the open-handed slap that Bones gave to his face.

Bones, agitated, let the slap sit in for a second before continuing, "But I said, 'no'." He clicked his tongue as Donte remained silent. "I said, 'Donte will hold up'. You see, as much as I didn't trust you, I *wanted* to trust you. But Tee-Tee didn't believe in you, and unfortunately fo' you, he was right. Yeah, that's right, li'l nigga. Look around you."

For the first time since waking up, Donte noticed that there weren't any windows in the room.

"Detective Anderson..." Bones looked in the direction of the Detective before looking back towards his dumbfounded prey.

Donte watched as the tall white man that he'd confessed to, walked over to the far wall where the television was mounted. With the ease of kicking over cardboard, the Detective raised his right foot and kicked as hard as he could. The entire wall collapsed outwards and fell to the ground, spewing up dust from the other side of the wall. Part of the ceiling that was attached to the falling wall came tumbling down as well. Where there once appeared to be an averaged sized hospital room, a much, much larger expansion was revealed.

Donte lay inside of a façade of a room; a makeshift hospital unit. But now that there was an opening in the wall, it revealed a large, near dark void. Staring off into that newly created void, Donte roamed the darkness until he spotted what looked like a burning incinerator on the far side of the opening. It wasn't a good sign. He watched as someone – a person that he could barely make out – was pressing the bellows to stoke the flames. In front of the burning incinerator was a conveyer belt – used to roll heavy objects right into the blaze.

"That's right, mu'fucka'." Bones' smile lit up as Donte craned his neck to look. "It never occurred to you that it was too hot in here to be a real hospital? You know they keep the temperatures low to control the germs," he laughed a sick laugh. "It never occurred to you that Detective Owens here, never used a tape recorder to record yo' so called confessions." Bones laughed. He paused. That shit was almost as funny as the horror on Donte's face. "You are a fool, you snitchin' bitch."

"You ran from Loony and 'em..." Bones continued. "...which I might add, made the plot even that much mo' dramatic. But either way, you were goin' to get knocked unconscious; and either way, you were goin' to get rescued by my two officer friends; and either way, you were goin' to be brought here to the basement of this abandoned warehouse. And to think that I would waste my own resources to try and prove yo' loyalty. Who said I didn't care?" Bones shook his head. "You still feel like screamin', mu'fucka'? No? Well, I got somethin' that's goin' make yo' ass scream."

Tee-Tee entered the little alcove of a room from the hole in the wall and was standing by the bed mugging Donte. When Bones hopped up off the bed, he and the Detective lifted the bed off of its frame. With Donte in tow, they began carrying him over to the conveyer belt and burning incinerator with Donte kicking and begging for mercy.

They ignored his cries and laid him down on the motionless conveyer. Reaching for the straps bolted to the side of the bed, they began to secure him to the frame. Donte tried his best to resist, to fight for his life, but he realized how weak his body had become.

To be honest, I'm giving you a li'l extra, cause you look like you're in a lot of pain. But don't tell the doctors I gave it to you, alright baby. The extra morphine Nurse Betty had given him had made him too weak.

Donte released more tears. There was nothing else he could do, though he attempted to struggle all the same. He thought about what it was going to feel like once he entered the flame. He didn't want to think about it, but the excruciating pain that he knew was coming wouldn't allow him not to.

His skin would blister before the flame seared it to a crisp. He would writhe in agony, developing blackened blisters all over his body. His screams would drown out when the soft tissues of his tongue and vocals began melting away. Eventually, the blood in his veins would begin to boil and his organs would split open like the fried meat they would become. Luckily for Donte, he would be long dead before most of that.

The human body could not sustain combustion by itself, but Donte had the blazing inferno to ensure that he would remain burning. Before it was all said and done, he would feel excruciating pain for about two to three minutes before his body finally succumbed to death. To make matters worse, his mother and two little sisters would feel that same excruciating pain before they died.

When Tee-Tee and the Detective finally got Donte strapped in, Anderson reached into his pocket for his handcuff key. He retrieved his hand cuffs and shackles and tucked them securely through his belt; he couldn't afford to lose city issued property.

Bones grabbed the hanging control panel to the motorized conveyer belt. Smacking Donte hard across the face once again to make him stop screaming, he waited until the boy got quiet, before he spoke, "oysters, Donte, open completely when the moon is full. When the crab see's one, it throws a piece of stone or seaweed into it; it keeps the oyster from closing again so that it serves the crab for meat." Bones paused just long enough for effect. "Such is the fate of he who opens his mouth too much, and thereby puts himself at the mercy of the listener." Bones gave Donte a moment of silence after sharing one of his favorite quotes from the '48 laws of power'. "Any last words, my nigga?"

Only a dead man's cries filled the void.

"Any last words, Tee-Tee?" Bones asked, turning towards his protege. He had been on the verge of giving Tee-Tee bigger responsibilities for some time, now, so keeping him aware of what he was capable of was very important in this moment. When Tee-Tee declined to speak, Bones continued, "Well, let's pray. Bow y'all heads." Tee-Tee and Detective Anderson, shocked, stared at one another in silence as Bones actually bowed his head. Not wanting to disappoint the mad man, they too obediently bowed their heads. "Lord..." Bones began. "...protect me from my friends. I can take care of my enemies. Amen." With the controller in his hands, Bones pressed the green button.

They all listened to Donte's screams. When his feet touched flame, Tee-Tee was surprised at how much louder the boy's screams became. Tee-Tee, partially zoned out, could only watch the writhing expressions on Donte's face as the flames began to eat away at his flesh.

Bones heard noises coming from within the make-shift hospital room. The scene before them would all happen again and again. In retrospect, he wished he would've first made Donte watch as his family was burned alive before killing him; it would've been far more dramatic. But what was done, was done. Ready to go back into the hospital room – to finish what he'd come to do – he glared at Tee-Tee and the Detective both before speaking,

"A man's heart is the vision of fulfilled desires..." Bones quoted. "...and hell is the shadow of a soul on fire."

CHAPTER 11
CRISPY AND CLEAN

MARCH 24TH. 6:02am.
JAMES CACEY HOUSING PROJECTS
EAST NASHVILLE...

20 DAYS LATER ...

Kimani awoke suddenly. He didn't hear an alarm clock; Sasha didn't have one. He usually slept without incident in the early hours – especially when things were quiet – but strangely, it was that very quiet that awakened him. Perhaps it had something to do with him sleeping at Sasha's place for a change.

The early morning light seeped through the fringes of her translucent window curtains, casting a dim bluish haze throughout the small room. He lay there, staring up at the ceiling as the morning's ambience reign down on his being. Kimani hardly ever got up at the crack of dawn anymore, but this morning, his internal clock was reaching out to him.

Deep in his own thoughts, he rolled over to place his arm around Sasha. He moved slowly and with ease, trying not to awaken her from her sleep. He loved her. He understood that more and more as the weeks went by and wouldn't change it for anything in the world. At the first touch of her body, however, he jumped back with a quickness that should have awakened her but didn't.

Sasha was cold and stiff.

Her eyes – beautiful even in death – stared off into the abyss. Her mouth was agape in agony; an expression that announced to all that could see, her fright in the midst of death. She looked as though she was trying to scream, but her soul – long gone from this world – wouldn't allow her to.

Panicking, Kimani pushed up on his hands and knees to hover over his love, but it was too late. There was nothing he could do anymore; his baby was dead...

He opened his eyes.

It was daybreak outside, and the bright sunlight that flooded the room verified it. He found himself looking up at the ceiling as he always did upon waking in the mornings. Mankind, it would seem, were very ritualistic beings. When the details of his nightmare came rushing back to him, he reached over to feel for Sasha; she was warm to the touch, and to his relief, she opened her eyes.

Sasha reached over to wipe the sweat from Kimani's forehead. She saw that familiar look in his eyes.

"Another bad dream, baby?" she asked. "You look like you just saw a dead body or somethin'."

Why would you say that? Kimani thought to himself. He stared at Sasha, at a lost at her prophetic inquiry. He still hadn't told her about the dreams. For the past two and a half weeks now, he had similar dreams; all of which, Sasha was...

He realized his heart was pounding and rolled over to lie on his back.

Sasha moved over to place her arm, and half of her body, across his. She stared into his nearly void eyes. Nine months ago, she never thought that she would be in love with him the way that she was. But things had changed.

Kimani held on to her, wrapping her body up into his own. He enjoyed the warmth of her. Since having the dreams – or nightmares for a better word – he had become more and more aware of his feelings for her. The more he tried to deny them, the stronger they became; he was only human. He simply recognized his love for her the more those dreams revealed themselves.

It was these very dreams that caused him to sleep over at her spot to begin with. He didn't want to leave her side for too long. While he had more than enough money to get them their own place, he knew that they weren't quite ready to make that move yet; but soon. He was young, on the verge of graduating high school, and living under his mother's roof. For now, that was all that anyone needed to know.

Kimani leaned over, and kissed Sasha on her lips.

She smiled and hugged her arm around his chest. She was already aware that he was a perfect lover and hoped that he would someday be a perfect father to their one day off-springs. Despite him being a banger and doing the things that bangers did, he made her happier than anyone ever had. She wanted a life with him, and she wouldn't have it any other way.

Contemplating, Kimani attempted to gather himself. As of habit, he tried to think about the things that he had to do that day, but the dreams of Sasha were twisting his thoughts. He had responsibilities that he needed to be focusing on, but the wires in his brain wanted to create their own path.

He was falling in love with this girl, and to him, it was the strangest thing ever. It all seemed to be happening at once; in an instant; the feelings were just there. He reached down and gave her a long kiss on the forehead, before getting up, grabbing his shower gear, and heading towards the bathroom down the hall.

It was forty-five minutes later before he was dressed and ready to step out to meet the world.

"Baby?"

Kimani heard Sasha calling from down the hall. "Yeah," he answered.

"Come here, please."

Kimani walked down the short hallway and back into the bedroom to find Sasha still lying on the bed.

"What's up, baby?" he asked.

"I was just wonderin' where you was goin'."

He walked over to the bed and laid down next to her, being careful to keep his shoes off the covers.

"I'm goin' be wit' C-loco fo' a li'l while." He said. "We gotta head outta town to take care of some business." Without realizing it, he was rubbing Sasha's stomach.

"Why you gotta go outta town fo'?" She asked, curious.

"We gotta take care of somethin'. I ain't goin' be gone too long. We should be back in a few days."

Sasha stared at him. She didn't know what he was up to, but she didn't want to have to keep questioning him to find out, either. She learned to let things be with him when it came to certain situations.

"Well..." she began. "...I just got off the phone wit' Kim. She on her way over here. She said she was leavin' twenty minutes ago."

"What, you want me to stay till she get here, or somethin'?" He knew that this was the very thing that she was implying, but he always tried to encourage her to express exactly what it was that she was trying to say.

"You don't have to if you don't want to. I got yo' cell number. She should be here any moment now." Sasha gave him that puppy doll face that he'd become so accustomed to.

"Well I guess I'll just ride out then." Kimani started to get up to leave.

"Aight, yes." Sasha, grabbing onto him, began pouting. "I want you to stay here until she gets here. Dang!"

Kimani smiled at the defeated look on her face. He simply wanted her to say what she felt. What he'd yet come to understand was that she simply wanted him to be able to read her thoughts and whims. Eventually – if the universe was kind – they would learn to live somewhere in the middle. He briefly played with the idea of them spending the rest of their lives together, and just as quickly wondered where in the hell the thought had come from. Nonetheless, he held her close to him, and asked, "where would you like to move to once I get things situated?"

Sasha backed up off him and gave him a funny look. He had never asked her anything like that before. "Do what?" She laughed nervously, before realizing that he was serious. "I don't know, baby..." she admitted. "... I guess I ain't never really thought about nothin' like that. Why you askin' fo?"

"Cause, I been doin' a whole lot of thinkin'..." He paused. "...and I think it's 'bout time we buy us some land. I ain't doin' what I'm doin' out here just to stunt. I'm doin' this shit so I can build a life and live comfortably. You feel me?"

"Baby, what's wrong?" Sasha asked, sensing his mood.

"Nothin'." He lied, as he stared into her eyes. He knew what she was alluding to. Something in him had changed. For reason's he couldn't explain, he knew that time was running out. He continued: "Most nigga's I know don't want shit but clothes, bitches, golds, and cars. Me... I'm just lookin' fo' a foundation, somethin' real to live fo'."

Sasha was about to speak, but he interrupted her.

"I know what you thinkin', baby. How we goin' buy some land wit' out the Feds bein' all up in our shit? I got all that situated." He paused. He knew that he shouldn't be telling her what he was about to tell her, but he decided to anyway. "Look, I know this big time businessman, stay out there in Brentwood. Somebody that I know, knows his daughter. When she drinks she talks a lot and found out that he been buyin' up shares out the ass and sellin' others right befo' they flop. Wit' a li'l work, I got enough info' on his illegal in-house tradin' schemes that I've convinced him to let me save his life."

"What?" Sasha cocked her head back. "I don't understand. Why you goin' save his life?" She was confused.

"I'm goin' save his life fo' everybody to see, just fo' looks. In return, he goin' feel obligated to give a nigga a li'l dough. I give him 'bout three-hundred stacks, we go to the bank and he wire me the same amount from his account... interest free."

182

"Is this the reason why you leaving town wit' C-loco... to extort some old white man?" Sasha didn't like the sound of all of this.

"Nah, baby. We on somethin' else." Kimani assured her. "Don't even worry yo 'self 'bout this. Everything goin' be aight. I promise you. Prolly shouldn't even told you."

Sasha stared at him. She would've never thought to do something like that, but she reluctantly trusted his judgment. She would go to the end of the world with him if need be. So, instead of trying to see if it would work without incident, she closed her eyes, laid back down on his chest, and thought about what type of house she wanted to live in.

"I'll give it some thought, baby." She said. "I'll look some up while I'm at school and we'll decide together whether we like it or not. Aight?"

"You do that." Kimani stated. "All I ask is that it's somewhere away from the city. I won't have my kids growin' up around here." *Damn, did I just say that?* He thought to himself. He noticed Sasha smiling from ear to ear. If it made her happy, then so be it, he was content.

He didn't have to tell her not to say anything to anyone about his plans; he taught her the power of secrecy a long time ago. Not even Ms. Reed would know anything if he didn't want her to.

Having that money wired to his mother's bank account, he would place the down payment in her name. He knew that she would consent; especially after some wealthy man gave her three-hundred thousand dollars for the heroic efforts of her son. His only dilemma would be trying to convince her to also move in a house of her own. For some reason that he couldn't explain, she loved the community where she lived; trying to coax her to change her environment would be an uphill battle.

Knock... Knock... Knock... They heard the rap on the door downstairs.

"That must be Kim," stated Sasha. "Make sure you keep yo' phone on, baby. I might need to call you fo' somethin'.

"Aight," he consented. "You just make sure you call me if you need anything. And I brought in that Moose tracks ice-cream you wanted last night. You better save me some, too."

"Thank you." Sasha was still smiling. "Be careful, and I love you."

"I love you too, girl." And there it was. He had finally said it. He watched as Sasha paused and stared at him. She looked just as shocked as he was. With the astonished expression still on her face, he leaned over and kissed her before picking up his backpack, going downstairs and letting Kim in on his way out the front door.

Kimani walked out onto South 6th Avenue and suddenly came to an abrupt halt. Out of nowhere, a small crowd of kids – age's six to ten – jetted out across his path.

Where they had come from was a mystery to him because he never heard them approach. Nonetheless, he watched as they ran off in the distance appearing to be having fun.

They laughed, tagged one another back and forth, and attempted to trip each other as they went. It was something that he hardly ever saw anymore. Now a days, the basketball courts were filled with drug dealers, and the playgrounds were filled with cluckers. To see children playing without worry brought a smile to his face. It appeared the world had potential after all. He watched as the kids ran around a building and out of sight.

The day was bright; not a cloud in the sky. Grown-folks and cut throats roamed the area. His temporary state of calmness came to an abrupt end and his senses were back in overdrive as the truth of his reality reared its ugly head. Getting back to the business at hand, he could only hope that C-loco hadn't forgotten about the day that they both had to do their laundry.

He continued his journey and headed for South 8th Avenue where he knew C-loco had stayed for the night. Hoping that the homie hadn't forgotten to get the rental car that they would need to get out of town with, he clutched his backpack and imagined every detail of their plan. Instinctively anticipating anything that could possibly go wrong, he had to force himself to stop over-thinking the situation.

Walking between two buildings, Kimani heard the echoes of a ringing cell-phone chirping off in the distance and turned to seek out the source. Realizing that his vicinity was void of life, he slowed his walk to better peep his surroundings; you could never be too careful in this neighborhood. With his gun hand at the small of his back, he listened as the cell phone went off again.

This time he realized his paranoid stupidity. With his backpack off his shoulders, Kimani unzipped the bag and shuffled through the bundles of hundred-dollar bills to recover his phone. If the muffled sounds of his own ringing cell phone in his backpack could cause him to be jumpy this early in the morning, he knew that he was in for a long day. Without missing another stride, he answered his phone placing the device to his ear.

"Hello."

"What up, nigga? Fuck you at?"

"I'm on my way. You in the same spot ain't you?"

"Yeah, I'm waitin' on Trina to get her fat ass up. She actin' like she tired and shit..."

"Bitch always actin' like she tired," said Kimani. "Did she get the rental?"

"Yeah, I made her get it last night."

"It ain't got no tints, right?"

"Nah, nigga. We good over here on this end. Where yo' ass at?" asked C-loco.

"I'm comin' out on South 7th now. Make that bitch get her fat ass up. I'm tryin' to be out this mu'fucka' by nine." Kimani reminded him.

"I got this shit, Cuz. Just remember, nigga, you takin one fo' the team next time." Demanded C-loco.

"Shit, I ain't never goin' spend the night wit' a fat bitch, nigga." Kimani admitted, laughing. "You did yo' thing though, boy."

"Fuck you, petty ass nigga." C-loco returned. "How much you got, anyway? I got like two-hundred."

"Shit, 'bout the same. I'm a be there in 'bout ten minutes. Tell Trina I said what up."

"Yeah, fuck you, nigga. I'll be here when you get here."

"Aight, fool."

"Aight, then."

Kimani broke the connection and placed the phone back into his backpack. He would handle his business and have fun while doing it. Have fun, clean some of his bread, and start putting his life together.

It was 9:43 before they broke the city's limits heading west on I-40 towards Tunica, Mississippi. Trina was at the wheel humming the hook to some song, while C-loco and Kimani both recounted their money. Kimani, in the back seat of the vehicle, knew that they'd brought Trina on this trip for one reason; to make sure that they got from point A to point C.

They drove for nearly four and a half hours before they reached Tunica. Being his first time in the city, C-loco used his GPS app to find the hotel they'd be staying in. Parked, they got out of the car, checked into the hotel and immediately went to their rooms. Kimani and C-loco prepared to hit every casino in the city while Trina wondered if C-loco was going to let her come along. Kimani, knowing his homie, already knew the answer to that.

Entering their first casino of the night, Kimani had to reveal the first of many fake Tennessee State I.D.'s he'd prepared before entering the gambling grounds; being underage, he had to improvise. They both purchased seven thousand dollars' worth of chips a piece, and then went to their respective areas. While C-loco went to only God knows where, Kimani went directly to the craps tables.

Their plan was to, of course, win. But if they came across a streak of bad luck, they would stop gambling and immediately cash in their remaining chips for a check. If they won, they would simply cash in their winnings, and receive a check before moving on to do it all again. From casino to casino, the duo would keep the checks coming in increments of approximately five to nine thousand dollars. Before they were done, they hoped to have at least laundered about seventy-five percent of their money with legit casino checks.

Kimani had several bank accounts set up to stash his winnings. When it was all said and done, and finding ways to funnel those accounts into a single business account, he would officially be another two-hundred thousand dollars richer, give or take. After doing nothing but saving his money over the years, he had to come up with alternate ways to clean it. Even at a young age, he knew that he had to make it legit.

The streets didn't last forever.

CHAPTER 12
PLOTS ON PLOTS

APRIL 3rd. 10:02am.
METRO NASHVILLE
POLICE DEPARTMENT
CENTRAL SECTOR/ DOWNTOWN ...

Detective Mark George analyzed the data streaming in from the lab at Quantico, Virginia's F.B.I. headquarters. After the local police's database failed to reveal any results from its fingerprint's bank, he was forced to use a national database to obtain the information he sought. When they discovered that the possible Sound Music bombing suspect entered Krystal's shortly after the blast, they immediately had a warrant served and went to the restaurant to confiscate the in-house surveillance footage.

Unexpectedly, the security video revealed that the same glare that obscured the perp's face in the previous footage continued to obscure his identity. Not understanding what was causing it, one thing was clear, they still couldn't get a facial. They were, however, able to observe the suspects strange behavior. Specifically, the way that he turned his entire body towards the camera as he pressed his hand on one of the restaurant's windowpanes as if to say to the law, *catch me if you can*. With the suspects fingerprints submitted, the Detective watched as a frontal and side-view picture of one Jesse Booker was frozen on his computer screen.

Their suspect was a forty-eight-year old African-American man with a limited high school education. A single prior checking fraud conviction occupied the file. His last known residence was 3399 Pullen Avenue on the east side of the city. According to the recent data, he never stayed in one place for long. He had no off-springs and grew up in a single parent home.

Having a limited high-school education was of no surprise to Detective Mark George, considering how easy Jesse Booker made it for them to figure out who he was. If it wasn't for the fact that the surveillance footage alone was not enough for them to convict him, they would've immediately issued a warrant for his arrest. But as of now, the Detective knew that he had to play this one like the criminal he was trained to defeat; nifty and methodical. Using his keyboard, Mark backed out of his files until the words, 'please enter password', popped up on the screen.

Detective Anderson sat at his home computer. He pulled the keyboard closer to him, cracked his knuckles, and then typed in his password, cov_f2_839_%_ert. The computers mother board immediately accepted his password and a variety of icons popped up on the screen. He quickly selected the one that he was looking for and watched as page after page of information on Chauncy Tiriq Learns was revealed. Not many people knew the original name of the man that was known to most people as Bones, mainly because Bones had his identity changed many times over the decades. The Detective was very good at doing his homework. It was a dangerous game that he played, but in the end, the man with the most information was usually the man who survived that game.

The Detective typed in newly gathered information that he recently obtained on Bones; information that could no doubt get Bones convicted and sentenced to death. In the event that something went wrong for the Detective, and he could no longer type in his password and reset the twenty-four hour countdown timer, the sequenced program would immediately find its way through the proper channels and the domino's would begin to fall. Of course, if that first domino did fall, it would be because the Detective was either dead or on his way to his death. A man had to have fail-safes of this sort when dealing with someone as powerful as Bones; such contingencies were critical in this game.

It took the Detective nearly an hour and a half to type, categorize, and save the new information. When he was done, he backed out of the program, reached for his briefcase, and headed out the front door on his way to another day's work. He was so sure of himself that he never noticed the pin-sized hole in the ceiling directly above his computer. Two minutes of ceased movement was all that was required for the hidden camera to shut itself down, save recording space, and wait to be reactivated when its motion sensors detected movement.

The room was silent and still.

Bones had his runners. Some were more or less simple runners, used for miscellaneous errands. But others were the ones that he used for more important shit; shit like what he had lying on his desk in front of him. As usual, of late, Tee-Tee sat directly across the desk from him.

Tee-Tee reached out his hand to accept the package that Bones was handing him. It was a manila envelope. When he upturned its contents, several large photos fell into his lap.

He picked them up and began examining them one by one. What he saw caused him to pause. What baffled him even more than that was that the dates on the photos were more than a month old. Tee-Tee knew that Bones knew the occupants in the photos for who they were; knew that the hood had been infiltrated by undercovers. Yet, even after a month, nothing had been done about it. The why was a fact beyond his comprehension. It all made him uneasy. Instead of asking the many questions that he wanted to ask, he simply stared at the O.G., wondering what was running through his complex mind.

Bones smiled and spoke calmly, "three very familiar faces. One belongin' to Detective Anderson, and the others belongin' to... well, you get the picture." Bones steepled his fingers in front of his mouth in thought, and then continued, "one wearin' a Detective's shield, and the other two... after bein' spotted walkin' into the Northside precinct, I had to get confirmation; their Narcs. It actually shocked the hell out of me when I first made the discovery, and I'm hardly ever surprised. But I've had a lot of time to do a lot of thinkin' since."

Bones got up and walked over to the bar to pour two shots of Hennessey for Tee-Tee and himself. The office was checked for bugs every morning, but only he knew of the electronic tech he had installed that prevented their conversation from being transmitted; a luxury that gave him the privacy he needed. Since some of his most recent discoveries, he had to get newer and far more advanced equipment. He had an idea the type of game that Detective Anderson was playing, but he too, had weapons of mass destruction. He realized that until he set his master plan into motion, the two factions would be at a stand-still.

Plots on plots on top of plots.

Tee-Tee gulped the shot of Hennessey as soon as Bones gave it to him. He barely felt the sting as his mind raced for answers.

Bones leaned back in his chair, and then continued the conversation. "I'm sure you're probably wonderin' why I haven't made the usual decision and executed these mu'fucka's? But the truth is, these are shaky grounds we're on." Bones contemplated what he was about to say. "I've thought about doin' that many times, by the way, but I've been knowin' Detective Anderson for a while, now. And I've learned that he's very cunnin' and persistent. If I did decide to execute these bitches, then I'll only have to go back through the process of filterin' out the next set of spies he'll send my way; rest assured, he'll send more."

"However, if I leave them in the position that they've worked themselves up to then *we* can control the information that gets back to Anderson." Bones paused again for thought. "Of course, I could always murk the Detective as well but in doin' so I'd be eliminatin' a much needed asset. In this case, I have to balance the need against the risk. Until we no longer need him, we'll keep him right where he's at."

It all began to make sense to Tee-Tee; everything was coming to the light. Bones was always one to think before making a decision and his admiration for the O.G. began to grow on sight. He wondered what else Bones had running through his head but quickly realized that he didn't want to know; the greed to know everything could destroy a man and he planned on living a longtime.

Tee-Tee listened as Bones continued…

"I'm tellin' you this, Cuz, cause you're around these bitches just as much as I am. I need you to be very careful what you say around them; don't reveal a damn thing. We don't want to give them the idea that we know. So, I'm goin' need you to act the way you would any other time. You're the quiet type and probably won't say shit anyway – which is why I like you so much. But I need you to recognize that you have an advantage needed for a man in your position. The secret to a well-designed chess match is to know everything about your opponent – habits and tactics – while revealing nothing of yourself."

Tee-Tee only nodded his confirmation. It was just over a month ago that these fools were promoted by Bones to be where they are. By the date stamped on the pictures, Tee-Tee now understood why. Keep your enemies close, and your friends closer, was the old adage.

This time it was he who got up and poured two shots of Hennessey. He sat down, gave Bones his shot, and immediately drained his before he spoke, "what do you wanna do 'bout Jesse?" Other than his name, Tee-Tee really didn't know much about the man, which is why he didn't trust him. Knowing that Bones would have far more information on Jesse Booker than he would, including how the investigation was proceeding, he had to ask, "do you want me to send out a party?"

Bones smiled at the idea of sending a squad after Jesse. They would be in for a rude awakening. Instead of revealing what he knew of the man, he said, "so far, the investigation on him hasn't gone anywhere, and Jesse ain't got a damn clue that he's a suspect." Bones snickered at the lie. "In the event that it takes a turn fo' the worst, then I know from experience, the boy can hold water; it's not somethin' that we have to worry 'bout."

While Bones portrayed his lack of care for Jesse, on the inside, he gave him much thought. He was closer to him than anyone knew. To keep from fretting over his well-being he simply changed the subject.

"Tell me, Tee-Tee, what's been goin' on out on the grounds?"

"Everything's been runnin' as smooth as usual." Tee-Tee updated the O.G. "I had Trilly split up half his team and move them into Boo's spot at the bottom of the hill. It's not jumpin' as good as Boo had it jumpin', but it's better than nothin'. Trilly decided to leave Loony in charge at the top of the hill." Tee-Tee picked up a file he had lying at his side and began leafing through it. "As you requested, I had gunners stationed in selected spots for ten blocks." He thought about the drive-by and expected retaliation. "Also, Chino got loafers over in U.C. to keep a watch on their activity; if they're plannin' to make a move, we'll know about it in time." Tee-Tee continued to scan his documents. "It's been a month since we blasted them fools, but nigga's ain't sleepin'. Ain't no tellin' how long the red flags will delay their retaliation. It's only a matter of time. The protocols fo' security has been established, and everyone's on alert. When them unicorn ass nigga's decide to make their move, we'll be ready."

The derogatory term 'unicorn' was usually reserved for times of all-out war; these were such times.

"Monetary?" asked Bones, putting the status of his gunners aside for now. He requested to know about the very thing that really kept the hood a factor.

"Bottom of the hill is down thirty percent since it lost its most active group, but Loony vowed to have it back above the rest. Top of the hill is actually up ten percent since last week's inventory. 4th and 9th are both up fifteen percent since then too. The rest have been leveled out fo' three weeks now, but considerin' that most of the groups are on the bottom and top of the hill, everything is lookin' good. With the pressure that I've put on the lieutenants, we should see some better results by the end of next week."

One of the main roles that Tee-Tee had learned to manage since obtaining his status was that of treasurer of all product revenues; a vast leap for a former soldier.

"That's what I wanna hear. You keep up the good work, and I assure you that in time I'll make you a worthy opponent."

Tee-Tee nodded. Coming from Bones, it meant a lot to him. From this point on, he knew that he was on the fast track. He took in everything that he could from his mentor; tried to learn every nook and cranny. He quickly came to realize that it took a lot to keep a tight-knit family together. The most important aspect of being a big-homie that he'd learned long ago was that the status wasn't the privilege that 90% of the people thought; it was a responsibility. It wasn't about calling the shots or being the man, it was about maintaining order of the ones below you; it was about realizing that the support and will of the lowliest of individuals was what kept a family solid; that the bricks at the bottom of the project building's walls were what kept those very project buildings upright. Without them, those buildings would crumble.

Bones took good care of the hood, and the people loved him for it. But more important than having someone's love, was having their fear. So he ruled with an iron fist. In return, he would protect them from narcs like Terrence and Donte. The expenditure of a soldier meant very little to him, but that was one of the attributes that made him the ferocious leader that he was; the reason the 90's maintained their dominance around the city.

"Get caught up on yo' duties." Bones directed. "Fo' the next week, we're goin' to be spendin' a lot of time out on the grounds checkin' up on everybody. Never fo'get, a leader has to be seen by his followers. To stay cooped up all the time will portray timidness, and we can't afford to give the people the wrong idea."

Tee-Tee began to notice how Bones spoke in terms of, 'we', when speaking to him. He was being schooled by one of the greats. As Bones shut down all of his devices and prepared to leave, Tee-Tee did likewise. Contemplating on everything that had taken place thus far, he came to realize a truth that most could only dream of.

Every day, with conversations and encounters like these, he gained more and more respect for the man known to his followers, as Bones.

CHAPTER 13
WORDS FROM THE PEN

APRIL 5th. 7:36am.
JAMES CACEY HOUSING PROJECTS
EAST NASHVILLE...

Ms. Johnson hummed the melody to "Amazing Grace" as she stood over the stove cooking breakfast for her son and her – hope to be one day – daughter in-law. She liked Sasha. For one, she was respectful and pretty. For two, Ms. Johnson knew how happy she made her son. She also felt that they would be married one day. Mother's always knew these things. She was in the process of flipping over three pancakes when Kimani walked into the kitchen and kissed her on the cheek.

"Good mornin', momma," Kimani said.

"Good mornin', baby." Ms. Johnson smiled. "I know y'all hungry, so I want you to go and get yo' self-cleaned up and tell Sasha that I said to come here."

"Aight..." he said, giving his mother a sideways look. He left out of the kitchen without another word, wondering what his mother wanted with Sasha. He was already surprised that his mother had let her stay the night, but now she wanted to talk with her in private. There was no doubt that was her reasoning for him to get cleaned up after sending Sasha to her.

It had been nearly two weeks since he and C-loco had gotten back from Tunica, Mississippi, and while still in the process of organizing all of his accounts, he was content with how things were turning out. He found Sasha sprawled out across his California king-sized bed. With her long silky hair, she was beautiful laying there the way that she was. Wanting to capture the moment, Kimani stood there in the threshold of his bedroom staring at the love of his life in silence.

As though she felt his presence, Sasha looked up and gave Kimani her best smile. Playfully, she threw the pillow at him. He easily caught it and threw it back at her before going over to the bed and lying down beside her. He rested his head on her stomach.

Sasha, still smiling, unconsciously rubbed the top of his head. "Good mornin', daddy..." she said in her sexy voice.

"Good mornin', baby girl. Did you sleep aight?"

"Boy, stop playin'. You know good and damn well I didn't get no sleep last night," she laughed, unable to hold back.

The broken lamp still lying on the floor was a testament to the kind of night the two had. It was then that Kimani wondered if that was why his mother wanted to talk to Sasha alone. She had to have heard the lamp shattering last night.

"My momma wanna talk to you," he said.

"For real?" Sasha's expression changed in an instant and she stopped rubbing the top of his head. "What she want?"

"Shit... yo' guess is as good as mines. She just told me to tell you to come here."

Kimani rose up to get a look at Sasha and immediately began laughing when he noticed her looking at the broken lamp shattered on the floor. Sasha hit him with the pillow one last time before getting up and attempting to put the lamp back together. That made Kimani laugh even harder. Leaving Sasha at her task, he left out of the room and headed towards the bathroom down the hall.

Getting the lamp together as best she could, Sasha left the room and went to rendezvous with Ms. Johnson in the kitchen.

"Hey, Ms. Johnson. Kimani said that you wanted to talk to me? You sho' do got it smellin' good up in here." Sasha complimented her. She didn't need to ask what was for breakfast; her nose gave her the answer she needed.

"Thank you, baby. You wanna help me set the table?"

"Yes, ma'am." Sasha agreed. Before Ms. Johnson could give any directions, she was at the sink washing her hands. Drying them, she went to the cabinet and grabbed three sets of cups and plates, placing them on the table. When she was done, she began helping Ms. Johnson bring the food to the table; pancakes, eggs, turkey sausage links, muffins, biscuits, and strawberry and blueberry bits in cream. From the looks of it, they would be eating well for their morning breakfast.

It suddenly hit Sasha; she was doing most of the work. She dared not say anything to Ms. Johnson about it, though.

They talked for a while about all sorts of things. From life and future plans, including how many kids Sasha wanted and her plans after college, to past relationships she had been in and what they were like. Sasha felt like she was being blitzed. She had been through it before with Kimani, so she already knew what to say. He always tried to – or did – get her to talk about her past relationships.

Thinking of Kimani, she looked up just as he was walking into the kitchen. He stopped in his tracks, picking up their conversation in mid-sentence.

"... he was so adorable at the time. I wish you could've seen him. As a matter of fact, I'm sure I got some picture around here somewhere."

Sasha placed her hand over her mouth to try to keep from laughing out loud. Looking over at a bewildered Kimani, she was barely able to do so.

He just stared at the two, wondering what all they had been talking about for Sasha to be looking at him the way that she was. Knowing his mother, it had to be something embarrassing.

"Hey, baby!" Sasha got up from the table and gave Kimani a peck on the lips before easing him into his seat. One way or another, she was going to show Ms. Johnson that she could be the woman that her son needed in his life.

They conversed about a variety of different things as they ate; with his mother and Sasha doing most of the talking. Kimani was just thankful that it wasn't anything embarrassing; he was grateful, at least, that they had gotten that part out of the way before he entered the room. With all of the plates on the table empty, and all of their belly's full, his mother and Sasha began taking the dishes to the sink.

"By the way, baby..." Ms. Johnson paused and turned towards her son. "...you got some mail from yo' uncle. It's in there on the living room table."

"Fo' real?" asked Kimani. He always loved hearing from his uncle.

"Yeah, my brother is always writin'," answered Ms. Johnson.

"That's what's up."

Though he was anxious to hear from his uncle, he didn't immediately get up to leave; he sat there for a minute to see what his mother and Sasha would talk about next. But when they remained silent, he conceded, and got up to leave the room. Just as he knew that they would, the two began talking as soon as he left. Women! He didn't understand them; he wasn't sure that he ever would.

Walking into the living room, Kimani looked down on the coffee table where all the mail sat; the letter from his uncle Kalonji was on top of the stack. Grabbing the letter, he walked to his bedroom and closed the door behind him. He scanned over the envelope. On the back of the kite were stamped the words...

The Department of Corrections
has neither inspected nor censored
and not responsible for the contents

Anxious to know what his uncle had to say, Kimani opened the scribe and began reading...

Kimani,   *April 1ˢᵗ*

Hey! What's good with you, nephew? You have to forgive me for not writing you in some time. Often more than I should, I allow this place to get me out of my character. I'm working on that, however. How's everything going with you? I hope that you are in the best of health. Your mother told me that you're involved with some girl. She said that she ain't seen you this happy since you were a kid. She also said that she was happy for the both of you. If she consents, then that's more than enough for me. I'm happy for you, li'l homie.

I'm constantly in the law library here, working on my post-conviction; they've threatened to pursue the death penalty if I ever got my case overturned, but I never let threats deter me. The time, needless to say, is irrelevant to me. All that matters is, right here, right now. Because it goes without saying... that heaven and hell is a state of mind; so it don't matter where you're at, but how you choose to live your life. Even out there on the streets people are locked up and suffering, but only because – or partly because – they are grasping at the wrong things; doing the wrong things. But then again, maybe there are no choices; nothing to choose from. So what do we have but hope? And I say, fuck hope, "just" praying and dreaming; it's time to wake up and start doing! Because God is not just going to fall out of the sky and make everything alright. We've got to start where we're at; right here, right now. We've got to wake up the next man; we've got to resist our true enemies in this covert war; and we've got to stop being afraid to die!

What I'm really trying to say is that it's about to go down. I'm a soldier of the first order; living to die. I've figured out why my life is so seemingly fucked up: I haven't been doing what I've been put on this earth to do; picking up where the greatest left off – Malcolm X, Nat Turner, John Brown, Huey Newton, George Jackson, Jonathan Jackson, Bobby Seale, Bob Marley, Tupac Shakur, Assata Shakur, Lumumba, Mao, Shaka, and yes, Trayvon Martin and George Floyd, to name a few.

I've been studying here lately, nephew: capitalism, communism, Amerikkka, (and how it created wealth), Che, Mao, Fidel, Marx, Sun Tzu, £umumba, guerrilla warfare (art of war). Shit that's relevant. Shit that I've studied before but now I'm paying particular attention to. I won't go out like a Jew; I won't be easily killed. Because what I'm about to do is extremely dangerous...

... I'm about to live!!!

Forget what I said about hope. Because in my world and in your world, hope and vision is all we have. The current state of affairs – the current system we live under – does not benefit us. The system – or whatever you want to call it (which includes working for wages, credit inflation, recession, that is, capitalism) is not designed for our benefit. Nothing in this country is. They say, "If you work hard enough and pull yourself up by the bootstraps, that you can make it and live the Amerikkkan dream." But that's a fucking myth, for the most part! It's all lies and propaganda. The media specializes in distraction and confusion. We are portrayed as monsters and fools always dancing around and grinning with gold chains around our necks (our ancestors were forced to wear chains!) Who can respect a brother like that? Somebody needs to talk to 90% of these cats in the rap game; these fools are lost! There's enough of us in a position to make a drastic change, but instead, we choose to worship the same shit that got us all fucked up in the first place... CAPITALISM!

Question:

What is a man with money, Kimani? Is he a man or a puppet? Hurricane Katrina and other disaster survivors saw what a world was like without money; a world where you could no longer go to the local grocery store to purchase your food when you're hungry; or drink fresh water from an uncontaminated tap. How many cats do you know who can truly "survive" off of the land (food, wate,r shelter)? Truth is, because of our lack of true survival skills, we are all prisoners inside of this unfairly balanced capitalist system. Unable to survive without the currency that fuels it – or the crooked individuals who decides how much of that currency is circulated throughout the local population –

we will forever be prisoners of this system. We as a people don't have the know-how to survive without this system; slaves confined to a controlled allotment. Think about it, we are no different than Katrina victims.

In the beginning of time, our ancestors were hunter/gatherers. They spent eighty-five percent of their days hunting for food just to survive. Because of this, there was no time for them to sit around in a group to devise ways to advance their civilization; because they had to spend so much time hunting, they didn't have the time to better themselves as a people. It wasn't until the invention of agriculture – the means to have food and sustenance in abundance – that our ancestors had that extra time to then enable them to take that leap forward and advance as a people; building cities as a result!!!

In the same manner, the current system "we" live in is also designed for us to be hunter/gatherers the majority of our day. On average, day-in and day-out, we sweat and toil for this system for the crumbs needed to survive. As a result under such a system, both parents often have to work long hours daily leaving their kids to be raised by social-media, the media, and the public school system. We remain forever stagnant with no time to advance. In the end, whoever has control over our only means to survive – money – ultimately controls us...

Kimani, as usual, thought hard about what his uncle was telling him. He knew that if he'd been caught with all of the money that he'd been making over the years, that he would be locked away for a long time. It was illegal to be making tax-free money the way that he was. Yet, if he'd been abiding by the law the way that the system had intended him to, he'd probably be making minimum wage with little or nothing to survive with; the system's way of keeping a man down in the dirt.

It was no secret that he didn't know how to survive off the land – he didn't know anyone who could. Reading what his uncle had to say gave him a new perspective about his place in the world that he lived in.

He continued, picking up where he'd left off…

To a capitalist, Kimani, money is God... If there was no profit motive, there would've been no slave-trade, no nuclear weapons, prisons, and police (they only protect the interest of rich capitalist). Without a profit motive, there would've been no holocaust, the depression, internet porn, disease, crackkk; you get the picture? The want and love for money makes mad-men out of some and slaves out of the rest.

These robots that guard us here in this prison have no marketable skills and don't get paid shit. But I have to keep my eye on them; I don't converse with them. They legitimize the wholesale kidnapping (warehousing) of the poor. 90% of whom are

here for economical profit. The saddest part is that most of the robots are poor like you and I, and most of them don't have a damn clue that they are imprisoned like the convicts that they are charged with housing. The best prisoner is a prisoner that thinks he's free.
But a new day is coming soon!!!

Love, your uncle
Kalonji

Kimani stared at the letter from his uncle for some time. As always, it had him captivated. His uncle was given two-hundred and twenty-two years over a decade ago for a triple homicide. The penitentiary had changed him since then. Some people it drove mad, and some – his uncle among them – it only made stronger; releasing the inner warrior that it was meant to destroy. Kimani reread the letter a couple times before neatly stacking it among the others he had accumulated from over the years. Like this letter, they all spoke volumes of real shit.

His uncle never spoke of the day that he hoped to be released; he never spoke of a future life of happiness. He always lived in the now. It was a strength that Kimani – at such a young age – didn't have the experience to measure.

He would log onto J-pay and wire his uncle five-hundred dollars to his books. Even though his uncle never asked him for money, he always made sure that he didn't need for anything – attorney fees and all.

Walking into the kitchen, his mother and Sasha had become quiet when they noticed his presence. Sasha was smiling as always, and his mother was looking at him as if he had interrupted the world. He was absolutely sure that he would never be able to understand women. Conceding, he decided to leave them to their gossip and exit the house all together. His mother had stolen the show and that was something that he just couldn't compete with. Shaking his head as he left the house, he secured his pistol at the small of his back and locked the door to the apartment behind him.

CHAPTER 14
CHILDREN OF THE DIRTY

APRIL 5th. 8:46am.
JAMES CACEY HOUSING PROJECTS
EAST NASHVILLE...

For a change, Kimani found himself posted up on the block with Caccy-Laccy, and a few of his other homies just getting a feel for the streets. It had been months since he stood out on the block for more than a few minutes, but today, he felt the need to get a good look at the hood.

From where he stood he witnessed three different groups working the streets down the avenue. Cats from thirteen to thirty ran back and forth, to and from vehicles before those vehicles even had time to stop. With elbows spread wide to prevent anyone from hi-jacking their sell, they collected their money, sent the buyer around the corner and out of sight, before heading back to the curve to wait for the next sell; they never had to wait long.

Prostitutes walked up and down the avenue to catch any wanted eye. They didn't collect money, however. The money was collected by Turk who sat in a parked van just a hundred yards down the block. Once paid, he would signal the chosen prostitute to follow the payee to one of the many abandoned apartments. No prostitute ever got into a vehicle to be driven away. That wasn't the way things operated in Cacey Homes.

There was a book-house that Kimani could observe from where he stood. There was a ten-dollar entrance fee. People would enter in the front and exit out the back; a rotation that would often reverse. Payees could gamble as much as they wanted so long as they did not break the rules. Numbers were also played at the book-house, along with bets on anything from sports and statistics – that varied depending on the spreads – to whatever a person felt like betting on. Money in Cacey Homes was being made from every possible angle.

Tabs were being logged as to how much money was being made also. No one was ever foolish enough to try and cheat Bones. But the structure was in place all the same. Though drugs were the number-one money maker in the hood, the other establishments – including the ones that not many knew about – were not far behind.

It all made Kimani think about his uncle's letter. It was that same capitalist system Kalonji spoke of at work here; only on a much smaller scale. Instead of the government and the bankers being in control of how much money circulated, it was Bones himself. He was the overall reason the hood ate and survived or burned and crashed. In this neighborhood, *he* was god!

Without such a system, it would be chaos here. Thoughts of such chaos made Kimani feel for the pistol at the small of his back. It was an involuntary reaction.

"Fuck you do, nigga... get demoted?"

Kimani turned towards the voice but knew who it was before he spotted C-loco getting out of a 760 beamer.

"Nah, nigga. Just keepin' the streets close to me," stated Kimani. "Stay away too long and people'll fo'get who I am and what I stand fo'. Feel me?"

"No doubt!" C-loco walked over and the two men chucked up the N's. "I heard you gotta piece on those flat-screens... nice li'l chunk, too."

"Damn, where you hear that shit from?"

"You ain't the only one that keeps the streets close. Feel me?" C-loco reminded him.

Kimani shook his head before speaking, "shit ain't even up and runnin' yet, and nigga's already know the business." He was too often surprised at how fast the streets talked.

"You already know what it is, Cuz. What they goin' fo', though?"

"Shit... 'bout fifteen a piece. But fo' you, give me five-hundred."

"How big are they?" C-loco asked.

"Ninety-six-inch LG's."

"That's what's up." C-loco reached into his pocket and brought out a wad of cash. He handed Kimani five-hundred, thought about it, then handed him five-hundred more. "On second thought, let me get two of them things. I'll get up wit' you later on to pick 'em up. Right now, I got somethin' to do."

"Bet that." Kimani took the cash. "What ever happened to ole-girl?"

"Who, Trina fat ass?"

"Nah, Kim, nigga. Sasha's homegirl?"

"Man, Cuz, you know that bitch was already slizzard." C-loco was smiling from ear to ear. "We went straight back to her crib, and I promise you, the bitch one of them wild ass freaks you only see on TV; she on the slurpies and some mo' shit."

"Aw, shit." Said Kimani. "So, what's up wit' y'all, now?"

"Didn't you just hear me just say that bitch a wild ass freak?" C-loco's smile changed to a frown. "She tried to pour some hot wax on me, and I had to call it a night. I ain't seen the bitch, since."

"Damn, Cuz." Kimani was laughing. "She doin' it like that? Yeah, that's some freaky ass shit, aight. She done turned my nigga out..." Laughing at his homie's expense, Kimani changed the subject. "So what you 'bouts to get into?"

"I'm tryin' to close this deal with a clothing warehouse up in New York. If shit go right, I'm goin' open up a spot on Main. All I gotta do is get them sucka's to come down off they wholesale; everything else a go."

"That's what's up." Kimani Congratulated. He could tell that C-loco was ready to leave. "You keep yo' head up out here, nigga."

"No doubt. You too, Cuz."

"Aight then. N's up."

"Aight, fool. N's..." Again, the two men chucked up the hood. Kimani watched as C-loco got back into his vehicle and headed off down South 7th Avenue. Having cleaned money paid off, but, you still had to be careful. Kimani hoped that C-loco knew that. After their Tunica Mississippi visit, they were in a much better position to make moves. But unlike C-loco, he just wasn't quite ready to bust open yet.

Kimani heard his cell phone ringing and reached into his pocket to answer the call. "Hello?" Nothing. Silence. "Hello? Fuck is this..." Still, nothing.

Kimani started to disconnect the call but could barely hear someone giggling on the other end. He looked at his screen and saw that the number was unlisted. Placing the phone back up to his ear, he attempted to identify the laughter, but to no avail; he simply couldn't determine who it was.

Listening closer, he began to realize that it wasn't just one laughter. It was a number of different laughter's – one on top of the other – that he could barely tell the difference between. So close, in fact, that they sounded more like echoes than anything else. Someone was toying with him. But who? He began to think that maybe it was Sasha but quickly tossed that idea aside; she didn't play like this.

Kimani wanted to hang up the phone – to end this silly matter – but for some reason he didn't. Heart racing, he listened closely, feeling the electricity in the air. What in the hell was wrong with him; why wouldn't he just hang up the damn phone? Just as he sought out those answers, the laughter on the other end of the line rang out in crescendo; each louder than the one before.

"Man, who the fuck is this..." Becoming agitated, he demanded to know.

"Tyler Butler... Andre Robey... Tacarra Lambrey..."

The whispering voices seemed to scream from the phone all at once. Kimani could hear them as clearly as if they stood right before him.

"...Nichole Aubrey... Jason Whitley... Natasha Abraham..."

He listened helplessly, unable to do anything else; including move.

"Tyler Butler... Andre Robey... Tacarra Lambrey... Nichole Aubrey... Jason Whitley... Natasha Abraham ..."

The echoes repeated again and again; never-ending. The whispers went on chanting in his ear; all in hypnotic fashion. Kimani wanted so badly to make it all stop – wanted to simply hang up the phone – but his mind was paralyzed. He clutched the phone to the point of breaking it, hearing the cracks in its structure. His panic was becoming frantic, his nerves on end, but still he continued to listen to the echoes in his ear.

Then, as suddenly as the chanting started, it stopped; just like that. The voices were gone, and the phone went dead.

Kimani snapped out of his reverie – took a few steps to keep from falling over – and tried against all rational sense to star-sixty-nine the number. What in the hell was he doing? He was going mad. Pausing to look at his screen, he was shocked – if not relieved – to find that his phone was no longer working; the cracked screen was dead black.

He looked around and noticed that Caccy-Laccy and a couple of other people were staring at him. He wondered what his expression looked like in the eyes of those people. Further scanning his surroundings in search for answers, he attempted to see if maybe someone had been pranking him. He figured he would be able to see it in their eyes if they were. But to his dismay, no one else was watching him.

He was just out of his mind.

Kimani realized how hard he'd been squeezing the phone and forced himself to ease up; it was a struggle. Wiping away the sweat that accumulated on his forehead, he placed the broken phone in his pocket and walked off in the random direction that he'd happened to be facing. He was walking towards South 8th Avenue.

Somewhere in his subconscious mind he recognized those names – all six of them – yet, he couldn't remember where. What bothered him more than that was the way that those chanting names echoed in unison; separate, yet together. He couldn't explain it any other way.

Though his phone was now dead, he felt like he could still hear those names echoing in his ear, carried by the breezy winds around him. The temperature was moderate, but he was sweating from every pore in his body as those names softly echoed off of the buildings.

Without remembering how it happened, Kimani had the cell-phone out once again pressing the power source with his thumb. Still, the phone would not come on. He slipped it back into his pocket and continued to walk without any general direction. He simply felt the urge to keep moving to get away from the madness.

It wasn't long before he was in a part of the neighborhood that had been abandoned for as long as he could remember. No one stayed within two-hundred yards from here. Project buildings stood where they seemed like they should be falling. Some apartments had doors that barely hung on, while others didn't have doors at all. Windows had either been busted out or boarded up. For years now, the only people that roamed this part of the hood were junkies and the homeless.

And now him.

The only problem was that he didn't remember how he got here. His thoughts were roaming quicker than his mind could process; the mental blackouts he was having was proof of that. He walked over to the nearest building and took a seat on the steps to allow himself to calm down and to slow his breathing. His mind wouldn't stop thinking about those six names. For reasons that he didn't understand, he felt a strong urge to remember them.

Tyler Butler... Andre Robey... Tacarra Lambrey... Nichole Aubrey... Jason Whitley... Natasha Abraham...

He'd heard them before, if only he could remember where. Every other thought vanished from his mind as the chanting names continued to echo all around him.

He was going mad.

Tyler Butl...

It took him a second to realize that he had the phone out again and was futilely trying to get the power to come on. His hands were shaking uncontrollably. Inspecting the phone closely he noticed that the charger input was blackened and burnt as though a high-power source had surged through it; the plastic surrounding the charging-port was slightly melted and rolled back on itself. He'd seen in the news where cell-phones were catching fire, he just hoped this one didn't explode. He wasn't an electrician, but he didn't think that this amount of damage should be possible.

With more effort than it should've taken, Kimani was able to put the phone back into his pocket.

Tyler Butler... Andre Rob...

He heard a distant conversation echoing off of the buildings; it was a conversation separate from the chanting he'd been hearing. In a desolate area such as this, hearing someone holding a conversation seemed out of place. Wanting to be by himself, he got up to leave – to go back the way he'd come – but was surprised to find himself walking *towards* the conversation.

As he rounded the nearest corner, Kimani froze... Just before him was a playground that he knew should not be operational but was somehow fresh and new. The playground was equipped with swings, a merry-go-round, a slide and even children that played amongst it. Kimani knew that this place should be broken down and busted just like everything else in this part of the hood. None of it made sense.

Suddenly it occurred to him that no child should be in this part of the hood. It was places like these where kids came up missing, never to be seen again. He went to go and tell them this, and to escort them back to population if that was what it took, but stopped before he could take his first step.

There were six of them...

The kids laughed and played with one another, oblivious to his presence. Starting to panic, Kimani forced himself to count again as he tried to slow his frantic breathing. He was relieved to see that there were only five.

"Hey! Mister... Mister..." Kimani looked down at his right to a child staring up at him. "Can you push us on the merry-go-round?"

He watched as a young boy about nine or ten years of age stood next to him; how the boy got beside him without him knowing, Kimani had no clue. He was taken aback when he saw the scar that went across the child's face. The scar extended from just above the child's left eye to the right corner of his mouth. The kid seemed too young to have a ghastly scar like that.

Heart racing, Kimani suddenly realized something else... the young boy with the scar on his face put the count back up to six.

"Hey, Mister, I said will you push us on the merry-go-round?" little-man with the scar asked.

Kimani squatted down to get eye to eye with the kid, but also because he felt like he was about to pass out. With the nervous fear that he was feeling at that moment, he had to make himself look the child in the eyes. They were the most innocent eyes that he'd ever seen; so deep that it felt as though the little boy was looking through him instead of at him. On top of all the madness, the depths of those eyes seemed to be all knowing as if they knew something that he didn't.

Kimani had to force himself to speak.

"What... What's yo name, lil Cuz.?"

"My name?" said the little boy. "My name is Tyler..." Kimani's heart nearly stopped beating.

The name had to be a coincidence. A lot of people named their kids Tyler – well, maybe not a lot – but this couldn't be the same Tyler that echoed inside of his head. Kimani couldn't stop shaking. His hands were shaking, his knees were shaking, and being in the squatting position that he was in made it worse. In the grips of this little ten-year-old child in front of him, he attempted to breathe slowly to control himself before he spoke, "why... Why y'all out here like this, Tyler?" Kimani asked. "Y'all do know this part of the hood off limits don't you; that this a dangerous place to be in?"

"Aw, what you think goin' happen to us, Mister?"

"I don't know, li'l Cuz..." responded Kimani. "...it just ain't safe out here. Y'all shouldn't be out here by y'all self."

Kimani stared Tyler in the eyes. He couldn't look away. They had a grip that brought fear to him, but, it was what happened next that scared the living shit out of him.

Tyler's demeanor changed. Even the tone of his voice changed from that of a semi high-pitched voice of a kids, to one of a scraggly old mans,

"Is this what you wanted?" Tyler suddenly screamed, his expression showing anger. "IS THIS WHAT YOU WANTED???"

Startled, Kimani jumped backwards. Before he had time to realize what was happening, he was flat on his ass about fifteen feet from where Tyler stood. He watched Tyler from that distance as the boy stared back at him. And as if nothing had happened at all, Tyler's voice returned to normal. "What's wrong, Mister? Are you aight?"

"What did..." Kimani was panting, barely able to control his breathing. "...what did you just say?"

"I said, what's wrong? Are you aight?" Tyler repeated.

"No. no, no, no... what did you say befo' that?" Without knowing it, Kimani was tearing chunks of grass out of the ground with his bare grip; a ground that was somehow ice cold to his touch.

"Aw," Tyler began matter-of-factly. "I said, will you push us on the merry-go-round?"

Us.

Kimani remembered. He risked taking his eyes off of Tyler just long enough to glance towards the playground where the rest of the kids played. The playground was ragged, rusted, and broken down. Not believing what he was seeing, he wanted to scream; this shit couldn't be real. Not only was the playground dilapidated like everything else in this part of the hood, but there wasn't a single child in sight.

Kimani hurriedly turned back towards Tyler, not wanting to lose sight of him. "What's yo' last name, li'l Cuz..." He needed answers, anything that could help him understand what was wrong with him, but Tyler too, was gone.

Kimani was all alone.

With the ability of a world class athlete, he got up off the ground and hauled ass as fast as his shaking knees would allow.

CHAPTER 15
WHAT THE FUCK IS REAL

APRIL 26TH. 8:37pm.
UNIVERSITY COURT
SOUTH NASHVILLE...

THREE WEEKS LATER...

It was raining; an unusually hot and muggy day. Hot and muggy days tend to make him irritable, but he had no time to focus on that at the moment. It had been over a month since their hood had been road on, and they were as close as they would get to knowing exactly who the culprits were. It didn't matter though. The window was narrowed enough to guarantee that the choices he made would bring those responsible to judgment.

The hood's interests were between two potentially warring factions – the Golden Valley Boys, and the Rollin-90 Crips – both of whom were out east. The red flags the culprits wore really took its toll on U.C.'s resources as neither of the potential culprits wore red. But tortures were very prominent in the investigations, and the few deaths that resulted were considered nothing more than collateral damage.

For the price of three of their member's dead, and many more injured, it was an act too foul to be left unpunished. Just over a month was too long a time without repercussions, nonetheless, people knew that things were being done. Tortures left signatures and death's left messages. Their primary target was finally coming into view.

Sirius puffed on his half smoked blunt and looked at his list of eventualities; economical and otherwise. The tensions with the Golden Valley Boys were always on edge, but that first pawn had never been officially moved. They were a small hood and could be totally decapitated within a months-time if he chose to make that call; no serious threat. The price of war with them would hardly dig into their coffers. But the downside to that was that to strike at them would make University Court appear in the eyes of many as bullies. In the long run it could cost them future business prospects. Bullies were cowards and no one wanted to do business with an apparent coward. If the Golden Valley Boys were in fact the culprits, then they would have to be dealt with regardless of that downside.

Those Rollin-90 nigga's, on the other hand, had been known enemies for twenty-five plus years. It had been an unspoken cease-fire for the last two of those years. But once again, it had always been unspoken. Sirius knew of the death of that 90 nigga the night before the drive-by, which made them the more likely candidates. But disappearances and subtle deaths had also occurred in Golden Valley. They, too, would have reasons to retaliate.

He understood that war on a large front with the baNgside 90's would cost U.C. much, both in soldiers and monetary. They were large, and both resourceful and skillful at the art of war. But the act of idleness in the face of such opposition was much more costly. The decision was made.

There was going to be a lot of killing after this; killing he hadn't seen since serving his tours overseas. Such were the things that he had to ponder when the lives of so many below him were at risk.

Sirius decided to flank the Golden Valley Boys with light cavalry to keep them contained, while going at them Rollin-90 Cats with a volley of multiple hitters. Spies and imposters were all a part of intelligence and infiltration. Things were in place, and loose ends were being tied tight. It had been over a month too long, but things were quickly coming to fruition. Weapons were being readied, and war for them had finally been declared.

Nails were being pulled free from crates, wooden lids were being lifted, and AR-15 fully automatic rifles were being organized along the tabletop. These were the very type of weapons that the government was trying to outlaw. Cousin to the military standard M-16 223 caliber assault rifle, it allowed one to spit a high volume of rounds into their intended targets with little effort.

There were two teams of four, and a clean-up team of ten. With the drivers of each vehicle only toting hand-guns, it left a count of sixteen M-16 rifles to be used in the assault. Maybe it was overkill, but overkill sent messages and often ended wars. There were twenty occupants who stood in the abandoned garage, and they all had a critical role to play for there to be success with this mission.

Sirius, the only one not on the front line, knew that he'd planned well. Serving two tours in Afghanistan and one in Iraq, he could go toe to toe in tactics as good as anyone. By the time the night was over, he would make sure that hell would visit his enemies.

"We've been over all of the details, bra. We know what's gotta be done." Sirius' raspy and slow drawl of a voice silenced all. The last few AR-15's were being silently laid on the table and the soldiers were focusing their full attention on what was being said. The moment had finally come. He continued, "this shit's been a long time comin' bra, and like you, I'm ready to handle this wax and show these fools how we bang. Fuck hidin' who we are; unlike them, I want these bitch ass nigga's to know who we are and what we stand fo'. So, bang bang, my nigga. Watch them bitches fall."

Sirius listened as his men uttered rallying calls.

He knew soldiers didn't need to know the full details of war, and he didn't bother telling them either. Each team had their on directives. All that they needed to know was all that they needed to know; they were the Rollin-90 hitters.

Each hitter picked up a random assault rifle drum and immediately began – with gloved hands – loading the drums with .223 caliber projectiles. The weapons were new, and like most new weapons, the barrels and housings were overly oiled. They were hardened men, all accustomed to the smells of warfare. They were also accustomed to the agonies of death; bodies could lay dead for days in the hood before the proper authorities came to pick up its decaying mass.

Sirius continued:

"Timin' is critical. Precision is critical. Mu'fucka's goin' be talkin' 'bout this shit fo' a long time to come. I want y'all to make examples out these bitches fo' any mu'fucka who even think about fuckin' wit' the U.C. No trespassers shall go unpunished." He paused for effect. "Y'all nigga's know the price fo' every heartbeat that no longer go bump. So do yo' thang, bra, and lets show 'em what that U.C. be like." As always, Sirius looked each one of his soldiers in the eyes as he spoke. "B-ride? You got point, bra."

B-ride rose up from where he had been lounging on the back of a large utility truck Sirius had acquired. It had been stolen some days ago and painted – thus far – with a fresh pearl-white coat. It had a large opened cabin in the back with a set of double doors that opened outwards from behind. As Sirius looked on, the finishing touches and designs were being applied to the utility truck.

Turning his attention back to the matter at hand, he approached a now standing B-ride.

"Directives have been issued, bra, and team leaders have their instructions. Everyone needs to be in constant contact until the mission's been completed. Show me what you got, bra, and let's make this shit happen." Sirius said what needed to be said. He made his umpteenth count, and once again went over the individual details. On his way out of the abandoned garage, he shouted, "U.C. FOREVER," and was answered with a series of like responses. The only sounds afterwards were the sound of nigga's making small talk and drums being loaded.

****

Kimani lay on his back, staring up at the ceiling in thought. It had been weeks since his last episode and he hadn't heard from Sasha since. He knew that it must be driving her crazy; the messages and notes that she had been leaving with his mother for him was a testament to that. She was hurting, and it wasn't a good feeling knowing that he was the one causing that hurt.

Ms. Johnson definitely didn't approve of how he had been treating Sasha, but as a mother, she didn't want to get involved in her son's relationship. She couldn't be the one to work out their problems, whatever those problems may be. So up until now, she kept a watchful eye and remained silent.

The previous weeks had been a downer for Kimani; the episodes he'd been having frightened the shit out of him. He went from the classroom, to straight home. For the most part, his days were mostly spent at home, thinking.

He hoped Sasha would hold out. She was strong where he was not. He felt that she would be there when he was ready and even hungrier for the absence; everyone craved for the sun during long days of rain. Being honest with himself, he was missing her just as much as she was him. But right now, things were moving too fast for him. There was simply no room for her in his fucked up thoughts.

Tee-Tee had come to pick up his pager a week ago, so he was currently off roll-call and actually apathetic about it. He just didn't care. More important things were going on in his life.

He often read books or saw movies where mu'fucka's were hallucinating and seeing shit – crazy shit – but that crazy shit wasn't supposed to be happening to him. He didn't know what was going on, but he knew one thing for sure, what he had been going through over the last month or so was real. The six names still rung in the depths of his mind. Tyler's features were still prominent in his overloaded memory; that gruesome scar running down the boy's face along with eyes that seemed to capture its prey with ease. Kimani still got cold chills every time he thought about that day. Something was going on with him that he didn't want anyone knowing about. It was the type of shit that people got thrown into mental asylums for. He couldn't let that happen to him.

Graduation day was nearing; just a few more weeks and he could gather himself, go off to college somewhere, and get away from the madness all together. Sasha was already in college – a T.S.U. Tiger – but he was sure that she would be willing to transfer somewhere else away from the city for her junior semester next year. He had to get away from his surroundings, and he wanted his girl to go with him.

Things were pretty much quiet in the hood, at least from his perspective, being cooped up in the house all day.

He still ran his financial transactions, but only from a shadowy distance. He didn't watch TV; he didn't even play the X anymore. The only game he played was chess; with the way that his mind was roaming, he had to find ways to focus. Anything that kept him from thinking about the things that he didn't want to think about was a plus for him...

Kimani was startled, nearly jumping out of his skin.

As he looked up, he was surprised by the presence of his mother standing in his bedroom door. There was no telling how long she'd been standing there. She was often as quiet footed as he, if not more so. She didn't say anything, she didn't move, she just watched her only son. She waited for Kimani to rise up in a sitting position; it was her silent permission to enter. Walking over with the confidence of a mother, Ms. Johnson sat down next to her son's semi-lying body and lovingly observed him before speaking.

"What in the hell is the matter wit' you, boy?" She was never one to sugar-coat shit. "You've been cooped up in here for more than three weeks, now, like you're scared to face the world or somethin'. You act like you ain't got no life fo' all the world that's out there. I've been knowin' you all yo' life Kimani, and even *I* can't recognize you. You're changin' right befo' my eyes."

Ms. Johnson always imagined that change would be good for her son, but she never imagined this.

"You've got a perfectly lovin' girlfriend out there in Sasha whose pullin' the hair out of her head cause of the stranger that you've created. And trust me, I know. But you actin' like you too dumb to see it. I won't get in y'all business, cause that's fo' you and her to figure out. But let me say this, men fo'get, but never fo'give. Women fo'give, but never fo'get. You keep up this fo' too long and that girl goin' be someone else's girl."

Ms. Johnson paused, pressed her lips, and then continued:

"I like Sasha, she's a good girl. But like I said, I won't tell you what to do. That part is all up to you. You just remember what I said, women never fo'get." She let that sink in for a while. She was about to get up and leave but could tell that her son had something that he wanted to say. "Well, what is it? Come on out and say it, cause I got these greens on, gettin' 'em ready fo' tomorrow. What you wanna say?"

"It ain't her," Kimani paused. "It's me..."

"Oh Lord. Jesus Christ. Please don't let..." Ms. Johnson began praying that there wasn't something terribly wrong with her only son.

"...I just been stressin' a lot lately." Kimani finished. He stopped and stared at his mother's demeanor and the way that she continued to thank Jesus over and over. He was beginning to understand women less and less. Instead of trying to figure her out, he shook his head and continued, "I don't know if I'm doin' too much or what. It just feels like everything is crashin' down on me. I don't wanna think; my mind don't wanna process nothin'. It's just easier fo' me to shut everything out, I guess. I don't think I'll be like this fo'ever, but right now it feels like the right thing fo' me. I know you always said I should never get out of character fo' no-thing, momma, but even that seem like it don't apply. I'm just tired. My mind is tired." Kimani shrugged his shoulders thinking about the unspoken.

"Well, the mind certainly has reason to be tired, it never rest." Ms. Johnson offered. "Even while the body is sleep, the mind is busy dreamin', busy all the time." She brushed her sons arm out of habit and love. "For most people, though, it's hard to think about one thing for longer than twenty seconds or more befo' their mind is off thinkin' 'bout somethin' else. You should try closin' yo' eyes, baby, and practice thinkin' 'bout one thing, one object, for as long as you possibly can. As soon as you realize that you're thinkin' 'bout somethin' else, as you often will in the beginnin', just go back to thinkin' 'bout that original *one thing*. In time, if you stay at it long enough, you'll train yo' mind to stop roamin' and to be still."

Kimani thought about the prospect of him meditating. What would it be like? Did he have the patience for it? And could he maintain the discipline long enough? He would have to see, because his mother had never let him down when giving advice before.

Ms. Johnson Continued:

"Imagine a puddle of water that has just had a stone thrown into it..." she pondered. "... the ripples that the rock creates will keep you from seein' yo' reflection in that puddle clearly. But once that puddle of water has been stilled, once it has stopped ripplin', you'll be able to see yo' reflection clearly. Still yo'self, baby boy! Too many people out there doin' too many things too fast and can't see death when it's starin' them right in the face cause of it. Not my son; no, no, no. I've worked and nurtured too hard for that. So, you hear me good, Kimani. Don't let the world drag you down wit' it."

Ms. Johnson knew that her son was not only hearing her, but, listening as well. It was more of a feeling than anything. She patted him on the arm and rose up to take her leave, thinking as she went. They never had a problem with communicating with one another. If Kimani was quiet it was because he was thinking, not because he didn't want to talk. Most of their conversations were simple and to the point, like this one. Simple and sweet.

Kimani was rising up off the bed as his mother was leaving out. The analogy she had made with the water puddle was one that made a whole lot of sense, as did a lot of the things that she had to say. He would have no problem with establishing what that *one thing* would be, either; he'd been thinking about that gruesome scar on Tyler's face for weeks now.

So much for wanting to get them out of his head. The problem with that was that they all – all six of them – were too damn prominent in his memory. To try and establish something else as his one thing would definitely be interrupted by the thoughts of them. He would never learn to still his mind.

Kimani stood up and stretched. His muscles were a little stiff due to his three weeks of idleness, but he was sure to be good before long. The floor to ceiling mirror allowed him to examine himself fully. He didn't look lost, just drained. He would force himself to keep on pushing; force himself to build momentum. He needed to get out of the house.

Walking over to his dresser, he opened the drawer that contained his boxers. Pushing aside the clothing, he hefted his .40 caliber. It was the Glock edition; a slide that never jams. With the intentions of getting back out into the world, he thought about his love. He desperately wanted to see Sasha, only he wasn't quite sure how to approach her after three weeks of silence. How would she respond? Would she understand him? Would she hate him? He knew that there was only one way to find out.

Looking at the .40 caliber in his hand, he thought about what his mother had just said about stilling his mind, and reluctantly – but assuredly – lowered the .40 caliber back into the drawer. He turned and began walking towards the bedroom door before abruptly stopping in his tracks. He was once again startled by the silent presence of his mother. She had to quit sneaking up on him like that. Walking over to her in the doorway he could only hope that she didn't see the weapon that he chose not to carry.

Ms. Johnson held up a new cell phone in her hands as Kimani approached. "I went and picked this up a few weeks ago," she said. "The technician wouldn't take my word for it when I told him that it surged on it's on; he seemed to think that you tried to plug it directly into a wall socket or somethin'. I almost smacked him when he said that most kids did stupid things. Hell, he don't know my child like that." She allowed herself a silly laugh. "Anyway, the warranty covered the damages, so it didn't cost me a thing, thankfully. But it don't matter. Here…" She handed him the cell phone. "… they put the same Sim Card in this one, so it's still programmed wit' all of yo' numbers from befo'."

"You know you didn't have to do this, momma."

"Boy please." Ms. Johnson corrected him. "I picked the thing up a li'l over two weeks ago, now. I just didn't know if you were quite ready for it, yet; wit' you bein' all cooped up in the house and such."

Kimani reached out for the phone and took it. Upon contact with the device, chills immediately shot through his fingers and up his arm to his spine. It was an eerie feeling; one that reminded him of the things that he didn't want to remember. When he took the phone, Ms. Johnson reached over to him, pulled him close to her and gave him a big motherly hug. She hugged him tight, and he didn't hesitate to hug her back. He was use to moments like these with her, and at that moment he simply needed the love.

"I love you, Kimani." Ms. Johnson proclaimed.

She pulled back from her son and continued to speak. "You remember what I said to you and be good to that girl. I know when you got a good thing. You may not know it yet, but that's aight, you're young. I can see it a mile away. There are not many women out here that'll give her mind, body and spirit to a man; especially not in this day and age. But that girl really does love you unconditionally." She grabbed Kimani by the shoulders. "That rap music you listen to, Kimani, may teach you how to be hard on ho's, bitches, sluts, and all that other madness. But what it fails to teach you is how to recognize when you got someone on yo' team and how to truly treat them like they're on yo' team."

She gently touched Kimani on the cheek before turning around to leave his room once more. While walking down the hall, she spoke to him over her shoulders. "Now, teachin' you what's real, that's what I'm here fo', and fo'ever will be." Ms. Johnson always said a lot by saying little.

Kimani paused for a minute to look back at his dresser drawer, but his gaze didn't linger for long. He placed the heavily burdened phone into his pocket, walked down the hallway of the apartment and headed for the front door. He had to get out. The world never waited for no man regardless of what that man's perception of the world was.

The block was pulsing as usual. Traffic went up and down the avenue, to and from their destinations. Caccy-Laccy had been having a good ride with Donesha these last few days, but he knew that it was coming to an end. It would soon be time to move on to other things. He leaned up against his ride with her pressed up against him and thought about the time that they had spent together, thus far. As fine as she was, he understood that it wouldn't last forever.

Donesha was a half breed; mixed with Korean and black. She grew up in the city, a third generation American, and was as hood as ever. Thick as hell, with medium-large breast and long limbs to accentuate her every move, the girl could steal the show at any beauty contest. Her smile was radiant, perfectly straight and white. With the two glistening golds on her upper teeth – one next to each fang – she was simply beautiful where most girls were just pretty.

These weren't the only attributes she had that drew the attention of Caccy-Laccy, though. Ole girl was a straight up freak, and her head game was on fire. Of course none of it was free – going out, shopping, etc. – but that was usually a part of the game.

Donesha leaned back and tried to kiss Caccy-Laccy in the mouth, but he quickly pulled away and kissed her on the neck instead. He was tipsy from drinking twenty-two ounce bud-ice, but he wasn't that tipsy. He knew the game too well than to let a slut like her kiss him directly in the mouth. Last night with her was one long fuck-fest and tonight would more than likely be the same. But making love to a ho was just too dangerous now and days. A couple more nights with this bitch and it would be time to send her on her way.

His cell phone rang, and he pushed Donesha up off of him to answer it. As he pulled it from his pocket, he never had time to read the caller I.D.; the phone exploded into a million pieces, sending shrapnel in all directions. Caccy-Laccy was temporarily stunned for a moment as the block erupted into chaos with the sounds of ear shattering gunfire.

Donesha screamed and tried to run for cover, but Caccy-Laccy – quickly coming out of his reverie – grabbed her and pulled her back to shield himself from the onslaught of raining bullets. He then dove behind his own vehicle. With his body safely behind his ride and his hands covering his ears from the deafening sounds of close combat, he watched as Donesha's – now lifeless body – fell limp to the curb riddled with bullet holes. Her life's fluids quickly spilled from her body and her eyes stared out into the after-world, but Caccy-Laccy had no time – nor did he care – to close them.

He rose from his squatted position with his weapon in hand to return fire with the rest of his *Conrad's*. The intruders were in drop-tops and were wearing their hood's flags around their wrist and tied to the ends of the barrels of their assault rifles. It was eerie how a man could pay so close attention to such details during the heat of battle. As Caccy-Laccy blasted his weapon, he counted his tenth and last round to the .45 automatic he carried. The slide to the weapon was locked into a cocked position waiting to be reloaded. Only there was no need; the assault was quickly over, and the intruders were now far down the block.

While most of his *Conrad's* continued to blast their remaining rounds at the disappearing off-brands, Caccy-Laccy turned to assess the damage. People were still ducked off behind cars, concrete walls, and laid out flat on the ground hoping to avoid a deadly bullet. But some of his *Conrad's*, unfortunately, would never be getting up again.

There was no time to wish them good luck in the after-life. While his *Conrad's* still had their attentions down the block towards the retreating off-brands, he noticed that another wave of assault was coming from up the block.

Caccy-Laccy quickly threw down his spent weapon and attempted to duck back behind his vehicle again while trying to scream for his homies to take cover. It was a warning that he never got to give. As the loud gun blast coming from the second drop-top drowned out the screams, Caccy-Laccy felt a piercing sting to his back. He fell to the ground, helpless and alone. His *Conrad's,* unaware of the new wave of assault, dropped one after the other from projectiles to the back.

The second assault vehicle had three gunners firing fully automatic rifles, spitting out fire that lit up the night. With two gunners firing from the right and left flanks of the vehicle, and a third gunner firing from the rearguard, the scene in James Cacey Housing Projects was akin to that of a slaughterhouse.

He got out of the car, and with gloves on, opened up the trunk to retrieve a tri-pod to set up on the curb in the dark alley. It was late, he was alone in enemy territory and he was ready to get this done. He reached back into his trunk and pulled out a large digital bullhorn. It had been preprogrammed to emit police sirens, and to increase in volume until it reached its climax. That climax would hold until someone figured out how to turn it off.

He mounted the digital bullhorn onto the tri-pod. The second volley of gunfire had already sounded off in the distance and that was his cue.

His job was easy, set up the bullhorn, activate its program, and then go home. He didn't know the full details as to why, nor did he care to know, but he knew from experience that Sirius always had a reason for everything that he did. The art of war was deception, but the art of deception was surprise.

****

The second assault vehicle pulled into the vacant parking-lot. There were no streetlights; their actions hidden under the cover of darkness. The occupants of the second assault vehicle pulled in right along the first one and got out of the car. The men immediately began pulling the flags off the barrels of the rifles; a symbol to all of who they were. Someone, preparing for what was to come, began dousing the vehicles with a five-gallon jug of jet-fuel. The fuel was expensive, but it burned ten times hotter than regular fuel. The AR-15's – bullets and all – would be left in the drop-tops when they burned. Though they were careful during the preparations not to touch the rifles or the bullets with their bare hands, it didn't matter; the extremely hot flames from the burning jet-fuel would make any leftover residue irrelevant to CSI. The bullets that would be left behind would eventually explode, keeping the fire fighters away just long enough for the flames to consume all of the evidence.

Once the vehicles were fully doused, the last man, jug in hand, left a wick-trail one hundred feet from the drop-tops. He walked towards two awaiting vans where he and his accomplices would wait for one other vehicle before setting them all on fire. From the sounds of heavy gun fire off in the distance, that wait wouldn't be long.

Kimani hit the steps of his building. The night stank of city air and project piss, but his nasal senses were used to the onslaught. His senses were always kicked into over-drive, as were most people in this neighborhood, when out in the open. When things around him were quiet enough, he could hear the heartbeat of the city; it would often become musical if he listened long enough.

He looked around, as he always did upon leaving his building, before stepping down onto the sidewalk and making his way towards the block.

Sasha was on his mind. He knew he would have a lot of explaining to do, but that was the price to pay when you loved someone. She was everything that his mother knew her to be and he considered himself lucky, even blessed, to have her on his team. She made him think about things in life that no one else made him think of; like the future, or just the essence of life in general.

He'd read somewhere that what made humans stand out from other creatures was that humans were conscious and aware of themselves; but he wasn't so sure. He wasn't so sure if humans *were* conscious or if they were just made to be and act the way that they do; programmed to be who they are. In that case, who were the programmers and who were the programmed? Are gang-bangers, killers, and drug dealers really what they consciously choose to be, or do they do what they do simply because they have been programmed to. A perpetual unbroken cycle. Do humans do the things that they do simply because they *believe* they are supposed to. After all, sons of doctor's and lawyer's often become doctor's and lawyer's. So, are human's conscious, or are they programmed slaves to a designed environment?

Kimani felt some of this shit definitely belonged in the movies, including the shit he was going through. Sometimes he felt that his life *was* a movie and he was being watched on the big screen. He sometimes felt that his life was similar to that of the Matrix, but he somehow took the wrong pill. Maybe he was just crazy and everyone else knew it but him. They probably whispered behind his back and smiled when he passed. Or maybe he was tripping; his conscious failing to distinguish what was real from what was fake.

In that case, what *is* real? Is it what the eyes can see, or the ears can hear? Is it what the nose can smell, or the fingers can touch? Because if that's what was real, then real was fake as fuck! He came in contact with fake ass nigga's every day; he heard fake ass shit coming out of their mouth's all the time; and he too often saw more fake shit than he did real. Maybe it all revolutionized the big question; if real was defined by what a conscious human could smell, hear, see or touch, then what the fuck is real?

He realized life was full of fucked up shit, fucked up situations, and fucked up thoughts. But these were only a portion of the things that circulated through his mind. If his thoughts got into the wrong hands, he would probably end up in a psyche ward somewhere surrounded by the real and fake ass nigga's in his head; trying not to answer his own questions. It's said that is what determines whether or not a man is crazy. But maybe that just depends on who defines what crazy is. As for a crazy person, how would *they* define crazy?

And what about normal? What *is* normal? That is, what's normal to one man may not be normal to the next. Is normal a universal concept that's universally perceived and accepted by each man independently from the next, or is it simply *programmed conscience*? Is normal, normal only because a person was told it was normal? Most people were taught good from evil, right from wrong, normal from abnormal. But how do they truly know that the good, right, and normal that they were taught is accurate? Maybe normal is nothing more than a man-made concept decided and set forth by those in power and programmed to those who are not. How do conscious humans know that the person who taught them the concept of normal were normal themselves? Not necessarily their parents, but yesterday's masters who brainwashed their parents, parents, parents!

What if killing was normal; on the streets just as it is to soldiers during times of war? What if robbing someone of their possessions was normal? What if humans were taught that concept from day one – from the day that they were born – that killing, robbing, and stealing was normal? They would probably believe it with conviction. Though he didn't necessarily believe that these things *were* normal, he still had to ask the question: How normal would normal be, then?

If one man believed that the sky was green, he would most likely be thought of as abnormally crazy. But what if the same color that one man *sees* as green, another man actually *sees* as blue. But because that first man was *taught* that the same color that he sees as green was called blue, he too, then calls it blue. Two men, perceiving the same color differently, but programmed not to. Who's to say that one man's perception of reality is *truly* the same as another's; or that it has to be? But only because of *programmed consciousness*, the human mind has been tricked into being held in check. The human's porous and easily influenced mind is often – that is, more than not – programmed to have a false sense of reality; METU NETER!

Maybe the real question was, why should a man be punished for doing what's normal to him? Because it's normal in the hood to see a man get killed; it's normal in the hood to see a man get held up at gun-point because another man believes he has what should belong to him; it's normal in the hood to see men run up and down the block all day trying to market their product; and it's normal in the hood to see a man toting a gun because most others have them too. There are a million other things that are normal in the hood, so why should men be punished for doing what's so damn normal to them?

Kimani continued to walk towards South 7th Avenue with his conscience in over-drive. He dug into his pocket for his phone to call Caccy-Laccy as he thought about these concepts, among other things, and wondered how other people's thoughts compared to his own. To his dismay, he would soon find out.

He came out on top of the hill on South 7th Avenue just as a drop-top, with three gunners with rifles hanging over the side, quickly passed him by. Putting his phone back into his pocket, he regretted leaving his .40 caliber at home. There was an old motto in the hood – it was better to get caught with it than to get caught without it. He watched as the block below him exploded with gun-fire right before his eyes.

There had to be at least forty people down below running for safety, or trying helplessly to fire back with their automatics or occasional fully. People even laid flat on the ground hoping that the deadly bullets would pass them by.

Kimani, knowing that it was futile, began running towards ground zero. A second fast moving drop-top assault vehicle – fortunately, oblivious of him – passed him by. This advance, he predicted, would be far worse with his *Conrad's* having their backs to the approaching assault. He continued to run but his screams and warning cries were muted by gunfire as the enemy sprayed their deadly ordnances. He screamed, nonetheless, as if his homies lives depended on it.

The scene below was a massacre in the making.

Looking at all of the bodies dropping, the splattering of blood and hearing the screams of the still dying was too much for Kimani to cope with. There was nothing he could do. He slowed his run and came to an abrupt halt. Dropping hard to his hands and knees, he regurgitated his stomach's contents. Tears welled up in his eyes and the muscles tightened in his abdomen. Bowed down on hands and knees, he forced himself to look at the scene before him. With the taste of acid burning his throat and throw-up dripping from his lips and chin, he tried to regulate his breathing and calm his palpitating heart; at that moment, they both had a life of their own. He helplessly watched as the last of the drop-tops past him by.

People – those that still could – were getting to their feet and trying to look every which way at once; no one wanted to be caught off guard a third time. Kimani had no idea who had perimeter watch in the direction that the vehicles had come from, but chances were they were dead along with so many others; it was the only way that the off-brands could've gotten so far in-hood without warning.

His heart and breathing were sporadic. His hands and knees were aching from the rough concrete. And his eyes were blood-shot from the tears that would no longer come. He watched as people tried to help the screaming and wounded, hollering for someone, anyone to call the paramedics. There were many non-bangers on the block as well, and most knew nothing of what should be done next.

Sirens echoed off in the distance which slightly eased the panic, while the Young-Ones – most of them eight and nine years of age – came out of the cuts and nooks of the avenue with large gym bags. They began pulling weapons out of banger's hands, dead or alive, and putting them in the bags that they carried to get them off the block before the authorities arrived. Though the hood had surely never been hit this hard before – at least not in his lifetime – protocols had to remain intact and strict discipline was second nature.

Kimani never liked the idea of Young-Ones having to live such incorrigible lives, but decisions like that were never left up to him. He thought about the things that he was forced to experience at such a young age, just as one of the Young-Ones began running in his direction with a bag full of weapons. The sirens in the distance were getting louder and louder and seemed to be getting closer, which meant that help was on the way. It was a blessing, considering that it usually took the proper authorities forever to respond to the hood's needs. He began climbing to his feet as a Young-One neared.

Though the night was still muggy and quite warm, Kimani got cold-chills as he dried his mouth with the back of his hand. It was more than the massacre down below that drove him mad; it was more than the look in a child's face in the aftermath of warfare; and it was more than the mother's, children and baby-mothers who would continue to suffer long after everyone else learned to live with the loss of a *Conrad* or friend. It was the knowledge of knowing first-hand that life was never a given. Kimani didn't fear death, he just feared not living.

The reward of ignorance was bliss, but the privilege of understanding was pain.

An ambulance drove past him and headed towards the carnage below. Its flashing red warning lights lit up the night with an eerie ambience, making the reality of the massacre all that much more gruesome. The chills continued to surge through his body, and his mind continued to process in over-drive. He stared at the ambulance in silence as it neared the dead and wounded of his fallen *Conrad's*.

There were hushed whispers all around, but he paid them no mind. People impatiently waited for medics; the dying was still dying. Time was of the essence. Along with the whispers in the night, Kimani listened to the still blaring sirens off in the distance while staying vigilant to everything that was happening. He had witnessed death before – had heard of it many times – but not like this. The whispers all around him continued to crescendo until they threatened to drown out the sirens and the cries of the dying.

Residents of the hood began making their way out onto their porches with babies in their arms or little-ones clutching their leg. Those that still feared to come out of their homes, kept watch from the safety of an upstairs or downstairs window. One thing was for certain though, people – whether aware or unaware – tended to be drawn to the axes of evil.

Kimani listened as the whispers began screaming their way into the confines of his head. Had it not been for the whispers interrupting his thinking, it would not have taken him this long to realize that something wasn't right. It wasn't until he sprang into action that those screaming whispers came to an abrupt halt.

Reaching out, he snatched the Young-One just before he was able to run past him. Grabbing the bag from the child's resisting hands, he urged the Young-One to keep it moving. Reaching into the cache of weapons, he brought up a fully automatic Uzi. He could only hope that he had enough ammo to ward off the coming assault, for there were two things that did not compute. One, the authorities never responded quickly to the hood; and two, the paramedics never arrived before the police; they were usually stationed, while the police were out on patrol.

He didn't have time to think further. The doors to the back of the paramedic vehicle burst open and armed off-brands stormed out of its cabin. People once again began screaming and running as gun blast shattered their eardrums for a third time. Kimani raised the Israeli-made weapon towards the cabin and squeezed the trigger. The fully came to life. His face and eyes lit up in the dark from the fire emitting from the nozzle, but those were details that he had no time for. The last five occupants in the cabin went down before they knew what hit them, which left Kimani with five additional targets that he had to search and destroy.

The occupants in the ambulance were surprised and temporarily confused to be taking on gunfire at this juncture in their attack; intelligence said that all weapons would be taken off of the block. There wasn't supposed to be any resistance, but change was often the case in any battle; things changed without warning. Of those still in the cabin, three were dead and the other two were incapacitated with severe wounds.

Kimani attempted to target those outside of the cabin as they all focused their fire on him, but the Uzi he was firing was now spent. Ducking behind a broke down deuce-and-a-quarter, he quickly reached back into his arsenal of weapons and came out with another Uzi. He got a very short burst before it, too, went silent. Frustrated, but trying against all odds to hold his composure, he came back up with two automatic handguns – one, a 9mm, and the other, a .38 Glock automatic – and immediately began firing at his targets from the cover of the broke down hoopty. Like the sounds of thunder, enemy fire reign down on the vehicles body.

The off-brands were making their retreat back into the ambulance while maintaining their cover-fire. In battle, it was often plausible to allow an enemy to retreat – to spare lives – while giving yourself the opportunity to regroup. Kimani stopped firing and lowered his head completely below the bulk of the hoopty. He struggled to control his breathing while counting off the seconds in his head.

He listened as the ambulance sped away. Knowing that it could be a possible ploy to goad him out of hiding, he waited a few more seconds before easing his head up above the car. Fortunately for them all, the off-brands were gone from the block.

Kimani eased back down and allowed his head to rest on the bumper. This was not the life he wanted to live. This was not the life he wanted anyone to live, especially the Young-One who watched him just fifteen feet away. Locking eyes with the child, unable to say anything, Kimani just stared. There was not an essence of life in the kid's eyes; no emotion whatsoever; shear apathy. The child had eyes that reminded him so much of Tyler's. Was *this* normal? He wondered, taking everything into perspective. Without a care in the world, the child walked up to Kimani, took the guns from his hands to put into the bag, and ran away in the direction that he was originally headed before he was so rudely interrupted.

EPILOGUE
RUN NIGGA, RUN

MAY 2nd. 8:42am.
METRO NASHVILLE POLICE DEPARTMENT
CENTRAL SECTOR/DOWNTOWN

Detective Mark George popped a piece of gum into his mouth. He often savored the initial taste of fresh gum on his tongue. It was something about the sweetness of it that made the nerves behind his mandible tense up. Keeping a fresh pack handy was a must as he hated once the taste became dull; like so many other things in his life.

The office was alive early this morning. Everyone seemed to have something to do. He was busy watching everyone else as he observed phones chirping and co-workers hollering for one thing or another. The Detective wondered if this was what it was like to be a stockbroker on the New York Stock Exchange. One thing was for certain, he would be making a hell of a lot more money than what the MNPD was paying him. He knew things would be changing soon, though, and for the better.

He watched as a new face appeared on the floor; it was Detective Anderson. Mark noticed that he had been coming to the central precinct a lot lately. It wasn't an oddity to see an officer walk into a police station, but Anderson worked the drug unit at the east precinct, and he was visiting the organized crime unit downtown. Officer's sometimes visited other precincts on official duty, but it wasn't very often – they simply didn't like each other – and he noticed that Anderson came in more often than not. From clear across the room, the Detective watched as Anderson took his usual seat in front of Detective Cecil's desk; something he did each time he came there.

Something wasn't right with these two. Detective Mark George didn't know what, but he knew that it *was* something.

Maybe it was the way that Detective Cecil began to look over his shoulders upon Anderson's arrival that sparked Mark's interest; or the way that Cecil seemed irritated by the unannounced pop up visit. One thing was certain, these two were up to something.

He watched as the two Detectives began talking to one another, but Detective Mark was no lip reader. Could he see the urgency in their expression? Yes. Or the suspicious way that the two began to scrutinize the people around them as potential eaves droppers? Definitely. But it wasn't enough to tell Mark what he really wanted to know: what in the hell these two were up to?

Fast to react, he picked up the phone line and quickly called officer Davenport's call-desk. It was the rookies first day on the job, and like every other rookie at this precinct, he spent most of his days directing incoming calls; a job Detective Mark remembered and hated.

"Metro Nashvil..."

"Davenport?" Mark interrupted. "This is Detective Mark over at your three o'clock. How's your first day on the job?"

"It's a little bit busier than I initially thought that it would be." Officer Davenport looked over his right shoulder to search out Detective Mark George and saw him waving fifty feet across the room. "Is there anything that I can do for you, Detective?"

"Yeah, in fact, there is. I just ran off some copies of a case load that I have to file. If you can do me a favor and go down to the printing room and pick them up for me? I promise I'll owe you one."

"I don't know, sir. What about the calls?" Davenport asked. "I can't direct them if I'm running errands. I don't want to get in trouble on my first day on the job."

"Don't worry about it. Look, you're not the only one directing call's here..." Mark lied.

"I'm not?"

"...of course not. Just put this particular call on speaker, I'll stay on the line to make sure that it doesn't hang up until you get back, and any incoming calls that come through will automatically redirect to some other station."

"Well, I didn't think of that," admitted Officer Davenport, not wanting to disappoint. "Alright, I'll do it. But where exactly is the printing room?"

"Just down the hall on your left; on the other side of the vending machines. There's a plaque on the wall that reads, 'copying/printing room.' And Davenport, I appreciate this one. I'll never forget it."

"No problem, Detective Mark."

"Just call me Mark. We're family here."

"Alright, Mark. I'll be back soon." Davenport promised.

"Thank you, Davenport. And remember, put the line on speaker. We don't want to get you in any trouble."

"Sure thing Detect... ah, Mark. I'll be right back."

"Alright."

The Detective listened as the speaker phone came to life. He reached for his computer keypad and brought up an expired caseload. It was large enough to keep Officer Davenport busy for some time. Mark immediately pressed print.

He couldn't afford to miss out on opportunities; missing out could cost him. The early bird got the worm, they say, but Detective Mark knew that the wittiest bird was usually rewarded with the best worms. He looked back towards Detectives Anderson and Cecil while turning up the volume on his desk phone, putting it on mute to prevent any noise from emitting from the other end. He could barely hear his targets conversation, but that was only because Cecil's desk was a full one station over from Officer Davenport's call-desk.

Listening closely, Mark picked up in mid-conversation, "... just not enough funds circulating, right now. I don't know what to tell you. You say one thing, but my man's screaming foul play."

"Foul play?" Protested Anderson.

"Yes. Foul play." Cecil returned.

"Well, you need to remind your man that I'm the one that brought his sorry ass to life. If it wasn't for me, there wouldn't be any him; he would be dead in the water. Do you hear me, Cecil?"

"Look, I hear you, but you need to realize that things are not always what they appear to be. They only let you see and believe what they want you to see and believe. You may have thought that you hired them, but I can tell you from experience that they hired you, old friend." Cecil paused to let that sink in. "Besides, it was someone on your end that choked up. Everything was just fine until that goddamn boy of yours got the fucking hot head."

"You don't have to worry about him anymore. That's been taken care of."

"You know just as much as I do that it doesn't matter one way or the other what I think. I'm not the one calling the shots here. You know what has to be done."

"Well, tell your man that I said..."

"That's no good. You know that messages are no good in our line of work. You wanna get something done you have to do it yourself. But take advice from an old friend, Anderson, you should just cut your strings on this one; they're already too long as it is."

"Damn it!" Expelled Anderson.

"Yeah. We've all said that one before."

Mark watched as Anderson leaned back in his swivel chair and laced his fingers behind his head. So far, he had no idea what the conversation was about, but knew that it was enough to turn a curious ear. As a Detective, he always had an investigative approach to things; more out of habit than anything else. For instance, every time Anderson came to the central precinct, it would always be to visit Detective Cecil. Habits and reoccurrences were things that made for an easy investigation; even if it was on one of your own.

He continued to listen, "what about last night?" Asked Anderson.

"What about it?" responded Cecil.

"Any suspects? Anything to go off of?"

"Not as of yet, but to be honest, no one really cares. They should all just kill themselves anyway; it'll make our jobs a whole lot easier."

"Cecil, my friend, if they did that then we wouldn't have jobs to begin with. Without them, there would be no us. We just have to keep them busy so that we can pay the bills. Busy, busy, busy."

"You're right, of course." Detective Cecil paused, thinking about the obvious. "So, how's the cuckoo's egg? Is everything up to par so far?"

"That's small potatoes; nothing to worry about. They're right where I need them to be and they'll hatch when I tell them to."

"And Bones?" Asked Cecil.

"Watches too many gangster movies, if you ask me. He's a tough one, though."

"You watch that one closely, Anderson. He's not like the rest of them, or like any we've ever had before. He makes me nervous."

"Cecil, you have always feared the things that you don't understand," teased Anderson.

"You call it fear. I call it self-preservation."

"What's the difference?"

"The difference is life and death, my friend. Don't let that old brain of yours get too old; old things tend to break down."

"I hear you, Cecil. I hear you loud and clear. But don't worry yourself too much. I can handle my own affairs. Besides, I have contingencies set in place just in case. And in the event of that something happening, well hell, we'll all be finished anyway." Detective Anderson allowed himself a smile. He knew how to rattle Cecil's cage.

"If you say so, Anderson. You just keep in mind that you're not the only one involved in this. There's a lot more at stake here than you could ever imagine. I don't know about you, but I value family above all. Our handlers won't be happy to find out about your fiascos. If they're as sharp as I think they are then they already do. You remember Smitty, don't you? How could anyone forget? Get yourself together and pull yourself up by the bootstraps before somebody else does it for you."

"Is that a threat, Cecil?"

"Not a threat, a promise. I was solving cases when you were still a scratch in your daddy's nutt-sack, and I'd be damned if I'm forced to retire because of your incompetence. There's nothing, and I mean nothing, we can't accomplish if we just stick to the plan. Deviate just a hair and you not only stir up your own house, but the one next to it. Are you listening to me, Anderson?"

"I'm listening." Anderson was no longer smiling.

"You ever stop to ask yourself why they're so damn compartmentalized with their daily affairs? Why we never know who "they" really are? It's so that when schmucks like yourself goes off and fucks things up, one domino doesn't affect the other. Better to lose the finger than the whole fucking body, right? Only the finger we're talking about is your life, my life, and everybody's life that we ever fucking loved. So, if you so much as even value anything I'm telling you right now, then you get your goddamn head out of your ass and get it together." Cecil paused to let it all sink in. "Do I make myself absolutely clear?"

"I hear you, Cecil. Like I said, there's nothing to worry about. Everything will realign itself. I just need a little longer."

"Good. I'll see what I can do. Until then, there's a matter of importance that I need for you to take care of. Do you have any idea who..."

"Detective... ah, Mark. Here you go." Officer Davenport sat a large stack of file papers on Detective Mark's desk. "That new printing machine is a real piece of work."

Mark, recovering from being startled by the Officer, laid the phone across his shoulder.

"New printing machine?" The Detective asked. "What new printing machine?"

"The one that the department just replaced the old one with. It copies a hell of a lot faster than the old one. Everyone's down there talking about it."

"Really?" Mark, hating the new printer, looked back over at Cecil's desk. "Well, thanks, Davenport. I'll never forget it."

"No problem. Look, you wanna stop for some drinks after work... "

"Now's not a good time, Davenport." Said Mark. "Maybe some other time. I'm just really, really busy right now."

"Well, maybe we can... "

"Davenport, man! Not now. Some other time." Mark exclaimed, anxious to get back to work.

Davenport, seeing the frustration on the Detectives face, put his hands up, palms out, and walked back to his call desk, defeated.

Mark hated rookies. They created unnecessary employment; that was money that he himself could be making. The world was just better off without rookies. The one reason he and his wife transferred to Nashville was because of its high metro pay, relative to its low cost of living. But getting a decent raise out of the city was all but impossible; they would much rather hire rookies and fund a larger roll-call. Putting the phone back up to his ear, he listened in for the few seconds it took for Officer Davenport to reach his desk and disconnect the line. The last words that Mark heard was, "ungrateful son-of-a-bitch," before the phone went dead. Well, that was settled; he wouldn't be getting any more favors from that rookie.

He watched as Cecil and Anderson talked for another fifteen minutes before the latter got up to take his leave. He couldn't make sense of the conversation – had no idea what the cuckoo's eggs were, who the hell Bones was, or what handler they referred to. But he knew that it represented something other than what it sounded like. As of now, he knew nothing; but even nothing was something.

"Mark? We got him!" Connie came running up to Mark from behind and sat down on the edge of his desk.

"Got who, Connie? What in the hell are you talking about? And why does everyone keep creeping up on me?" Mark put the thought of Anderson and Cecil out of his head for now and turned to his partner of two and a half years.

"What in the hell's wrong with you, Mark?" Connie watched her partner. "Look, never mind that. We got Jesse Booker, that's who. I have Williams following him as we speak."

"Williams?" Mark asked, sitting up straight.

"Yeah, Williams."

"Who else knows about this?" Mark asked.

"Just the two of us, for now," said Connie. "Williams doesn't even know who he's following yet, and I wanted to come and get you before we called our two agent friends. Williams is good at tailing. He'll hold 'em until then."

"First of all, we're not calling Batman and Robin."

"What? But Mark, they gave us specific instructions to notify them if anything came up. We can't just... "

"I know what they said, Connie, but they're just going to screw things up." Mark protested. "It's not illegal to just walk into a fast food joint while things around you are blowing up. If we don't figure things out on our own and catch Jesse with something incriminating, then we may as well just forget about apprehending him in the first place. Trust me on this, Con'. If it doesn't pan out, then we'll call your boys in. Until then, let me run point on this one."

"Alright, Mark." Connie thought about the dilemma. "But if it doesn't work out the way that you plan, you'd better be coming up with something to cover my ass. I like you and all, but I like my job a little bit more."

"Trust me on this one. Have I ever failed you?"

"You're the man, Mark."

"That's what I wanna hear. Now, where are they?"
"They're mobile. But if we hurry, we can catch up to them in the car."

"When we're done with this, Con', I'm going to buy you some pussy."

"Shit, I don't need you to buy me pussy. I get way more pussy than you, and I'm twice as ugly." Connie joked.

Mark immediately reached for his keypad and backed out of his computer. His screensaver was a picture of money blowing in the wind. Grabbing his gun holster, he followed Connie to the elevators and out of the office. He couldn't help but notice the evil-eye that Officer Davenport was giving him as he hurried behind his partner.

What Mark didn't notice was the attention that Detective Cecil was giving him. One thing was certain, that old bird didn't miss much.

****

Driving down the boulevard, Jesse turned down the volume to the radio. 101.1 The Beat, wasn't playing anything worth listening to, but that wasn't the reason for him wanting silence. He had company. He first noticed the tail back on Two Rivers Boulevard; but that was ten minutes ago. Since then, he had driven in a couple of circles and even through a mall parking-lot, but to no avail. There was no telling how long he had been followed prior to that. Had it not been for the heavy traffic, he would have known for sure. His tail was in a blue Chevy Impala – newer model – which made him immediately think the Narcs. But there was just no definite way of knowing for certain; it was a hostile world out there and the police wasn't the only ones carrying guns.

Once his tail had been established, Jesse quickly made his way down Gallatin Avenue. He needed to get to his spot, and fast. In the movies, the tailors' always had tinted windows; but not this tail. It made it possible for Jesse to see a forty-something year old black male at the helm. Assassin? Maybe. But if so, he had plenty of opportunities to make his move.

The tail kept his pace – eight cars back and two lanes over – trying to remain incognito. Jesse too kept his pace; he didn't want to alert the tail that he was on to him. For now, that disguise was his only advantage.

As he pulled onto Briley Parkway, Jesse sped up to the posted speed limit of fifty-five miles an hour, while keeping his eye on his tail. Turning south bound on Ellington Parkway, he kept at a steady fifty-five, trying to buy some time. He made his exit on Trinity Lane a short time later, driving a bit of a distance before entering Shepherd-Wood subdivision. It was a middle-class white neighborhood where he had been operating some two months now.

The traffic was less dense here, and as expected, the tailor lagged back about a half a block to try and compensate for the lack of vehicles to blend in with. He was good, Jesse noticed, but expertise was no good when your cover was already blown.

He pulled onto his block on Teardrop Drive and eased into his driveway. Without turning his head, he noticed that his tail pulled off to the side of the road some ways back. This was definitely the narcs, Jesse realized; unlike his tailor, an assassin would be scoping out his surroundings for every possible exit. Jesse nonchalantly got out of the car, walked to his mailbox to retrieve his junk-mail, and then went to his front door to let himself in.

"Talk to me, Williams. Where are you?"

"I'm out her in Shepherdwood, on Tear Drop Drive. Where are you?"

"We're still inbound; about fifteen minutes out," stated Connie.

"We're?"

"Yes. Mark is with me."

"Well, you mind telling me who this is that I'm following, and how it is that you knew exactly where I could find him?"

"I got an anonymous call; some old guy, from the sound of him."

"An anonymous call?" asked a bewildered Williams.

"Yes. Go figure."

"So, who am I following?"

"It's probably best if I don't tell you."

"What the hell, Connie?"

"I don't know. It's just strange." Connie admitted.

"What do you mean, strange?" asked a curious Williams.

"The old guy... he not only knew where the target was but knew that *you* were in the vicinity."

"What type of shit is this, Connie?" Williams was becoming frustrated.

"Yeah, like I said, strange."

"That's beyond strange. That's downright creepy."

"Who're you telling?"

"Well, what should I do? Should I call for back-up? Are we going in?"

"No. No back up." Interrupted Connie. "We just need to watch him; find out all we can about him. This is just reconnaissance. What can you tell me about him, so far?"

"Well, he seems to live here; saw him get some mail out of the mailbox. Even used a key to get in the front door. Can't see any other vehicles, but that doesn't mean that no one else is inside. I can tell you that he doesn't have a clue that I'm here. What do you want me to do?"

"Just wait until we get on the scene, and then we'll take over from there. If he leaves, notify us immediately. Other than that, just sit tight."

"Got you. I'll be here when you get here."

"Alright, Williams. And thanks."

"Anytime, Connie."

"Alright, bye."

"Bye."

****

"Nine-one-one, what's your emergency?" The 911 dispatcher answered the call.

"Uh, yes. There's a black guy parked right outside of my home on one-thirty-five Tear Drop Drive," said the caller. "I saw him pull up about five minutes ago. He has a gun, and I've seen him handing people something outside of his car window as they walk by. I believe he's selling drugs."

"Drugs, sir?" asked the dispatcher.

"Yes. I do believe that's the case."

"And you said that you saw a gun, sir?"

"Yes. I definitely saw a gun. I work too hard to have this type of activity going on in my neighborhood."

"I understand, sir. And what type of vehicle is he in?"

"It's a blue... looks like a Chevy."

"You said a blue Chevy, sir?"

"Yes."

"And what model is this blue Chevy?"

"It's a newer model."

"I see," said the dispatcher.

"I believe he's one of those gang-bangers in my neighborhood, the way he looks. He's a black guy."

"Yes. I understand, sir. Just sit tight. I'll get someone on it, right away. Thank you for calling, sir."

"I work too hard to have black gang-bangers run my neighborhood selling drugs."

"I understand, sir."

"What's next? They're going to want to come and start doing drive-bys while listening to gangster music, that's what? I work too hard for..."

"Sir, the call has been made. There are officers on the way to handle the situation. Now, if you'll excuse me, I have other calls that I need to dispatch."

"Well I just wanted you to know that I'm a hard-working American. I deserve a..."

"Goodbye, sir."

"You just... "

"Sir, I'm hanging up, now."

The line with the 911 dispatcher went dead.

Jesse discretely stared out of the window at the car parked down the street. The occupant simply kept an eye on his house; definitely the narcs. All of his years of being under the radar, and he allowed himself to get too sloppy. How could they have known exactly where he was in real time? He had to be more careful, he was so close, closer than he'd ever been.

He hated coming into the cities. There were just too damn many cameras, and cameras were dangerous. He was too close to his end-game, and taking chances was something that he had to risk. There was no more shifting from place to place – city to city – trying to do things incognito; the war that had been brewing for more than two and a half decades was now finally reaching its climax. He was running out of time. If he wanted to survive the next few days, he knew he had to pull himself up by the bootstraps and dig in harder.

It would be his only salvation.

Right now, he had to get out of the city, and fast; there were too many cameras. While he didn't blend in well with rural America, it was better than going up against a thousand eyes. With all of that in mind, he knew that he wouldn't have to wait long.

This particular safehouse wasn't used for much – but it was no longer safe. It only had a bed, a vital laptop, weapons, a couple of throw away cell phones, a few items of clothing, passports, and roughly fifty thousand dollars in cash. It was a getaway package; a contingency designed for situations like these.

In calling 911, he felt he'd did a perfect impression of a white guy. In this city, like most others in America, it was the only way to get something done fast. Looking down at the multiple passports he laid out before him, he double checked to make sure that everything was in order before placing everything in a military duffle-bag.

He heard thunder off in the distance, but the day was hot and sunny with not a cloud in the sky; an indication that it was show-time. Right on cue, in a neighborhood full of white people in distress, a helicopter swooped in from the heavens just as police interceptors rushed down the street from both directions with engines revving. Like a man on a mission, Jesse picked up his duffle bag with all of its contents and headed out the front door.

Outside, the uniformed officers had their guns drawn on the blue Chevy Impala and screaming for the occupant to step out of the car with their hands up. Jesse heard his mark telling the officers that he was a cop, but the white pigs already had their minds made up.

Getting in his car, he threw his duffle bag onto the passenger seat and started the engine. He quickly drove his way down Tear Drop Drive in the opposite direction of the arresting officers. The last thing he saw in his rearview mirror was his target face down on the ground with white police officers handcuffing his black ass.

****

"Oh no. No, no, no! What the hell happened?" Connie began to panic as their sedan sped down Tear Drop Drive in what appeared to be the preparation for D-day.

"Damnit, Connie. Williams? You chose Williams?"

"He was already in the area," Connie countered. "What else was I supposed to do? He was convenient and our only option. Besides, we don't know what happened. Hurry up and pull to the side. Here, here, here..."

Connie was half-way out of the vehicle before Mark even came to a full stop. As she approached Williams, she noticed the disappointment in his eyes and knew that the question she had would not receive a good answer. She asked him anyway.

"What the hell happened here, Williams? Where is our guy?"

"Your boy got away, Connie. Thanks to these cracker-jack motherfuckers over here." Williams looked at the officer's with scorn.

"What? What do you mean he got away?"

"These fucking uniforms swarmed in out of nowhere and dragged me out of my car like I was a fucking common criminal. I saw your guy leaving in a white Park-Avenue, while these dumb ass jerks here played Robocop."

Mark and Connie both looked in the uniform officer's direction.

"Hey, we were doing our jobs. We got a call over the radio saying that there was a guy in a non-hostile neighborhood with a gun selling drugs. We responded accordingly," the uniform stated with an attempt to defend his position. "Besides, it was screamed across the radios, you should've heard it and made your intentions clear."

Detective Williams launched towards the uniformed officer with Mark and Connie both grabbing onto him. Connie, wanting to defuse the situation, explained, "he's a Detective at central. He's on a totally different frequency. It's why you never see Detectives respond to house-calls; it doesn't fit our job description."

"Looks like a house-call to me." The uniformed stated sarcastically.

It was Connie's turn to launch at the uniform, while Detective Mark attempted to hold her back; one slap was all she wanted.

Detective Mark spoke, "what's your name, officer?"

"McConnoughly, why?"

"Have you been debriefed?" Mark asked.

"Yeah, I've been debriefed."

"Then you've got one minute to get into your squad car and be off of this scene, " Mark demanded. "One minute, McConnoughly."

McConnoughly looked around and noticed everyone looking at him. To try and save face, he stuck out his chest before getting into his marked vehicle and driving away. He simply didn't care one way or the other.

"Did anyone send out an APB to try and find Jesse? You did see the type of car he was... never mind. You said a white Park-Avenue. Did anyone send out the call?" Connie asked Williams.

"The helicopter went in pursuit..."

"Helicopter?"

"... but the car was abandoned three blocks over up in flames."

"They sent in a damn helicopter?" Mark asked in disbelief.

"You do realize that I'm a black man posted up in an all-white neighborhood don't you?" Asserted Williams.

No one said a thing. The three Detectives were still in shock over the whole ordeal. How could a simple reconnaissance go so damn wrong so fast?

"How did all of this get started in the first place?" Mark wanted to know.

"Someone called about a drug-dealer selling drugs and waving a damn gun while doing it." Williams explained.

"Because of the neighborhood, someone felt obligated to send in the whole fucking precinct."

"Anyone went inside, yet?"

"Inside?" Asked Williams.

"Inside the home." Connie clarified. "Has anyone gone inside to see if there's any evidence?"

"No warrant..." Interrupted Mark. "... and unless he has a warrant for his arrest... we can't just go barging into his home without one. So far as I can tell, the T.B.I. only wants him for questioning." Mark turned his attention on Williams.

"You said someone called nine-one-one about a drug deal in progress?"

"That's the story," Williams said.

Mark looked over at Connie at the same time that she looked over at him.

"Jesse!" they both said in unison.

"He must've spotted you, Williams," said Connie.

"What? Who? What are you two talking about?" Williams asked.

"I'm willing to bet that Jesse's the one that called nine-one-one. He used our own resources against us. How cute is that?" Connie said.

"Pretty damn cleaver if you asked me," admitted Mark. He was impressed, especially since he was the one that initially mistook Jesse as being incompetent. Underestimate a foe, and it could be the last thing that you did.

"Oh, shit! Shit! Shit! Shit!"

"What the hell's wrong with you, Connie?"

"Don't look, your six o'clock. Your T.B.I. friends just pulled up. You remember what I said, Mark," Connie warned. "Oh damn. They've spotted us. They're headed this way. You remember what I said."

"Why do you two have T.B.I. friends? And why are you so damn nervous, Connie?" Williams demanded. "Tell me what the hell is going on, guys?"

"We're guest to those two until we can find a way to solve this case," admitted Connie.

"What case are you talking about?"

"The studio explosion." Connie said.

"Holy shit? Jesse? Jesse Booker? They got you two on that?"

"Yeah, that's what we do, solve impossible cases."

"You had me following the guy that blew up a fucking building? You didn't think to tell me this shit?" Williams said.

"One, it was the situation that we were dealt," explained Connie. "And two, I didn't want you to screw things up by trying to nab him."

"But that's why we're here, isn't it; to nab the bad guys?" Williams, becoming frustrated, attempted to change tactics. "You know what, don't even bother. In fact, if it ever comes up, you make sure that whoever wants to know, knows that I know nothing about this shit. I let the studio bomber get away, for crying out loud. Not something that I want on my resume." Detective Williams shook his head in disbelief.

Connie was about to defend her position but was interrupted by the approaching Agent Benedict, "the entire central precinct is talking about a botched stakeout, Detectives. Mind telling me what the hell is going on?"

Connie began staring down Detective Mark waiting for him to tell the story that she hoped to hear.

"Well, Detective Williams here..." Detective Mark began.

"Williams..." Detective Williams protested. "...ain't got shit to do with this."

"Detective Williams, *here*..." Mark gave the Detective the 'shut the hell up' look, not being assigned to this case, Mark knew that Williams couldn't be held accountable. "...was working a case of his own when he came across a guy that may have looked like our guy. He called me about it and I had him follow the suspect back to this house..." Mark pointed. "...just in case. While he was staking out the home, someone called nine-one-one – that someone is believed to be our suspect – and reported someone selling drugs outside of a blue Chevy Impala." Mark nodded towards the vehicle Williams was leaning on. "When patrol arrived, all hell broke loose, at which time our suspect slipped away. By the time my partner and I got to the scene, Detective Williams here was still dusting himself off. And of course, Agents, we didn't want to bother you unless we were *sure* this was our guy." Knowing that it was best to try to keep a lie as close to the truth as possible, Mark pressed his lips together and waited in silence.

"And what was your position in this bullshit of a story, Detective Connie?" Agent Benedict asked.

"Well, sir, I was told that we may have our guy. I wanted to lend my support. I regretted not knowing if this was really our guy or not, but hopefully when the warrant arrives, we'll know for sure." Connie offered. Somewhere off in the distance, she could hear echoes of helicopter vanes as they rotated. They were loud and seemed to beat down on top of them all. She hoped that their story – while somewhat true – was good enough. She waited silently for the Agents response.

"Un huh." Benedict sneered. "And did anyone think about evacuating the neighborhood; a two-hundred-yard perimeter?"

"Evacuating the neighborhood, sir?" Mark wondered.

They were all interrupted as a large military helicopter swooped in from above, creating a strong whirlwind. With a precise maneuver, the large helicopter landed in the middle of the street in front of them.

They all looked in its direction as the door to the cabin slid open and an F.B.I. Agent stepped out onto the ground. Head ducked low, the man held up his hand and assisted a beautiful woman in full Navy uniform out of the chopper. As the helicopter vanes began to rev down the newcomer pressed her hand against the top of her head and began looking around as though she was in search of someone.

Agent Benedict stared in wonder at the woman before turning back to the problem at hand. Somehow, with the new arrival, he felt that this case was about to take a turn for the worse. He quickly made the decision to get the scene under control but with the helicopter vanes not yet completely revved down, he had to yell to gather everyone's attention:

"Listen up ..." he began. "...this home is ground zero. I want a one-hundred-yard radius marked off from this point, and I don't want a single citizen within its boundaries. We are dealing with a man that is highly capable of using high-grade explosives. He has no regard for human life. I want this neighborhood evacuated as of yesterday." Benedict stared at his audience. "Now, people! Get a move on it." The Agent turned back towards the Detectives as everyone else began running in all direction going from home to home. "You said that you believe that Jesse was the one that called nine-one-one on Detective Williams? How did you come to that conclusion?"

"It just seems highly probable. The story the caller gave was a convenient lie," admitted Mark.

"Then I want you to call dispatch and find out where that call came from." Benedict paused and turned towards his partner. "If it's from a cell phone, then have the FCC triangulate its current position and notify me at once."

Before the Agent could finish, Detective Mark had out his cell phone and was dialing numbers.

A uniformed officer came running up to them with an urgent gait. He interrupted them all, saying, "sir, ah, we did a sweep around the perimeter of the home and looked into a few of the windows."

"And," demanded the Agent.

"Well, it's strange, sir."

"Get it out, Officer. What is it?" urged Mark.

"Well, sir, there's a discharger with a ticking timer, but the discharger isn't hooked up to a bomb or anything."

"Did you say that it *isn't* hooked up to a bomb? Are you sure?" asked the Agent.

"Yes." The officer paused. "There's just two conjoined wires sticking out of it – one black, one red, attached to a piece of copper. There is some type of orange dusty substance sprinkled all around the floor throughout the home." The officer attempted to control his emotions; it was evident how inexperienced he was.

"You said there was an orange dusty substance?" asked Connie.

"Yes," said the officer. "It kind of looks like…"

"…Thermite." Interrupted their new arrival. Silence followed. They all turned to look at the woman in the blue Navy uniform. She'd found who she was looking for.

"…I was going to say, saw dust." The confused officer admitted.

"Did you see how much time was left on the charger?" The beautiful woman asked as everyone, including the T.B.I. Agents, looked on.

"Couldn't tell," answered the officer.

"Then I suggest you get the Fire-Department out here with the quickness if you wish to save the homes next to this one." Their newcomer offered.

"Now wait just a second." Benedict held up a hand. He had a feeling this was coming as soon as he saw the chopper arrive, but he still wanted to protest. He watched as the newcomer flashed her shield and handed him a signed affidavit.

"I'm Captain Roselyn Dotson. Navy Intelligence," said the newcomer.

"Navy Intelligence?" asked Benedict. "What the hell?"

"Affirmative. And it's not quite hell, yet."

"Can someone tell me what Thermite is?" asked the still confused officer.

"It's one of the hottest burning combustibles known to man," answered Benedict. "It burns at more than four-thousand degrees Fahrenheit. Once lit, not even water can put it out; you'll just have to let it run its course. Looks like our evidence is about to go up in flames." So you, officer, should be evacuating the neighborhood." The uniformed officer promptly turned to leave while the rest watched as Jesse's apartment became engulfed with flames and black smoke.

Detective Connie stared at Captain Dotson in awe, though, wondering what the hell a Navy Intelligence officer was doing at their crime scene. With the decorated badges of honor pinned to her Navy uniform, she reminded Connie of a heroine out of the movies.

"You must be Agent Benedict? T.B.I?"

"Yes." The Agent nodded. "Why are you here?"

"I believe you may have stumbled upon a suspect that might be vital to an on-going Navy Investigation."

"You mean, Jesse Booker?" Connie asked.

"Is that the name you came up with?" Dotson returned.

The two Agents and the Detectives all looked at one another. Williams – deciding that he'd heard enough – simply stood up and walked away.

Captain Dotson continued, "someone in your department ran a particular set of fingerprints through a national database. Those fingerprints are a calling card from the past. Allow me to be the first to tell you, Agents and Detectives, this... Jesse Booker is not what he seems. He's dangerous beyond all measures. If you, Agents Benedict and Swallows, plan on assisting me in this investigation, I suggest you put on your thinking cap and keep eyes at your six."

"Wait just a minute; we're so close to apprehending him," stated Mark. He thought this was bullshit.

"You, Detective, could not be further from the truth." Dotson continued, "As Navy Intelligence, and with the full backing of all of her resources, I've been close to apprehending him for more than two decades now. He's absolutely the best at what he does. If it was my guess, he's probably somewhere close by watching us as we speak." The captain paused before continuing. She couldn't help but notice how they all began looking around. "The man you seek is a trained Navy Seal. He was running special ops when some of you were still shitting in diapers. I know, because I've known him for longer than I want to admit."

"And why is Navy Intelligence searching him out?" asked Connie.

"I'm sorry, Detective, but that's classified information that you're not privy to know." Captain Dotson looked at Agent Benedict. "Agents, if you'll come with me..."

"With all due respect, Captain Dotson," Benedict said, "these two Detectives have been on this case since the explosion. I'm sure that there's something they may know that could be of assistance to you."

It was the Detectives turn to look at each other. Benedict was the last person they expected to speak up for them.

"Suit yourselves." Captain Dotson looked around to make sure that no one else could overhear. "What I'm about to tell the four of you is highly sensitive and classified information. That means that if you tell anyone outside of this circle, Uncle Sam will be kicking down your door with armed men to boot. From this juncture on, Navy Intelligence has jurisdiction over this entire investigation as this sworn affidavit from the Secretary of Defense indicates." Captain Dotson held up the sworn affidavit for all to see. "From now on, the four of you are to do what I say, when I say, and how I say. This is not going to be your around-the-mill investigation; it will be fast-paced and up-tempo. I cannot afford to have any of you lagging behind. Do I make myself clear?"

"Yes." The four agreed in unison.

Dotson looked back at her FBI liaison. He promptly came forward with a stack of papers before stepping back.

"These are legal affidavits stamped by Director Hager at the Department of Defense and legally binding to anyone who signs them. I need the four of your signatures before we can proceed any further." Dotson waited while the four of them went through the legal jargon. Once she had all four signatures, she continued, "once again, the assortment of information you will receive in the days to come will be highly sensitive. Your full cooperation is essential. Now, lady and gentlemen, if you will please follow me, we have a flight to catch." Dotson gestured with her hand in the direction of the awaiting helicopter.

"What about my vehicle?" asked Detective Mark.

"What I say, when I say, and how I say, Detective." The captain reminded Mark. "Quickly arrange to have your vehicle find its way back to the station. But hurry, we must leave now; as you know, the first few days are vital."

Shortly after, the six of them – the two Agents, the two Detectives, and Captain Dotson and her liaison – all loaded into the helicopter as the vanes began to increase its RPM's. As the pilot elevated the collector and the helicopter lifted into the air, they all looked out the port-side window as the rooftop to what was once Jesse's apartment caved inwards spewing burning cinders in all directions.

"I always wanted to fly in a helicopter." said Detective Mark.

www.ingramcontent.com/pod-product-compliance
Lightning Source LLC
Chambersburg PA
CBHW060522260626
47161CB00003B/731